Praise for the Cherry Tucker Mystery Series

DEATH IN PERSPECTIVE (#4)

"One fasten-your-seatbelt, pedal-to-the-metal mystery, and Cherry Tucker is the perfect sleuth to have behind the wheel. Smart, feisty, as tough as she is tender, Cherry's got justice in her crosshairs."

– Tina Whittle,
Author of the Tai Randolph Mysteries

"Reinhart succeeds in mixing laughter with the serious topic of cyber-bullying through blogs and texts, all the while developing a chemistry between Cherry and Luke that absolutely sizzles."

– *Kings River Life Magazine*

"Artist and accidental detective Cherry Tucker goes back to high school and finds plenty of trouble and skeletons...Reinhart's charming, sweet-tea flavored series keeps getting better!"

– Gretchen Archer,
USA Today Bestselling Author of the Davis Way Crime Caper Series

HIJACK IN ABSTRACT (#3)

"The fast-paced plot careens through small-town politics and deadly rivalries, with zany side trips through art-world shenanigans and romantic hijinx. Like front-porch lemonade, Reinhart's cast of characters offer a perfect balance of tart and sweet."

– Sophie Littlefield,
Bestselling Author of *A Bad Day for Sorry*

"Bust out your gesso and get primed for humor, hijackings, and a handful of hunks!"

– Diane Vallere,
Author of the Style & Error and Madison Night Mysteries

"Reinhart manages to braid a complicated plot into a tight and funny tale...Cozy fans will love this latest Cherry Tucker mystery."

– *York Journal of Books*

STILL LIFE IN BRUNSWICK STEW (#2)

"Reinhart's country-fried mystery is as much fun as a ride on the tilt-a-whirl at a state fair. Her sleuth wields a paintbrush and unravels clues with equal skill and flair. Readers who like a little small-town charm with their mysteries will enjoy Reinhart's series."

— Denise Swanson,
New York Times Bestselling Author of the Scumble River Mysteries

"Reinhart lined up suspects like a pinsetter in a bowling alley, and darned if I could figure out which ones to knock down...Can't wait to see what Cherry paints herself into next."

– Donnell Ann Bell,
Bestselling Author of *The Past Came Hunting*

"The hilariously droll Larissa Reinhart cooks up a quirky and entertaining page-turner! This charming mystery is delightfully Southern, surprisingly edgy, and deliciously unpredictable."

– Hank Phillippi Ryan,
Agatha Award-Winning Author of *Truth Be Told*

PORTRAIT OF A DEAD GUY (#1)

"*Portrait of a Dead Guy* is an entertaining mystery full of quirky characters and solid plotting...Highly recommended for anyone who likes their mysteries strong and their mint juleps stronger!"

— Jennie Bentley,
New York Times Bestselling Author of *Flipped Out*

"Reinhart is a truly talented author and this book was one of the best cozy mysteries we reviewed this year...We highly recommend this book to all lovers of mystery books. Our Rating: 4.5 Stars."

— *Mystery Tribune*

"The tone of this marvelously cracked book is not unlike Sophie Littlefield's brilliant *A Bad Day for Sorry*, as author Reinhart dishes out shovelfuls of ribald humor and mayhem."

– *Mystery Scene Magazine*

The Body in the Landscape

The Cherry Tucker Mystery Series
by Larissa Reinhart

Novels

PORTRAIT OF A DEAD GUY (#1)
STILL LIFE IN BRUNSWICK STEW (#2)
HIJACK IN ABSTRACT (#3)
DEATH IN PERSPECTIVE (#4)
THE BODY IN THE LANDSCAPE (#5)

Novellas

QUICK SKETCH (prequel to PORTRAIT)
(in HEARTACHE MOTEL)

The Body in the Landscape

A Cherry Tucker Mystery

LARISSA REINHART

HENERY PRESS

THE BODY IN THE LANDSCAPE
A Cherry Tucker Mystery
Part of the Henery Press Mystery Collection

First Edition
Trade paperback edition | December 2015

Henery Press
www.henerypress.com

Author photograph by Scott Asano

ISBN-13: 978-1-943390-37-3

Printed in the United States of America

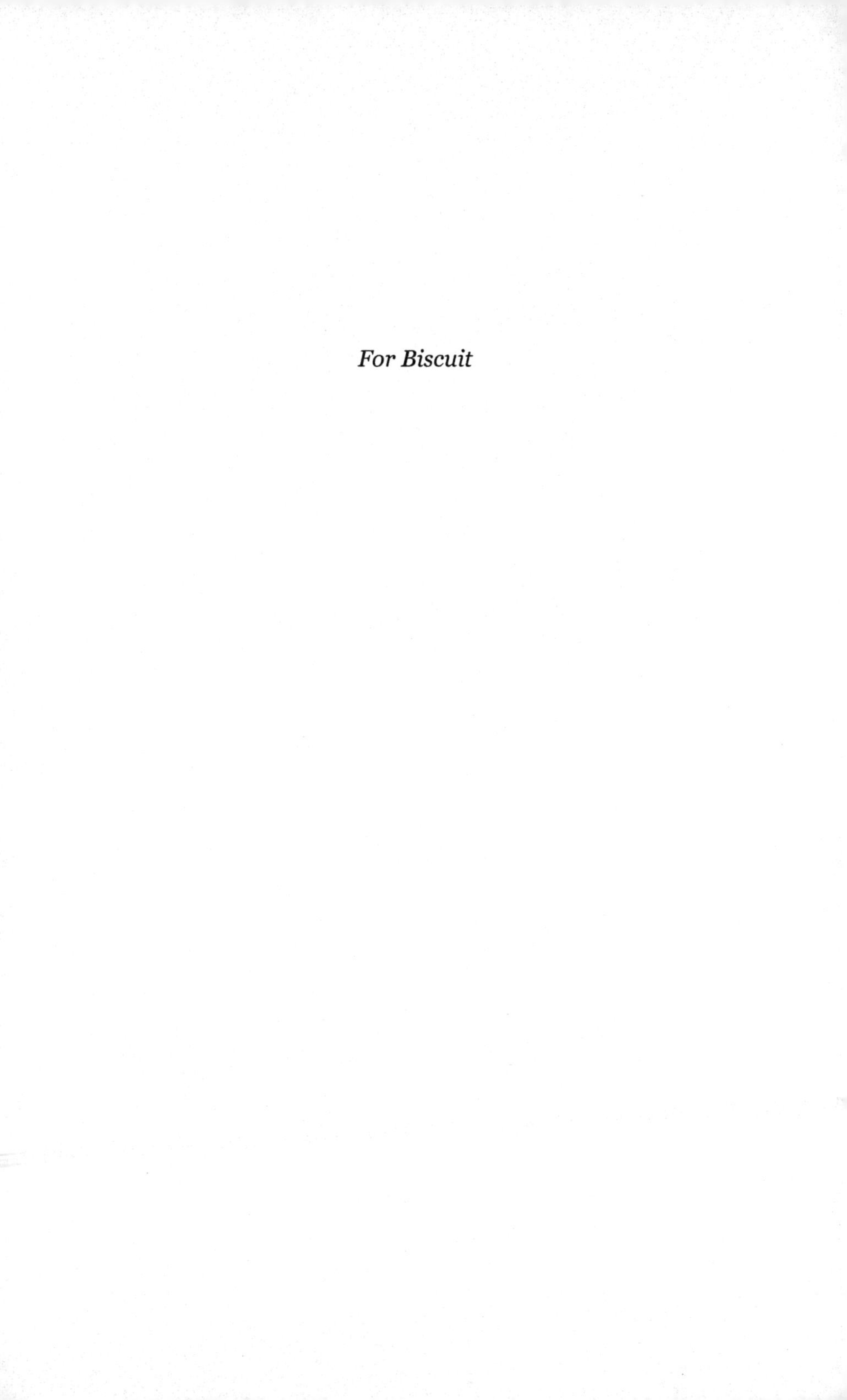

For Biscuit

ACKNOWLEDGMENTS

Thank you to my editors Anna Davis and Kendel Lynn. You are both amazingly talented, and I consider myself blessed to work with you.

Also to Captain Pye of the Peachtree City Police for his advice, entertaining stories, and for organizing the Citizen's Police Academy, one of the best classes I've ever taken.

To the Mystery Minions for all your support.

To Gina Niebrugge for all your help, Hailey for your assistance, Lily and Bill for the encouragement, and Lettie for the dog modeling.

To Fred and Demar Hill, thanks for giving me the inspiration for this book with your wild hog hunt stories, especially the one about the rock star.

To Flat Creek Lodge of Swainsville, Georgia. Thank you for all the assistance in answering my odd questions, for your wonderful hospitality, and excellent food and service. I will never forget your cheese platter. Nor the shrimp and grits. Or homemade jelly. And the local honey. I loved every minute.

And as always, my love and thanks to Trey, Sophie and Luci.

ONE

I found the body. Actually, if you want to get technical, I found his hat, then the body. I had escaped the guests at Big Rack Lodge to do a spot of plein air painting when my peaceful Monet-inspired afternoon took a nasty turn toward disturbing. Landscapes aren't even my usual genre. I'm a portrait painter. But how often do I get a free weekend getaway in the countryside that included a portrait commission?

I'll tell you how often. A big fat never.

I planned to take advantage of time away from the insanity currently running amok in my hometown of Halo for the autumnal splendor of rural Georgia. Watercolor landscapes are always popular with art buyers. And I was in need of the kind of tranquility brought about by a forest glen and the zen-like murmur of wet brushstrokes across heavy dimpled paper.

It's not easy for me to find peace. Especially in my current circumstances. But I had it all. Complete absorption in my woodsy surroundings, even with the damp chill. Total focus on color, form, and space. Bare recognition of the rustling of squirrels and other woodland critters. Or the song calls of birds who had not yet retreated farther south before the temperature dipped beyond nippy. The sharp scent of woodsmoke and the mustier smell of wet leaves hung in the air. But all my attention was given to ochres, umbers, and greens with the occasional sienna.

And then that spot of royal blue.

My position must have prevented me from noticing that dab of blue nestled in the background. I sat slightly to the side of my portable easel on one of those folding camp stools that makes your back ache after thirty minutes, even a back as young as my twenty-six years. I had stood to stretch and step away from the watercolor to check the depth on my middle ground when I zoomed in on that blue in the distance.

For a few seconds, I just stared at the incongruous color, not registering the form. Finally, it occurred to me that this unnatural blue was most likely trash.

Woodsy Owl had taught me well.

I trekked across the clearing to do my environmental duty, admittedly enjoying that sanctimonious high brought about by do-gooding. As I drew closer, I found my watercolor background was actually the border of a shallow ravine. The blue, a ball cap, lay on the edge of the ridge disguised by the accumulation of fallen leaves and pine straw.

I bent over to pick up the hat, smirking at the cursive white "A" embroidered on the front but stopped before actually touching it.

Not three feet from the cap, the ground cover had been disturbed. A skin of water-darkened deep ruts dug into the clay. Muddied tracks mangled the soft cover of pine straw and leaves. More mud and leaves had been churned into clumpy mush, exposing the chewed roots of a late growth of young ferns. My thoughts flew from the Braves cap to the impetus for this weekend.

Hogzilla.

My breath caught, and I took a longer scope on the feral hog rooting, switching my gaze from painterly to hunterly. I had my suspicions that the supposed giant boar terrorizing Big Rack's property and surrounding farms wasn't as large as famed, but the churned ground did give the appearance of something big.

Feral hogs had been wreaking havoc throughout the South for some time, eating crops and causing damage that cost American farmers millions every year.

Raised on my Grandpa Ed's dairy farm, I heard enough swine-induced horror stories to make me no friend to pigs other than what appeared on a dinner plate.

I didn't want anyone with a deer rifle mistaking me for an in-season creature while I painted.

The phone in my hand was also studded with crystals. The stick-on kind that tend to peel off when you shove your phone in and out of pockets.

While I waited for a "Rookie Holt" to speak to me, I watched the police and rubbed my thumb over the faux jewels, fighting the temptation to dial Luke Harper's number. His particular drawl was Southern Comfort to my ears. Strong and smooth with a potent heat that leaves you with a hint of sweetness.

However, I didn't want to be *that* girl. The one who ran to a man every time she verged toward Hot Mess-ville. My life was entirely too full of ramps toward that exit. And anyway, I'd tired of fighting the town's negativity pressing down on my family. About tired enough to give up on Luke. Dating the stepson of the family bent on incarcerating my brother felt like more than I could handle just now.

As much as I pined for Southern Comfort, I was on the wagon. For a girl who favored a nightly nip, it sure was tough.

"Miss Tucker?" A young deputy approached. Rain dripped off the edge of her navy Deputy Sheriff cap and her nose had brightened to match my fuchsia sweatshirt. The hat looked brand new, matching the "Rookie Holt" nickname her fellow officers had teasingly called her.

"Are you okay?" she asked. "Do you feel like answering some questions now?"

I nodded, more reluctant to leave the protection of the sweetgum than to answer questions.

After my initial statement, I had offered to wait in the woods with the local authorities. Because Todd had run back to get help while I stayed with the body, I assumed his interview had been done at the lodge.

"I'm fine. Glad to help."

She shook my hand. "I'm Deputy Deborah Holt. I understand that not only did you find the victim today, you met him last night?"

TWO

The Swinton deputies didn't bother with their rain gear although the earlier sprinkling had turned to a steady drizzle. Bierstadt might have enjoyed the atmosphere for one of his landscape paintings, but for the police, the weather conditions made for miserable work.

After photographing the body and surroundings, they stood in the creek bed, arguing over the best way to lift the stretcher out of the shallow ravine.

The police had immediately recognized the dead man, Abel Spencer, and figured the situation to have been an accident. It seemed Abel often trespassed through the lodge woods. And from their offhand mutterings, I understood they knew Abel as the town drunk. Which didn't make the situation any less sad.

I had met Abel the night before, not knowing his notorious nature. To me, he had not been unlike the grizzled, older men who hung around the farmer's co-op with my Grandpa Ed, talking about tractor parts and the price of seed.

Except Abel had talked about dogs.

I reflected on this as I stood with my back against a sweetgum, trying to stay dry as well as blend into the background, so I could watch the local police work. Although blending proves challenging when you're wearing a neon fuchsia and lime green hand-painted camo sweatshirt with the outline of a deer rack studded in mandarin-orange crystals.

I prefer to bling out my own version of hunting wear.

"Briefly. I had just arrived at Big Rack Lodge. My friends were stowing their suitcases and gear in their cottage, but I'm staying in the main lodge. While I waited for them, I took a walk around the grounds. I was heading toward the parking lot, actually."

"That's when you met the victim? What time was it?"

"We checked in around eight. Couldn't have been more than thirty minutes after, but I don't wear a watch."

She nodded and noted that dubious fact in her notebook.

"Mr. Abel was over at the kennels. Saying goodbye to his dog, Buckshot. He told me Big Rack sometimes used his dogs in hunts. They were real sweet together, Mr. Abel and Buckshot. He was sitting in the kennel with her. Gave me a start."

It had been dark, but the lodge grounds were generously lit. The kennels were located just behind the office, on the way to a parking lot where Max had parked his Range Rover. I couldn't find my sketchbook in my duffel bag and hoped to spot it in Max's fancy SUV. Abel's low murmuring had caused me to glance into a kennel where I spotted a grotesque form. After my heart had returned to my chest and I had convinced myself the lodge didn't keep Hogzillas as pets, I moved closer to the kennel and realized the lumpy shadow with additional legs and a tail had been man and dog combined.

"How did he seem?" asked Holt.

"Fine. A little concerned about his dog's comfort. That was real nice. Also very interested in meeting me. He came out of the kennel, wanting to know who I was and what I was doing. We talked for maybe fifteen minutes. I learned about Buckshot and the rest of the pack. He sure loves those dogs." I swallowed hard. "Loved those dogs, I mean."

The deputy kept her pen flowing over the notebook. "Abel raised hunting dogs for a living."

"He explained which dog was used for what kind of hunt. Sounded like a nice assortment of breeds."

"Did you notice anything else about Mr. Spencer? Any details are appreciated, even if they don't seem important."

"He was wearing the same clothes, near as I can remember. And he was extremely curious about the Hogzilla hunt contest, although I couldn't give him much information."

"What do you mean by extremely curious?"

"He asked a lot of questions, but once he realized I didn't know anything, he stopped."

"Was there anything unusual about his speech or the way he acted?"

I shook my head. Based on the chitchat I had overheard, she likely wanted to know if I'd noticed if Abel had been drinking. I wasn't sure why, but I felt a need to defend this man. There's something about knowing a victim, no matter how briefly, that creates a bond. Law enforcement becomes somewhat immune to this phenomenon. Having grown up around them, I knew flippant remarks worked as a defense mechanism created to protect that immunity. I also knew most law enforcement were more careful about letting those remarks slide in front of civilian witnesses.

Yep, that bothered me.

A voice calling for the deputy stopped me from explaining my headshake. She glanced toward the glen where I had been painting. Two men strode toward us. Mike Neeley, the Big Rack Lodge manager, I had met upon check-in. He wore a Big Rack ball cap and fleece jacket, and moved with his hands shoved in his pockets and shoulders hunched against the rain.

Mike was not local, unlike most of the other Big Rack employees. I felt for Mike, who seemed like a nice guy. The approaching storm had been an inauspicious start for such a huge hunting event. Then to find a death on lodge grounds just before the beginning of the hunt? A PR nightmare.

The other man I hadn't met. I shook the rain from my blonde ponytail and straightened my spine to my full five feet and a half inch. I couldn't help myself.

Call it an inherited defect from my floozy mother, but even if my heart consistently pounded for Luke Harper, the sight of certain specimens still made my pulse race.

Besides, I was an artist and appreciator of natural beauty, whether it be autumnal- or testosterone-enhanced.

He was decked in camo head to toe, but he wore Realtree real well. Nearly six feet of good ol' boy, minus any hint of beer gut, with a five o'clock shadow roughing up a strong jaw. The man looked impervious to the cold and rain. From beneath the brim of his Big Rack cap, serious brown ochre eyes flashed around the surrounds and zeroed in on the fresh hog rooting. He left Mike and the deputy to track the animal evidence, stopping before the yellow tape strung between pine trees near the ravine.

"Do you know this woman?" the deputy asked Mike.

I drew my attention back to the officer and manager. "I met you in the office when I checked in."

"I'm sorry you had to see this." Mike turned from me toward the deputy. "Deborah, Miss Tucker's a guest for the Hogzilla hunt this weekend. You're with the Avtaikin party, right?" He stumbled over Max's name but most did. Ex-Iron Curtain names did not occur naturally to the country vernacular of rural Georgia.

"I'm not hunting, though. I'm here to paint the winner's portrait," I said. "Bob Bass and Max Avtaikin both think they're going to win the hunt. They're calling it a 'kill portrait' and have a little bet going with the portrait as the prize."

"Mr. Bass and his party arrived yesterday too," said Mike. "The Avtaikin party arrived later. Around eight, I think?"

Rookie Holt nodded, probably noting that his reported time jived with mine.

Because I'm a curious sort, I asked, "Who's that?" and nodded toward the Realtree Hottie. Good looking he may be, but I liked knowing who tramped around a suspicious death scene, even if the local law enforcement didn't seem to care. I had learned as much from my Uncle Will.

"Jeff Digby, our head guide," said Mike. "How'd you find Abel?"

"I came out here to catch some quiet and paint when I spotted a hat over by that creek."

"Gosh, I'm sorry about this." Mike shoved his hands deeper in his pockets. "We've told Abel a million times not to trespass, but before the Woodcocks bought this land, lots of folks used an old logging path to cut through to town and across our fields. Can't break old habits, I guess."

"The Woodcocks?"

"Big Rack's owners," said Rookie Holt, and added with small town finality, "They aren't from around here."

"They've got a condo on the top floor of the main lodge units, but the Woodcocks don't come much anymore," said Mike. "They live in Atlanta. Corporate folks."

That explained the two thousand thread-count sheets and thin walls in my room. They paid for sumptuous bedding but skimped on contracting. The owners likely had tired of hearing their guests whoop about deer kills and stopped spending their weekends in their tax write-off.

"Did you alert them about Abel?" asked Rookie Holt.

Mike sighed and nodded. I got the feeling Mike didn't like alerting the Woodcocks to bad news.

"Gutersons probably cut the fence wire again. I keep blocking off that cut-through." The guide, Jeff Digby, paced toward us. His eyes sharpened on Rookie Holt. "Y'all got to get on them more."

"Who are the Gutersons and why would they cut your fence?" I asked, then shot a glance at Holt. My mouth often acts before my brain catches on.

"Neighbors," said Mike, flashing a harsh look at his employee. "Let's not get into this now."

"Sorry, ma'am." Jeff touched the brim of his cap. "Poor ol' Abel. He must have tripped or something. That guy was drunk as Cooter Brown, more than likely."

"Was that his hat? The Braves cap?" I looked at Rookie Holt.

"Yes, ma'am. Guess it came off when he fell."

I wondered why the hat wouldn't have fallen into the creek with poor ol' Abel. "You think he was scared by a wild hog? I noticed the rooting before I saw Mr. Abel."

"That's an old dig." Jeff's eyes gleamed. "And not our big boy, either. This morning I found his fresh wallow in the preserve, not far from the bunkhouse."

"You should check on the fence line anyway," said Mike.

Jeff nodded then hiked off, following the path I had taken to my painting retreat.

Mike glanced at the deputy. "Deborah, if you don't need me, I've got to tend to my guests. We've got one who still hasn't checked in."

"I wish I could do something for Mr. Abel's family." I chewed the inside of my cheek, remembering the old man who had given his dog a final hug before leaving her in the kennel. Neither had known the goodbye would be final.

"No family," said Rookie Holt.

"No friends either," said Mike. "Most gave him a wide berth, unfortunately."

I sucked in a breath. "Abel wasn't a criminal, was he?"

"No ma'am," said Rookie Holt. "Unless you count the trespassing. Abel was just a mangy ol' coot. Always getting into people's business. Kind of sneaky."

"He irritated a lot of people." Mike shook his head. "Plus he was drunk more than half the time. And look what happened. Such a shame."

Rookie Holt glanced toward her senior officers, now hoisting Abel Spencer's body from the ravine. Remembering her place, she cut off the hearsay and got back to her job. "You'll need to do an official witness statement at the station, then you'll be finished with this to enjoy your vacation. Thank you, Miss Tucker."

Dismissed, I followed her through the glen toward the waiting police vehicle. First impressions didn't mean much. The Abel I had met was not the man they described, but this wasn't my town. Maybe Abel Spencer acted differently with strangers. Sometimes familiarity did breed contempt.

Maybe he had just been unlucky enough to be born on the wrong side of the tracks, like me. I felt sorry for him. Whatever he did to tick people off in town, no one deserved to die falling into a ditch. Which made me a little curious to know more about the night of his passing. Did he tie one on after leaving his dog? And in that case, why was he found in the lodge's woods?

Because there was one significant problem with Abel Spencer drunkenly falling into that ditch without his blue Braves cap.

When I had met Abel, he wasn't drunk.

Three

The Swinton police station needed better coffee. Rookie Holt also needed a refresher on "establishing rapport with witnesses." A certain gray-eyed Forks County deputy (more of a light Payne's gray bordering on Blue Deep, although I still had not captured that color to my liking) had explained the importance of that interview strategy to me on more than one occasion. Like the time I suspected little Clayton Jeffries of pilfering from his sister's Girl Scout cookie cash box while she was busy talking up the Thin Mints to Mrs. Meyers. According to my personal deputy, my interview techniques with Clayton's best friend (and eyewitness), Jeremiah, could have used some work.

But that's neither here nor there. I'm not a professional. I can't say the same for Swinton's Rookie Holt. But she was young and eager to get her commander to sign off on our interview.

"Look, I appreciate your concern," she said in a voice that didn't mark any appreciation for my concern. "But expressing your condolences to Abel Spencer's people is not necessary."

"There's got to be someone. My visit with Mr. Abel might be a very comforting story for them to hear. Knowing in his final hours, he was caring for his dog and friendly to strangers."

She shook her head.

I pressed my point, hoping for at least one name who would be sorry that Abel Spencer had died.

There had to be someone who knew him differently. "I'm sure they'd like to know he hadn't been on some kind of tear before he fell. The Abel Spencer I met is not the Abel Spencer y'all described."

"Because Abel Spencer—" Rookie Holt zipped her lips in a firm line, probably remembering recent training in spilling too much info to overeager witnesses. "Look, I'm glad he was friendly to you. And he was good with his dogs. That's all you need to know. You're finished here. Unless we need you later."

"Look, I can't bring anyone a casserole, but I can shake a hand and say I'm sorry. It's not like I often meet people just before their accidental death. That's a remarkable event. My Uncle Will could vouch for me. He probably knows your sheriff pretty well since, as Forks County Sheriff, Uncle Will knows everybody. Particularly other country law enforcement."

"Are you threatening me?" Rookie Holt's spine cracked as her shoulders tensed.

"No, ma'am." My super-ego began butt-kicking my id. I had gone too far again.

"Let me tell you, Miss Tucker. Flashing your uncle's name around may get you out of tickets and such in your own town, but it won't work here."

"I was just trying to be helpful. And it doesn't get me out of tickets. Believe me on that one."

"Witnesses don't offer casseroles and comforting stories to victim's families they don't know. You're old enough to know that." She consulted my witness statement form. "Twenty-six years old, in fact. What's wrong with you?"

Well, I thought, my daddy died when I was a toddler. My momma took off soon after, and my moral compass, Grandma Jo, stopped moving about the time she passed. Which was when I was fifteen. As my brother and sister do act their emotional age, I thought I was doing pretty good.

Instead I said, "I was raised to bring casseroles and comfort the grieving. Although Red says my need to help victims of unfortunate circumstances is most likely a form of projection."

"Red's your therapist?" She clicked her pen and flipped her notebook open.

"Bartender. He just watches a lot of daytime TV."

"Thank you for your testimony." The air nearly frosted with her words. "That's all we need from you."

However, filling out a witness testimony sheet was not all I needed. Some could question my compulsion to learn more about the victim, but meeting someone just before they plummet to their death? That's an event you can't file under "weird shit that just happened" and go on about your day. I had to spend a weekend hanging with rich and famous people. Hopefully making a good impression so they'd want to hire me for future portraits. I needed my head in that game. But my head was in the "I just met a man before he died" game.

Not a fun game.

Particularly when I couldn't resolve the man I met with the man the police muttered about under their breath.

After a hot shower and change of clothes, I still hadn't thrown off the chill of finding Mr. Abel's body.

Unnerved, I grabbed my phone and let my finger hover over my favorite speed dial number.

Before I could give in to the impulse, the phone shook in my hand and sang "I Walk The Line." The personal ringtone for Max Avtaikin, a.k.a. the Bear. Not that he's hairy. Just big and scary. And able to score from shady dealings quicker than a grizzly snatches salmon.

But I've pretty much forgiven him for that trait.

"Hey, Max, sorry to keep you waiting. I'm heading downstairs," I answered, in my chirpy customer service voice. Always make the art patron happy. Even when you've found a dead man earlier that day.

"You must hurry." His growl almost disguised his Slavic accent. "I need your help with this rock star idiot."

"Come again? I thought Bob Bass was your friend. Why else would you bet to have a winning portrait made? Who does that?"

"He is the business associate." The Bear's growl took a turn toward abashed. "Our bet was the mistake created by too much vodka. In truth, he tries my patience. The man lives on flattery. That is not something I do well. He also likes to give too much—what you call?—trashing talk."

"Talking trash. Bob Bass is an international star and adored by every gun lover in the country for his stance on the right to bear arms." My voice shook. Meeting Bob Bass was going to be the high point in my wretched day. "Trash talk's natural with competitors."

"I also believe in this American right, but do you see me on the television proclaiming I am the hunting expert? In my country, we hunt to feed our family. I know hunting. Bob Bass grew up in Beverly Hills. What does he know?"

"Beverly Hills? I thought he grew up in the hills of Kentucky. Or was it a West Virginia coal mine?" I squeezed my eyes shut to help pry facts from my memory. "I know, a Louisiana bayou."

"Songs," Max spat. "His grandfather was lipstick tycoon and his mother was the actress."

"You are really bursting my bubble. I love Bob Bass."

"You love the idea of the Bob Bass. The real Bob Bass is Fortnum Robert Bassler the third. He hired the PR firm after his first album didn't sell. They discovered the rural population enjoys his music. So they reinvented Bob Bass as the big hunter."

"How do you know this?"

"I made it my business to know."

"What business?"

"My own."

I recognized the defensive tone disguised as swagger. "Bob Bass plays poker in your secret casino, doesn't he? You had him investigated. You better keep in mind, your friendly wager for the winning portrait might lose you a rich customer."

"I am spending much money on you this weekend, Artist. That does not include your advice."

"Very true," I said quickly. "And even though you have destroyed the enjoyment I once had in Bob Bass's music, I will do my best to flatter the rural interloper and get you through the weekend."

"Perhaps he will have you appear on the television show with the reality of himself."

"You mean his reality show," I corrected. Max's English sometimes disappeared between the Carpathians and the Appalachians.

"It is too bad Bass's filming of this weekend will portray his defeat."

I could imagine Max's icy blue eyes gleaming with excitement. A mocking smile would flash across his normally stoic features.

The man took to competition the way a cougar takes to a limping deer. I had a feeling this supposed "trash talk" was of the personal variety.

"My people, we have the history of great hunters..."

I switched off Max's rattle about the prowess of Slavic sportsmen and waited for a pause to change the subject. "I have a funny feeling about Mr. Abel."

"Who is Mr. Abel? Is he also in the hunt? My last count was six contestants."

I took a deep breath to block the image of a body from my head. "Mr. Abel is the man I found in the creek."

"Ah." Max paused. "I am sorry. Of course, you must be distressed over this tragedy. What is the funny feeling?"

"I don't know how to explain it," I said. "But I don't think Mr. Abel took a drunken spill into that ravine. For one thing, he would have gotten pretty damn hammered in a short amount of time, because when I met him earlier that night, he wasn't drunk."

"It depends on the drink and the person's condition."

I wasn't easily dissuaded. "And another thing. His hat fell off on top of the ridge, but the body was in the creek, facing up. He fell backward. How does the hat fall forward if the body falls backward?"

"What are you saying?"

"According to Rookie Holt, Abel wasn't liked by anyone."

"You suspect the foul play? You do have the habit of jumping the conclusions, Artist. A social misfit does not make the strong motive for murder."

"But I saw Mr. Abel's face, Bear." I fought back tears. "He looked scared. That also does not jive with the man I met earlier."

Max pulled in a breath. "Of course, if he fell..."

"And Hogzilla didn't scare him. The Big Rack's outfitter said the giant hog was on a different part of the property. The rootings weren't fresh enough."

"So the beast was spotted on property? Excellent." Max caught himself with a cough. "I see. The police are investigating? You told them your concerns?"

"Well, yes, I guess."

"Then you have done your duty. Do not worry yourself needlessly. It is sad thing, of course, but there is nothing more you can do. I will see you soon."

"But I need to do something. The police act like they're writing this off." I spoke to a dial tone.

I hung up and palmed my phone, ready to snap it shut, when I noticed my thumb, once again, hovered over Luke's speed dial number. I caught myself. This was a working vacation. Tragedy or no tragedy, the art show must go on. Instead, I left my phone to charge, polished my best boots, and practiced my happy customer service smile before heading out.

In the lodge elevator, mellow jazz played a version of "Blue Christmas."

Where was "A Holly Jolly Christmas" when you needed it?

FOUR

I hurried through the guest lodge foyer. The hunt activities officially started in the Twenty Point bar with a meet and greet, followed later by a fixed menu dinner. The rain hadn't returned and I could smell pork chops frying, giving me hope for a better evening. My nose led me across the stepping stone path toward the Twenty Point restaurant and its famed country cooking. Having brunched off property before my landscape painting debacle, I'd been looking forward to this meal for weeks.

And despite the tragic afternoon, I still did. My stomach was odd like that.

On the way, I passed quaint timbered buildings settled amid beautifully landscaped grounds. Behind the guest lodge, a set of luxurious cabins circled a large fishing pond.

The entourage stayed in the guest lodge. Todd, however, had somehow inveigled an invitation to stay in the Bear's cabin. A two bedroom and two bath with a full living area, small kitchen, full bar, and fishing porch.

And, I'm just guessing here, five thousand thread-count Egyptian cotton sheets.

Todd, the inveigler, flagged me from his spot under the eaves of the restaurant. "Everyone's here. Are you okay?"

"I won't pretend finding a body hasn't thrown me for a loop. I've got a lot of weird ideas buzzing around my head where there should be thoughts about networking with future portrait clients. How about you?"

"I'm fine. My thoughts aren't so weird, except for worrying about you. But that's kind of weird for me."

I hugged him. Sometimes Todd was a few peas short of a casserole. But he meant well.

"Did I miss anything yet?"

"Not really. Bob Bass didn't play a single song. But he sure likes to talk."

"The Bear thinks Bob Bass is a phony. He's from Beverly Hills, not West Virginia."

"I don't believe it. I was hoping we could jam together. I brought my sticks."

I glanced at the drumsticks poking from the pocket of his cargo shorts, just above the cherry tattoo. "Guess I should get in there and meet the contestants."

Todd held open the door to the Twenty Point. I dashed inside the foyer and bumped into something large, furry, and wearing Santa's hat.

"Jiminy Christmas." I hopped away from the bear, embarrassed by my startle. The bear wore an expression that didn't match his Santa hat. More snarly than jolly.

"You okay?" said Todd. "Not like you to be nervy."

"I was just surprised by the Christmas getup, that's all." My new role as witness seemed to have made me jumpy. "I'm sure the hunter nor the bear expected this fine specimen to be used as a holiday decoration."

"You think that's bad? Check this out." Todd hooked a thumb at the dining room.

Under the tin-roofed rafters, more stuffed animals played. Squirrels chased raccoons up the wooden beams bracketing the open roof supports. Racks from departed bucks hung on the walls. Above the entrance to the kitchen, a stage had been erected where deer knelt beside dancing foxes, rabbits played with pheasants, and quail popped from bushes with the aid of wires. A sweet tribute to lives lost to arrow or bullet.

And all were wearing Santa hats or tinsel crowns.

"I wonder if this was the Woodcocks' idea?" I shook my head. "Another example of how artists suffer for their work. The buyer's interpretation is often different from their own."

Todd shrugged. "I think it's kind of cute."

I turned toward the narrow bar on the side of the restaurant. There another crowd of creatures mingled. Some glassy-eyed. All nametag-stickered and clutching cocktail glasses. On my way to my room, I had gotten the contestant rundown after bumping into Bob's manager. I watched them for a few minutes, awed by the individual incongruities that formed a group with one goal in mind: to be the one who nailed a ginormous wild hog.

A rangy man fighting his age dominated the small group with a vociferous "aw shucks" attitude and blaring self-amused laughter. His black cowboy hat sported peacock feathers and his fingers sparkled with rings. Bob Bass. I would have recognized him even without the electric guitar swung across his back, bandolier-style. Electric, I noted, without an amp hookup.

Max stood next to him, pretending to listen while discreetly checking out the raven-haired beauty on Bob's right. In name alone, Peach Payne had given Bob a tabloid boost with flavor of the month jokes. Her gravity-defying cleavage and scarlet lipstick had caught more attention than just Max's. I feared our bartender might suffer a neck sprain from his ogle. However, Peach's focus remained on the phone she palmed while sipping a martini.

Another middle-aged man suited in a suede jacket and bolo tie alternately smiled and stole cagey glances at the other contestants. The scent of Atlanta money oozing from his pores told me this was Clinton Sparks.

His wife, Jenny, a blonde weighted in makeup and diamonds, spoke to an African-American girl of about eighteen. Junior Olympic Rifleman LaToya Peterson had a reputation as a crack shot and a destiny to become the next cover girl for *Garden & Gun* magazine.

At the edge of the group, appearing displaced and slightly dazed by the moneyed crowd, stood a thirtyish bubba wearing gaiters over his Wranglers. Not a bad looking guy, but his discomfort masked it well. The local raffle winner, Rick Miller, I guessed.

Already at the bar, Todd caught my attention, pointing toward the pint glass he had just ordered. I strode to his side, accepted the drink with thanks, and took a sip for luck before plowing through the crowd to meet Mr. Bass. Todd followed with his own beer and Max's cane.

All the fancy dress made me glad I had worn my bedazzled denim and a newly accessorized sweater for dinner. I had unraveled the sweater's edges and beaded the threads with tiny silver reindeer buttons. Silver pigs would have been more appropriate, but reindeer seemed more in keeping with the season. I assumed the odd looks the ladies threw me were due to jealousy. Not everyone can successfully bling out Walmart.

Todd leaned into my ear. "I still can't believe we're in the same room with Bob Bass."

"Let's hope Max misinterpreted Bob Bass's bio," I whispered back.

"Artist," said Max, lightening from his glower. "This is the singer with whom I have the portrait bet."

"Hey there, sweet thing." Bob's blinding smile looked as perfect as my deceased Great-Gam's set of purchased quality teeth. "Friends with the cripple here, huh? I see you brought his cane. Ha, just kidding there, Avtaikin."

"Nice to meet you, Mr. Bass. I'm a big fan."

"Course you are, honey. Call me Bob. I bet you're looking forward to setting your paintbrush to my handsome features next to a big ol' ugly hawg."

His harsh laugh caused a slight shudder in Miss Cleavage. "I don't see why you'd want to look at some nasty pig hanging on your walls."

"Peach, there's a pride you get from bagging such a fine animal, especially if this boar is as big as they say. Just wait until you center Mr. Hog in your crosshairs. Not that you'll get him, honey, but I'm sure you'll understand the feeling once we start the hunt."

Peach's nose wrinkled, but she raised her chin. "Whatever you say, Bob."

"You know it, babe." Bob smacked her bottom, causing her martini glass to slosh over the side.

I swigged my beer, disappointed by the ease with which celebrities fell off pedestals.

"We'll take the party to my cottage later, what do you say? Y'all are invited." Bob grinned. Light glanced off his teeth and refracted off my beer, spotting my vision. "What happens at Big Rack stays at Big Rack. Am I right?"

Peach spoke with her eyes on her martini-sticky phone. "Right, Bob."

"My wife and I are regulars at Big Rack," said Clinton Sparks. "We love it here."

"When we're not on hunting safari in Montana or Africa," added Jenny.

"Have you hunted here before?" I asked LaToya, hoping to find a normal hunter in the crowd.

LaToya shook her head. "No, ma'am. I'm from south Georgia. But we have a lot of problems with wild hogs there too. I've had plenty of experience and I'm feeling pretty confident about winning. I plan on bringing back a trophy."

The man in gaiters bobbed his head. At our recognition, Rick cast us with a smile that quickly disappeared.

"I guess you probably hunt around here, Rick, right?" I asked.

Light brown eyes blinked at me. "How'd you know?"

"I heard a local guy won a raffle and you're the last man standing, so to speak."

"I've never hunted in Big Rack's preserve. Not legally, anyway." He squeezed out a short laugh. "I mostly shoot squirrel and rabbit. Sometimes deer. The lodge is lending me a better rifle. I'm pretty lucky, I guess. I don't care about the trophy so much, but I could sure use that twenty thousand in prize money."

A wave of uncomfortable smiles flickered through the hunt party. Smiles used in polite situations to acknowledge gauche remarks. As a frequent recipient of that particular smile, I found it easy to recognize.

"Bob Bass." Max used a forced chuckle to move the conversation away from their discomfort. "Now that you have met the artist, I'm sorry Miss Tucker will not get the chance to paint you in the winner's portrait. Perhaps I should allow her to paint you as a gift. A gesture of goodwill."

"Goodwill my ass," said Bob. "I already said I'm gonna win, so no worries on the outcome of the contest. You're gimping around like an old man, Avtaikin. No way you can outshoot me. Yes, ma'am, you're going to see my face next to that pig's."

I found myself considering the perspective I could take. In my mind, I had already entitled the painting *Two Pigs*.

"We will see about that, Bob." Max raised his tumbler. "To the best man or woman winning."

The others raised their assorted glasses and murmured agreement.

Now I understood why Max refused the cane he so obviously needed. And why he wanted help with Bob Bass. Charming jackasses was an art unto itself. Although this artist lacked proficiency in that particular medium.

Behind Bob, his lackeys buzzed in a whispered conference.

"Excuse me. I'm Bob's publicist, Risa Rispoli," said a pretty young redhead. "We're outfitting Bob and Peach with GoPro cameras for the contest since the lodge wouldn't allow a camera team on the hunt. While I have you here, we need signatures giving permission to be filmed for Bob's reality program, *Rockin' The Hunt*."

I pulled a Berol number two from my embellished jeans pocket. "I'll sign."

"Are you one of the contestants?"

"No," I said. "But you could film me painting Mr. Bass's portrait. How about that?"

"We just want Bob hunting. Thanks anyway."

Max shook his head. "You do not have my permission. No television."

"We can keep your name anonymous," said Risa. "We could write, 'hunt contestant' under your face when you're shown."

"No."

"We could fuzz out your features."

"Or could you insert my face over his?" said Todd.

"No, we can't do that." She fixed her gaze on Max, pleading. "It will be almost impossible not to show you on camera unless we do minute editing."

"So you will do the minute editing." Max broke eye contact, ending the conversation.

"I don't know either." Jenny Sparks giggled nervously. "Wouldn't want to be caught without my makeup on."

"I'd need to call my sponsors first," said LaToya.

"Don't use my name either," said Rick. "I don't like appearing in pictures."

Risa exchanged a look with Bob. "Usually people are happy to be on the show."

"Don't worry about it, honey." Bob reached around Peach to give Risa a squeeze, causing more martini spillage. "Peach and I will be the stars of the show. And that giant hawg. I think we're dividing into groups anyway, so as long as my guide doesn't care about being on TV, I don't see a problem. More face time for me."

Risa's neck reddened and she busied herself pulling contracts from her briefcase. "Everyone needs to sign. Just check yes or no to the TV appearance, and write an addendum if you want your name used or not."

As the contestants examined the fine print of their contracts, I leaned into Todd for a whisper. "I don't understand why everyone is so spooked by appearing on Bob's reality show."

Todd nodded. "I'd do it in a heartbeat."

"Me too. That's rich folks for you," I said. "Always worried about appearances."

"Rick's not rich."

"True. It's almost like they don't want to get caught doing something on camera they shouldn't." I slanted a look at the party examining the paperwork. "Except for the ones wanting to be on camera doing stuff they shouldn't."

Five

Their paperwork finished, the group returned to sipping drinks and comparing hunt stories, which began to sound like episodes of *Deadliest Catch*. My mind was still on possible reasons for TV appearance refusals. On the off chance *Rockin' The Hunt* could be dubbed for Max's ex-commie homeland, I suspected a few people there might use the show for a Bear tracking device. Rick Miller, on the other hand, had surprised me. Folks of Rick's ilk normally chambered a "hey y'all, lookie here" whenever someone broke out a camera. YouTube was full of our willingness to look like idiots for the world to watch. And as for the Sparks, why would they care if the cameras caught them stalking Hogzilla? They had said they were regulars at Big Rack.

These people made not one bit of sense.

I turned to Todd as I often did in times of confusion. "You want to get out of here for a minute? I'd take another beer, but fresh air is much cheaper at this place."

He grinned and nodded.

"Maybe we can check on something while we're out."

I wanted a distraction. The local phone book had contained Abel Spencer's address. My lodge room had contained a local phone book. Some would call that a sign. Or standard hotel phone book practice. Either way, I felt a quick visit to Mr. Spencer's homestead was in order. Just to round out my curiosity on the man. I couldn't focus on schmoozing while my brain kept taking trips to what's-the-deal-with-Abel-Spencer land. I'll admit my brain doesn't always work like others. It runs along the tracks toward Morbidity and Inquisitiveness Junction. Often with a quick stop at Meddling-ville. We'll just chalk it up to my artistic nature and not to my need to fix lemonade from my life's constant barrage of lemons.

Anyway, Todd was used to my brain if others were not.

"How was your conversation with the Swinton PD?" I asked Todd while clinging to an armrest as to avoid whiplash on the rutted road we traveled.

Not a metaphorical road, mind you, although some might find that true as well.

We had borrowed the keys to Max's Range Rover and followed the dirt road from the lodge. Evening had not quite sprung, but the clouds had left the late afternoon in what felt like a perpetual dusk.

"Did they question your motives for being out in the woods?"

"No." Todd kept his eyes on the pocked road. "Why? We weren't trespassing, were we?"

"Not as lodge guests. But those Swinton police were a bit prickly."

"I didn't notice, but you are more tuned into that sort of thing."

"Well, offering to bring casseroles to victim's families makes Swinton police awfully prickly."

Todd cut me a quick worried look. "Baby, you don't know how to make a casserole."

"Exactly. That's why I thought a personal condolence more appropriate. Which is why we're headed to Mr. Spencer's home. Maybe some kin or friends are hanging about. I can give my respects and get on with the weekend."

We could hear the dogs before the sorry homestead came into view. Abel Spencer's property had been carved out of a bit of woods on the edge of Swinton. A house as big as a thimble with rotting steps and sills. The pine tar-stained roof had more depressions than the moon had craters. No vehicles in the drive, although a redneck smorgasbord propagated among the weeds. Old grills and dead lawnmowers. Assorted pipes and wooden wire spools. Even Piggly Wiggly shopping buggies.

This sort of image was not uncommon in my hometown of Halo. Everyone knows spare parts come in handy. Grandpa Ed threw away nothing. My alleged convict of a brother kept a revolving collection of broken-down vehicles in Grandpa's barn. True, the farm didn't have this appearance of a recent tornado touchdown, but I could cut Mr. Abel a break. It sounded like he had been a bachelor. Left to their own devices, men often needed cleaning up after.

"No yellow tape," I noted.

"I thought his death was an accident," said Todd.

"But still, any accidental death like this should require some investigation. Uncle Will usually traces the victim's steps back a couple days before their death."

"Maybe the police didn't make it out here yet."

"In that case, we better be careful. Don't want to leave any unnecessary evidence."

"I thought you were just looking to offer sympathies. You didn't say anything about looking around the man's property."

"Do you hear those poor dogs? I just want to check on them. Where's the harm in that?"

Todd gave me a look that said he didn't believe me for a minute but popped the Range Rover door. That's the good thing about Todd. He's got a sense of adventure. Even if he doubted my motives, he'd go along with me anyway.

We picked our way around the rusting junk, circling away from the house and checking for the mark of recent trampling so as not to disrupt any investigational clues. At least the drizzle had stopped, leaving behind a damp cold that seeped beneath reindeer sweaters and darkened already somber moods.

Behind the house, the weeds gave way to the soft matting of pine straw. I paused in wonderment. What Abel Spencer had not spent or maintained on his house and yard, he had on a dog kennel.

Rubber coated chain-link enclosed a half-acre that included a large cedar shed with doggy-sized doors that looked like a home where Snow White's small friends could comfortably reside. From behind the fence, an assortment of breeds watched my approach. A yelping beagle. Three galloping Labs. A springer spaniel. Some kind of pointer or setter paced the fence line. And behind them all, a Bluetick Coonhound wailed.

I ambled toward the fence, speaking in calm, low tones. The dogs greeted me, their eyes piteously sad, the heads drooping, tails pointed at the ground. My heart hiccuped, but I kept my voice strong and easy to buoy their mood.

"Hey there," I told the pack. "Are you missing Mr. Abel already? You're good dogs, aren't you?"

The tails wagged in agreement, but without joy. Slick noses pushed through the chain link and I put my palm up for each to smell in turn.

"We used to have a dog at the farm." I spoke to Todd, but meant my words for the dogs.

"I didn't know that." Todd's long fingers fondled a Lab ear.

"This was before Grandma Jo passed. Daisy was a mutt, not like these pedigrees. She was meant to be a farm dog, but Daisy liked the house. She stuck close to Grandma Jo.

"Grandpa keeps goats now," I told the dogs. "They don't like me much. Or they like me too much. I can't tell with goats."

All but the Bluetick queued up to drop their heads, reminding me of a receiving line at a funeral. They took the scratching without real enjoyment. Once petted, the group broke to resume their anxious wait for Abel.

"You poor dogs." I folded my arms to hug out the cold and leaned my forehead against the fence to watch them. "They must have really loved Abel. Glad someone did."

Daisy had succumbed to this sort of mourning when we had lost Grandma Jo to cancer. At the time, Daisy had been five years younger than my fifteen, so I had known Daisy the entire time I lived at the farm. Grandma Jo had been the mother my momma couldn't be and losing her felt like God had given up on the Tucker kids. He took the most tender of the pair that raised us. I tried to find comfort in Daisy, but she couldn't be comforted herself. Daisy stopped eating. Couldn't drink. She wouldn't move from beneath the kitchen table where she had watched Grandma Jo cook.

Daisy died two weeks later. Grief killed her. We never got another dog.

I watched this pack waiting for Abel and felt my heart shatter.

"They said Abel was a drunk and sneaky," I said. "But I bet these beauties never went hungry. Look, Todd. Mr. Abel put an a/c unit on the doghouse when he doesn't even have a window unit on his own."

The beagle cut her barking to growl, catching the attention of the Labs. They rushed the fence, barking. I turned. Rookie Holt stood near the edge of the house, watching us with her hands hovering near her belt.

"Shit," I muttered beneath my breath.

"What are you doing here?" She strode forward, her eyes narrowing beneath the brim of her cap. "You're trespassing."

"We were careful not to walk near the house and to watch for anything suspicious or recently disturbed," I said. "I just wanted to see his dogs. I thought maybe there'd be someone here."

"I told you there's no one. Go back to the lodge." Rookie Holt notched her chin higher. "And stay there."

"Why haven't you—"

"Yes, ma'am." Todd grabbed my arm and hurried me forward.

"Their water bowl is full," I called over my shoulder. "Mr. Abel's got one of those self-watering types. Their food bowl too, but I'm guessing that's because they're not eating."

The dogs began another barking frenzy. A moment later, the sound of tires churning on damp Georgia clay carried to our non-canine ears. Todd and I paused next to a rusted shopping buggy just short of the drive.

Rookie Holt halted next to us, then took three steps forward. "Who's that now?" she muttered.

We watched an old Blazer emerge from the forested lane and bump into the weedy drive. The Blazer jerked to a stop, reversed, and roared back down the lane.

"Why did they do that?" I wondered aloud.

"Saw the patrol car, likely. Rick Miller, that sumbitch." The words slid from under her breath. Catching her mistake, she flushed. Rookie Holt's rookie status was not improving. "You two go on and get out of here."

We did our version of hightailing under Rookie Holt's young eyes. I waited to voice my question until Todd had pulled out of Abel Spencer's weedy drive. "Isn't Rick Miller the name of the local guy in the contest?"

"I think so," said Todd.

"He must have known Mr. Abel. But the way Rookie Holt said his name, sounds like Rick Miller's about as popular as Abel Spencer." I worried my lip as I mulled that over. "I need to talk to him."

"Why?"

"Because I just don't understand how a body lands in the woods and nobody in this town seems to care. Something's not right here."

SIX

Back in the Twenty Point Bar, Todd and I found the contestants as we had left them an hour earlier, save for a few exceptions. Big Rack Manager Mike and Head Guide Jeff Digby had joined them. Rick Miller had disappeared. And an extra hour's worth of alcohol had been consumed.

I hesitated before taking our place among the inebriated, wondering if I could slip away again to look for Rick. Talking to Rick about Abel interested me more than mingling with this crowd. But a job was a job and I already had my designated coffee/find-more-about-Abel break.

"Do you think Rick followed us to Abel Spencer's?" Todd's disappointment in Bob Bass had eclipsed my own and he seemed just as reluctant to return to our station. "Why would he leave?"

"That, my friend, is a very good question." I pondered those queries for a moment. "Maybe Rick didn't know about Abel Spencer's death and heard about it during the hobnob? Drove out to see if it was true?"

"Who would have told him? The guy barely talked to anyone."

"The bartender? Why would Rick follow us? He didn't know us from Adam."

My eyes cut to Max's, where he had been silently signaling a "get the hell over here and help me" kind of look. Or whatever the equivalent of that was in his country.

We scooted to the bar to join him in the small cluster of hunters. I hoped I looked as abashed as I felt.

I had no right to put Abel Spencer's death over a patron's needs. No right. Just an overwhelming desire. I had taken this job partly to sit on the mental box containing all the crap from home. The death of Abel Spencer made for a more interesting cushion than celebrity hunters.

The Bear leaned into my ear. "You were gone longer than I expected, Artist."

"Sorry, just had to take care of something," I whispered. "I'm here now. Ready to dazzle Bob Bass with my charm and get him to forget that although he's lost a lot of money in your secret casino, you still want to beat him in this crazy contest."

"Your understanding is not accurate, but it is enough."

Max straightened, but not before flicking a crimson leaf caught on one of my dangling reindeer. "You have been in the woods again? Not the scene of the death, I hope." His voice fell into a lull in the contestants' conversation.

The party turned to stare at me.

"Sorry for interrupting. Hope we didn't miss anything." With their eyes on me, I felt the need to explain. "We were just visiting the house of the man I found in the ravine earlier."

"You went to Abel's house?" said Jeff Digby. "Why would you do that?"

"Pay respects." My mumble was lost in Todd's reply.

"Cherry thinks there's more to his fall than an accident." Todd rubbed his hip where I poked him. "No need to worry about her, though. She does this thing all the time. When she gets a notion something's not right, Cherry's like a terrier on a squirrel. Until it's proved one way or another, she'll keep barking up that tree."

"What do you mean there's more to it?" said Jeff. "That's not what the police said."

"The police can't say anything officially until they've finished their investigation," I explained.

"Then let the police handle it. Can we get back to our earlier conversation?" Jenny Sparks set her empty wine glass on the bar. "I want to make sure I understand what's going on with the hunt."

"We were just talking about the issue of weather," said Manager Mike. "We're leaving for the bunkhouse tomorrow afternoon. The contest will start Friday evening. But another front's moving in. It'll keep the hog from scenting us but may make it harder to track him. And harder to travel."

"The problem is mud." Jeff Digby let that fact hang in the air. Mud in Georgia is serious. We're mostly a red clay state, which is great for pottery and bad for pretty much everything else. "We've got five all-terrain utility vehicles to take everyone out to the bunkhouse. It's a long haul on a dry day. We're going to split up from there, each party with their own guide. But with the rain we've had and more coming, even the UTVs might get stuck. If we get the hog, we'll probably need to bury it out there too."

"Eww," said Peach.

"That means you," Bob pointed his rocks tumbler at me, "need to come out with us. I want my portrait done with that pig. Can't leave him long before he starts stinking, and I'm not standing next to him any longer than I have to."

"The weather sounds iffy for working outside. I could easily paint your portrait from a photo when you get back."

"Everyone knows it's better to have a live subject. What kind of artist are you?"

I kept my mouth shut when I longed to point out that half of the subject in his "kill portrait" wouldn't be "live."

"You are known for quick sketching, is it not true, Artist?" asked Max. "You make the winner's sketch out the doors and paint inside. Plein Air pig."

I sighed and nodded.

"Maybe I could hold a tarp over her," said Todd.

"Now you're cooking with gas," said Bob. "I like the way you think, boy."

Todd beamed. Unlike me, Todd easily suffered fools.

"What about the business of this death on property?" Clinton Sparks didn't seem to mind his abruptness, but his wife blushed. "Will the investigation interrupt the hunt?"

"Swinton police said by tomorrow afternoon, we should be good to go," said Mike. "Mr. Spencer's accident was not in the reserve, anyway. We've got target practice in the morning and we'll head out after lunch."

"Do you think it'll hurt Big Rack's business?" With his eyes on Mike, Clinton sipped from his scotch.

"What Clinton means," said Jenny Sparks, "is we're just such fans of Big Rack, we'd hate for anyone to think badly of the lodge."

"I thought Henry and Lois would be here tonight," continued Clinton.

"I haven't seen the Woodcocks yet." Mike forced a weak smile. "How about we get dinner started? Go ahead and take your seats in the dining room. We've got a specially prepared menu."

"I hope it includes those pork chops I smell," I said.

"Our new gourmet chef's taking on all the cooking for your weekend," said Jeff Digby. "Viktor doesn't recommend eating certain meats or dairy before a big hunt, though. Pigs have a great sense of smell and they'll get wind of the oils seeping through your skin."

"I guess a hog might be offended by pork chops," I conceded.

"I'm sure Viktor will have something better than pork chops," said Jenny. "I love his foie gras."

I didn't know in what world foie gras would be better than pork chops, but not the one I resided in. "I've heard a lot about your local cook. The housekeeper told me she makes some good chicken fried steak."

"That's true. Jessica's food is amazing." Jeff's gaze drifted to the ceiling. Probably recalling the delicious chicken fried steak he was now denying the hunt members. "But Viktor is very good at the foodie stuff."

"Let's see what Viktor planned for tonight's meal." Mike held out his arm. "This way, y'all."

The others began making their way to the dining room.

I caught Todd's arm. Ominous descriptions like "foodie" and "foie gras" didn't sit well after an afternoon spent with the police.

Particularly when my nose had sussed out pork chops.

"I don't know about this fancy food," I whispered. "I had French food once and they gave me snails. It was like eating erasers dipped in butter. I've been counting on pork chops ever since catching the scent, and my stomach's not so good with shocks to the system."

"Maybe we won't get snails," said Todd. "Foie gras sounds Chinese. You like eggrolls."

"I'll just sneak into the kitchen and see if this Viktor can let me eat regular food. I'll tell him my snail story and he'll be real sympathetic, I'm sure."

"I don't know, Cherry," said Todd. "They made a special menu for us. Now that I think of it, eggrolls sound pretty good."

"Todd, my sister and Pearl have had a kitchen war for months. Do you know what I had for Thanksgiving? Frozen pizza." I held back a sniffle. "Even Cody got served turkey in jail. His arrest ruined Thanksgiving and Thanksgiving's my favorite holiday. I haven't had a decent meal in weeks. I might end up cooking for Christmas too. Which leaves us with Cup o' Noodle as the holiday dinner."

Todd massaged my shoulder. "You act like you're selfish, but I know you're just worried about Cody."

"Maybe when it comes to food, I am selfish, Todd."

"It's not the food that has you upset."

"I'm not upset." I blinked away unwanted tears and slammed shut the mental box containing my issues. "I'm heading to the kitchen to see if I can rustle up something normal. I'll get something for you too. If they serve you a foie gras eggroll, you're going to get some kind of surprise."

I didn't tell Todd, but I had another plan. Besides food, kitchens also rustled up good gossip. Someone might know why Rookie Holt had so much antagonism toward Rick Miller and poor departed Abel Spencer. Were they friends? Or enemies?

And where was Rick Miller?

seven

I let my stomach guide me toward the kitchen. A pass-through blocked entry into the long, narrow area. Behind the stainless steel window, a thickly mustached man in a white chef's jacket and hat paused to look up from his task. Before him, a collection of plates held dry toast points sprinkled with tiny leaves and globs of mush. Even the pretty Gamboge Yellow Lake color could not disguise the globs as anything but goo. While I gaped in abject horror, the chef returned to shaving slices of what looked like a hunk of dirt on the plates.

"Are you Viktor?" I asked.

"Da," he said, his focus on the dirt. "What are you doing in these kitchens? We are busy with the dinner."

"Is that what you're serving the hunt contestants?"

He nodded, confirming my fear. Much worse than foie gras eggrolls.

I abandoned my line of questioning for stomach self-preservation. "I heard you were good. But I was wondering if you had something simpler. I've got real simple tastebuds. They like chicken and waffles. Shrimp and grits. Ribs and pulled pork. That sort of thing. Chicken nuggets, even."

Viktor's icy blue eyes cut me a scathing glance before returning to his hunk of dirt. "I have the carefully planned menu. You will enjoy."

I tried a new tact. "You sound just like my friend. Same accent. Where are you from, Viktor?"

"Friend?" Viktor's eyes narrowed. "Where is your friend from? What is his name?"

"I always get those countries over by Russia confused. But he's from one of them."

"I see." He set the dirt clod on the counter and crooked a finger to beckon me behind the pass-through.

Knowing full well the importance of following orders from someone at the head of my food chain, I trotted around the stainless steel shelf and stopped a few paces away. Beyond Viktor's station, three more cooks worked in the back of the kitchen. One dredged fish fillets in a flour mixture. Another stirred a pot that smelled like Brunswick stew. The last wielded a spatula over the griddle. My stomach barked its approval, but I refused it service to fix my attention on Viktor.

Folding his arms over his chest, he stared down the length of his nose. "You are friends with Maksim Avtaikin?"

"You know Max? He doesn't associate much with—" I stopped myself from saying "fellow foreigners."

"What does he not associate with? The cooks? Or the honest citizens?"

Max seemed to be losing a popularity contest on this trip. First with Bob Bass and now Viktor. I didn't care for the hostility that showed in the white-knuckled grip on Viktor's arms. I hated to think of what that negativity did to his food. Perhaps that was why he stayed away from the deep fryer.

I sought a new subject that might move his emotions in a different direction. "Viktor, did you know Abel Spencer? I suppose you heard about his unfortunate death. I wanted to express my condolences."

"I don't know him."

My best customer service skills did not seem to work on Viktor. "What about the contestants? They're an interesting bunch. Did you get to meet Bob Bass or Rick?"

"Not yet. I am accompanying your party to the bunkhouse in order to cook for the weekend. I will meet soon enough."

I opened my mouth to ask about specialized food requests when Viktor grabbed a sizable, gleaming knife. My mouth shut.

Viktor glanced at the knife, caught his reflection, and smoothed his mustache. He lowered the knife. “Tell your friend, Avtaikin, I’ll be very close.”

“How do you know Mr. Max?” I quickly prayed Viktor hadn’t lost significant sums in the Bear’s backroom gaming industry.

“You ask the Bear.” With a flick of his wrist, the knife tip pointed at my belly line of jiggling reindeer. “And tell him I will watch him carefully this weekend. You too. Any of the funny stuff and he will be reported.”

“Be reported to who?”

“To whom. Your English is not so good.” The gleaming knife flashed and aimed toward the door. “Now I must be preparing the dinner. Out.”

Back in the dining room, I found a seat between Max and Todd at the long table for the hunt contestants. I nodded at Bob and his entourage sitting across the table. Bob flashed me a smile, then continued his story involving a politician, a flamethrower, and a bag of marshmallows. Lowering my voice, I spoke to my untouched plate. “The chef knows you, Bear.”

Max raised a heavy eyebrow, scooped the orange mush onto a small piece of toast, and layered it with the dirt and tiny leaves. “Who is this chef?” He popped the bite into his mouth.

“A Viktor from your home country.”

He chewed for a long minute. “I do not know any chef Viktor in Georgia.”

“He sent a message warning you to watch your back this weekend.” I cut him a sharp side glance. “Via knife blade.”

“He must be the mistaken.”

Todd poked at the orangish blob with a fork and opted for plain toast.

“Maybe Viktor’s got Mr. Max mixed up with another Max.”

"Lord, I hope so."

"You should widen the palette," said Max. "Try the uni."

"I prefer to use a palette for paint, not for sustenance."

Across the table, Peach giggled.

I eyed her, wondering if extreme cleavage only caused the appearance of a drop in IQ points. "Where are you from?" I asked.

"California," she said.

"Had a gig at a gun rally," said Bob, dropping an arm on the back of her chair. "Peach snuck into my dressing room. Isn't that cute? She's been with me ever since."

"A long time then?"

Bob searched the ceiling rafters. "A couple months?"

"Since August." Peach switched her strained tones to a lighter octave. "Almost four months, Bob."

"Sorry, babe," said Bob. "Long time. Just think, the first time you met me you wanted to kill me and now you're going to star on *Rockin' The Hunt*. Must be love."

I dropped a dry toast point. "Peach wanted to kill you?"

Bob's laugh bounced around the roof timbers. "Peach snuck into my tent with a lil .38 Special. Told me hunting animals was mean. I said holding guns on people was just as mean. My bodyguard disarmed her and we've been together ever since."

"That was pretty funny," said Peach.

I didn't understand the humor, but maybe it was a California thing.

A glass clinked and we turned our attention to the head of the table where Mike stood with Viktor and a line of Big Rack staff.

"Excuse the interruption," said Mike. "I wanted y'all to meet the folks who will be serving you this weekend." He introduced each guide, housecleaner, and cook.

At Viktor's introduction, I poked Max, who showed no indication of knowing the disgruntled chef.

While Viktor ushered in the next course—another gelatinous goo, this time black, on a bed of lettuce declared by Jenny Sparks as the newest superfood—I popped from my chair with a ladies room excuse. Looking as pale as I felt, Risa the publicist scooted out of her chair and followed.

We stopped at the hall to the restrooms. "Not a superfood fan?" I asked.

"I go to the gym so I can eat burgers."

I laughed and left Risa to head to the bar.

"You've got to get me something to eat," I told the bartender. "Something edible."

He poured me a bowl of nuts.

"Where can I find the cook named Jessica? They didn't introduce her in the dining room. I'm desperate to meet her." I left off the part about desperate to try her food.

"Jessica's here. She's cooking tonight. You must have missed her."

Disappointed, I grabbed a handful of nuts, tossed them back, and ordered a beer. Politely turning from the bar, I spied a young woman with a large bakery box struggling with the vestibule door. I hurried to the front door to help her and her appealing-looking box.

"I need to find the hunt contest party," she explained.

I blasted her with a huge grin. "I'm with that party. Is this dessert?"

"I guess so. It's a cake. Was told to deliver here at six sharp."

"Regular cake? Made from flour and sugar and butter?"

"Red velvet, actually."

She looked surprised at my touchdown dance.

"I can take this to the table if you'd like." I trotted back to the dining room with the heavy cake and slid it onto an empty table. "Special delivery for our party."

Mike scooted from his place at the head of the table. "I wasn't aware of a bakery order. We try to make everything here."

"Is it gluten-free?" asked Jenny Sparks.

"Hope not," I muttered and flipped open the lid.

I froze for a moment, trying to get my senses to correlate the opposing sensations. The sweet scent of sugar, vanilla, and cream cheese triggered my drool glands, but the image hurt my gut and caused goosebumps to prickle my flesh. I slammed the lid shut and turned my back on the cake.

Mike reached for the lid.

I shook my head. "Don't open it."

"Wrong address? Although how anyone would get the lodge mixed up, I've no idea. Looks like it's from the bakery in town too." He turned toward the contestants. "Did one of y'all order a cake? That was real sweet of you."

I pulled on Mike's sleeve. "I don't think anyone here ordered this cake. And I need to talk to you privately."

"What's wrong?" he said, and before I could stop him, flipped back the lid.

"Is that dessert?" Returning from the bathroom, Risa strode up to the table and glanced into the box. Then screamed.

EIGHT

As the contestants crowded around the bakery box, Bob's manager helped Risa back to her room.

A cake shaped like a rotting pig's head complete with bloody looking jam, white chocolate maggots, and spun sugar flies was enough to make me lose my appetite too.

"Is this someone's idea of a joke?" LaToya's teenage toughness had lost its swagger. "That's disgusting."

"Almost too disgusting to eat," said Todd.

"We shouldn't eat this." I stepped aside to give Peach room to take a cake selfie. "The police might want it as evidence."

"Evidence?" said Mike.

"There's a knife stuck in the hog's head. The cake says, 'Death to Pigs.' No one here sent it. Don't you want this investigated?"

"This kind of thing happens to me all the time," said Bob. "Don't bother the authorities. No harm, no foul."

"People send you dead animal cakes with threatening notes all the time?"

"Hell, if I had a dollar for every time some activist threw red paint on me, I'd be a rich man." Bob laughed. "What am I saying? I am a rich man."

"So you think this was done by activists?"

"Sure, honey. What else could it be?"

"Wouldn't they want to advertise? Like stage a rally?"

"Usually," said LaToya. "Sometimes anti-gun people demonstrate at my rifle tournaments. They want the publicity."

“They’ve been at some of our hunt tournaments too,” said Clinton Sparks.

“But those were bigger venues,” said Jenny. “Big Rack is much more private.”

“Don’t forget *I’m* here,” said Bob. “I am your bigger venue.”

“I just thought activists demonstrated to draw attention to their issues. Not that I have any experience with activists; my art isn’t that controversial. Except for one local woman, Shawna Branson, who’s hated me since time immemorial. But she’s more drama queen than activist.” Realizing my digression, I continued. “So what’s the point of sending this cake? Besides ruining a perfectly good red velvet?”

“Perhaps the idea is to remind us of our own mortality.” Max’s Eastern European intonations produced a group shiver. “I like this cake. It is circle of life. The hog gives us life in his death. We have respect for his sacrifice because one day we are also covered in maggots.”

Hopefully not with a knife stuck through our heads, I thought.

“That’s a bunch of bull hockey,” said Bob. “You make Hogzilla sound noble. You didn’t sign up for this tournament to protect the countryside from a dangerous predator. You’re here to win, just like me.”

“Perhaps it is why you are sent disgusting cake,” said Max. “A good hunter respects life. And that is why you will not win this tournament.”

“Man almighty,” I muttered to Todd. “There’s a knife and threatening message and they’re still trying to out-piss each other.”

“Competition’s fierce,” he whispered back.

“Maybe Bob’s right,” said Mike. “Let’s just ignore the cake and move on.”

Bob reached for the knife, sawed off a chunk of cake, and shoved it in his mouth. “This is what I think of their message.” Bits of red spittle and crumbs sprayed from his mouth. “Delicious.”

“I think I’m done with food tonight,” I said. “And I think that’s the first time in my life I’ve ever uttered those words.”

* * *

At the guest lodge vending machine, I decided to skip the pork rinds. I hoped my food trauma would soon pass. I also hoped to figure out who sent that cake. If I was forever put off red velvet, I would need vengeance.

But I also couldn't shake the weird feeling I'd had since arriving at Big Rack Lodge. Before I had found Abel Spencer's body, something had seemed off. Even the staff seemed tense. In Georgia, you could usually count on amiable service, particularly out in the country. Generally you had to drive to Atlanta for tense.

I had written off my foreboding feelings to the troubles at home I'd hoped to suppress. But then I had found Abel. And now there was this wacky cake. One and one didn't make two in this situation, but one and one did cause me to search for a three.

I called Rookie Holt. She answered right away, once again proving her rookie status, as the law enforcement I knew generally let my calls roll to voicemail.

"Rick Miller didn't come to dinner," I said.

"That's why you called me?"

"Just thought you should know since you find him suspicious."

"I didn't say I found him suspicious."

"Someone also sent our party a cake. A cake with a threatening message."

"Threatening the party?"

"Not sure. But it had to do with the hunt. Check with the local bakery, but someone ordered a decomposing pig's head with a knife stuck through it. By the way, Swinton's bakery is pretty talented."

"I'll send someone over." Her reply sounded automatic.

"What are you thinking? Bob Bass and the other hunters say it's a protestor, but there was no credit taken by any group."

"I can't say without seeing it for myself. Are you always this familiar with law enforcement?"

My cheeks warmed. "My Uncle Will—"

"You told me about him. Anything else?"

"I just can't shake this odd feeling I have."

Holt's voice softened. "You saw something very disturbing today, it's understandable."

"It's not just that—" I stopped, knowing feelings didn't count as facts, particularly with police. "Has the coroner seen Abel Spencer yet? I just thought if your coroner is like ours, it's not like they have a lot of bodies to examine. Did they give a cause of death?"

"Blunt force trauma. His head struck the rocks in the creek when he fell."

"Was he drunk?"

"If you know procedure so well, you'll know it takes much longer for the BAC report to come back," she snapped.

"Sorry. Everyone thinks Abel took a drunken spill. I just wondered if they were right."

"Not everyone thinks that."

"What do you mean?" I tried to control the excitement in my voice. "Do you think differently? You know I didn't smell alcohol on him."

She pulled in a breath. "I think we've talked enough. Tell Mike one of us will come out to check on that cake."

Her hang-up came before any goodbyes could be said, but I was too stunned to care.

Sweet drippings of bacon, I had a suspicion that Rookie Holt had a suspicion that Abel's death was suspicious.

But were we alone in our suspicions?

Back in my room, I nibbled on peanut butter crackers and Coke, my thoughts hopping between bloody cakes, dead bodies, and troubles at home.

In the next room, a TV kicked on, blaring the local six o'clock news loud enough for me to hear the weather report. I grabbed my own remote, slid back on the bed, and caught the three-day forecast for clouds, rain, and storms.

"Those poor dogs." I wondered how quickly the police would find Abel's pack dry and loving homes.

The weather forecast reminded me of my soaked art supplies. The police had returned my easel, tackle, and watercolors. I had left the easel to dry in the bathtub but left the waterlogged pad and paintings on the desk. A smear of blue among the greens and browns caught my eye. Lifting the paper, I realized I had painted Abel's hat without knowing what it was. Just a daub of royal blue.

Lucky I chose that spot in the forest to paint, I thought, or no one would have found Abel's body before the hunt.

Not that anyone would expect a visitor from the contest to park herself in a glen to do a bit of landscape painting. The area I had chosen wasn't in the reserve across the road, but in the forested area ringing the lodge and its farm fields proper. Unlike Goldilocks, I hadn't wandered far. Followed a path of cleared trees until I reached a spot I liked, not knowing fifty yards farther, the clearing dropped into a shallow ravine.

Maybe too lucky.

I walked the curling paper to the bathroom trash and returned to grab my phone from the rustic nightstand. I flipped it open.

Behind me, the newscaster announced breaking news on Big Rack Lodge. I spun around to watch. An aerial view showed footage of the lodge grounds, then panned out to show the surrounding woods and farmland. Tiny cows ambled in a field and the metal blades of a windmill caught the sun, obscuring the camera's lens for a moment.

Old footage, I mused, since I hadn't seen the sun since arriving at Big Rack.

The angle tilted, then steadied on the spot in the woods where I had found Abel's body. The announcer described the tragedy that had temporarily suspended the big hunting contest. The view of the woods shrank a bit until it showed the triangulation between my landscape spot near the ravine, a small homestead of trailers, and the lodge cottages. Almost ninety-degree angles between the three places.

"One of those trailers," the reporter announced, "was the last known place the deceased, Abel Spencer, had been seen before his death."

I jumped as I saw myself leaving the Swinton police station, outed as the lodge guest who had found the body. More faces flitted across the screen. The Sparks, then LaToya with a brief description of her Junior Olympian status. Finally, several photos of Bob Bass were shown. Bob playing at a concert. Bob posing with his gun and guitar. Bob and a dead moose. Bob and Peach Payne. But no Max. And no Rick.

How did the Bear manage to get his name out of the local news? I pondered that detail but became distracted by a blurry night-vision video of a humongous creature nosing through a field. The massive hulking form, stark black against the white field, paused from eating the corn it had tromped and mangled. Twisting to face the camera, his small, piggy eyes glowed with an almost human malevolence. With an eerie abruptness, the giant pig disappeared, galloping out of the camera's range.

I shuddered, glad I had skipped the pork rinds.

The short news story had no mention of the police calling Abel Spencer's death suspicious. Only a sad fate. I sank onto the bed, tapping my phone against my knee, perturbed with the news story. Not just perturbed. Distressed.

The contest didn't bother me. I had grown up with hunters. Rational, responsible men and women with a strong moral code. Not the type who were sent hostile baked goods.

However, Abel Spencer's death troubled me. I thought his death also troubled Rookie Holt. But according to the news, no one else seemed troubled. Was the investigation of his death suppressed from the news or was there no investigation?

I didn't think Rookie Holt would speak to me again unless I had something worth talking about. However, there was another deputy who might have some ideas.

"Hell." I glared at my phone. "I'm looking for more excuses to call. And I promised myself I wouldn't."

Our last hookup, just before my brother's arrest, had started as a professional consultation too. But we both knew Luke's investigative advice had been an excuse to see each other.

Commercial break over, the news turned to security footage of a fight between two wiry meemaws over the season's favored Christmas toy at the local Walmart. I cut off the TV, opened my sketchpad, and drew a cell phone.

Broken hearts flew from the receiver.

Dropping my pencil, I flipped open my phone. And pushed the number five. By accident. Sort of.

Nine

"I wondered how long you could hold out," drawled the baritone that answered. "Where are you?"

"Big Rack Lodge," I said, picturing the man on the other end of the line. Dusky brown curls, gray eyes, and dimples. I sketched his lean, tall physique in the pose of the Ancient Greek Lysippos's bronze *Athlete* statue. One hand of the runner reached toward his curls where I sketched in a phone instead of a laurel wreath. The other dangled naturally in mid-stride, just as Luke was most likely pacing to a place of privacy.

"So," I continued, "I found a dead body today."

"You sure know how to throw cold water on a guy," said Luke. "It's been a long time since I've even caught a glimpse of you, let alone heard from you."

"Two weeks," I said. "I had pizza for Thanksgiving."

"I'm sorry," he said. "Thanksgiving was a bit tense here too."

"I'm sure it was hard for your family to nibble turkey while discussing how best to keep my brother incarcerated."

The silence on the other side reminded me how chilly the night had grown.

"Sorry. Still a touchy subject in my family." I rolled the pencil between my fingers. "Anyway, I was painting in the woods and found an older man who had fallen into a stream and hit his head. A local ne'er-do-well."

"How far was the fall?" asked Luke.

"About six feet, I'd say. Face up." I shivered.

"Fell backward? I'm sorry you had to see that, sugar. I guess you've been busy with the local police?"

"They deemed it an accident. Although my rookie deputy may think otherwise."

"Your rookie?" I could almost hear Luke's eyes narrow. "What's his name?"

"Deborah. I might have found my match in the not-good-at-keeping-your-mouth-shut department."

The tension in his voice eased. "What'd you do? Go out for a beer after your witness statement and got her to spill her suspicious death hunches?"

"Not even. I don't think she likes me. And she doesn't want to tell me her hunches. My hunch is they don't match her superior's. Around here, Abel Spencer is known as a sneaky gossip and drunk with no friends. I met an Abel Spencer the night before he died who was nosy, but not drunk. And he raised the sweetest dogs, Luke."

"You met the victim the night he died? Are you the last known witness?"

"I'm not sure," I said. "The TV news said he was at a nearby trailer. And I can't get a whole lot of information from Rookie Holt except when she slips."

"No wonder she doesn't trust you."

"Hey now. It's not like I'm a suspect. But I wonder if she does have a suspect? She sure doesn't like the local contestant in this hunt."

"You're probably reading more into it than necessary. You do have an imagination."

We mulled that fact for a long moment.

Luke's voice dropped. "How's things with your family?"

I thought about what Casey would say if she knew I was talking to the arrester of our brother.

"No change on that front," I said. "Let's not talk about it."

He sighed, then brightened. "You got space in that hotel room for one more? I could swap shifts and steal down to Big Rack on Saturday. No one would know..."

I drew a gigantic exclamation point. "That'd be too easy, wouldn't it? Todd is here, and of course, Max Avtaikin."

"What's Todd McIntosh doing at this hunt?"

"Todd's assisting Max," I said, drawing a tree on my pad. A heart appeared on the tree. I stopped before adding initials inside the heart. At this juncture, nothing seemed safe. "I'm worried Max is going to reinjure his bum knee cavorting around the woods. Of course, he doesn't listen to me."

Luke snorted. "Avtaikin's a grown man and an excellent hunter. But won't they be busy with the hunt? I could stay hidden in your room. We could order room service. I'd only let you out to paint."

To center my libido, I drew a tiny image of my brother behind bars. "You don't want room service here. Food's terrible. Besides, Bob Bass is insisting I accompany the hunters, hoping I can capture the image of fresh blood dripping from his trophy before it stinks to high heaven. Which means I'll be camping with the crew in the bunkhouse overnight."

"Better hope the bunkhouse is bigger than a deer stand."

"Judging by the fineries at the lodge, I'm sure we'll have hot water at least. But I wouldn't be surprised if there was a Jacuzzi."

"Nice." Luke paused. "I miss you, sugar. Can't stop thinking of you."

My heart throbbed. I snatched at saner thoughts. "Somebody sent a cake that looked like a decomposing pig to the party tonight. The hunters think it's from an anti-hunting fanatic."

"Lovely."

"Actually it was pretty disgusting."

"As our talks are few and far between, I hoped to keep death and disgusting cakes to a minimum." Luke's tone lightened. "How about I tell you about my day?"

"No death or cake?"

In the next room, someone had lowered the volume of their television. A phone trilled. At the booming "What's up?" I found myself third party to that conversation.

Then realized eavesdropping could go both ways.

I prayed his TV had drowned out my earlier conversation, squeezed my eyes shut, and focused on Luke.

"Five traffic stops and one with a pot bust," continued Luke. "Between them, I was thinking about you. How I'd like to take you out and then take you home. Want more?"

My eyes popped open.

"I don't care what you have to do..." My lodge neighbor must have been pacing, because the voice faded, then grew louder as he approached my wall.

"Okay," I whispered, securing the phone more tightly to my ear. "Where did you want to take me and what did we eat?"

I glanced at my sketchpad. I had drawn a deer wearing a hunting jacket, phone raised to his muzzle. This was the problem with accidental eavesdropping. Instead of sketching Luke, my artist subconscious had chosen my loud neighbor as a subject.

"...how do you think? Distract him," said my neighbor.

I added a mustache. And erased the mustache. My neighbor didn't sound mustache-y. Although he did sound youngish. I replaced the mustache with a hipster beard.

"What do you mean, what did we eat? Always thinking about food." Luke chuckled. "Wouldn't you rather hear what I'd do after I took you home?" I could hear his smile stretch until the dimples broke to frame his grin.

I jumped at the sound of a loud bump. No-Mustache had dropped or kicked something. On my sketchpad, the deer kicked off his field boot.

"Sure, tell me," I said, refocusing on Luke. I forced my hand to draw hearts and cupids. "What'd we do when you took me home?"

"First, I'd peel off that denim jacket you love to wear. And you'd kick off those old cowboy boots."

"Getting comfortable. Sounds good."

No-Mustache's voice oozed with condescension. "You know how. And don't tell me you don't like the benefits..." His voice trailed off as he began to pace again.

My deer now stood with his hooves on his hips, bearded chin raised. Below him, a bunny with drooping whiskers stared at the ground. I drew in a limp carrot.

"Let's see, you're still wearing that skirt I like." Luke's voice deepened and dropped to a caress. "What should we do about that?"

I scribbled out the limp carrot. "Um, how about your jacket and boots?"

"You want me to take anything else off?"

"...is good," said No-Mustache. His voice grew louder. "But I'd rather see him dead."

"Dead?" I exclaimed. Then realized No-Mustache could hear me.

And so could Luke.

"Shit," I said.

"Sugar? You okay?"

In the next room, a door slammed.

"Fine, fine." I dropped my sketchpad, ran to my door, and cracked the door to peer into the hall. "Where'd he go?"

"Where'd who go?" said Luke.

I opened my mouth, then shut it. Curiosity was one thing. Admitting to spying on your neighbor while your sort-of-boyfriend-but-not-really thought you were concentrating on nekkid fantasies was a whole other deal.

"You're breathing hard. And not in a good way." Luke's voice switched from sizzle to snap. "What are you doing, Cherry?"

I swapped my attention back to the phone. "Nothing. Where were we? Do you still have on your imaginary pants?"

"Are you even in your room?"

"Of course I'm in my room."

"Then why are you asking yourself about where some guy went?"

Dangit.

"That was nothing. The TV." I glanced at my dark TV. "In the next room. The walls are paper thin at this place."

A young man in a knit beanie and skinny sweats stepped through an open door at the end of the hall. He balanced an ice bucket under one arm while he checked for his room key in his pocket.

I shut my door before he caught sight of me. "Soul patch," I whispered. "Not a beard. But definitely no mustache."

"I don't have a beard. Or a soul patch," said Luke. "Are you spying on your neighbor?"

"Possibly." I rolled my eyes at my own idiocy. "I'd say I couldn't help it because he was loud and saying crazy stuff, so I wanted to see the face that matched the voice. But I know that's not a good reason."

"What's a good reason?"

"That we shouldn't be talking like this, so I'm distracting myself. Just like I'm distracting myself with Abel's death so I don't have to think about what's going on at home."

"Sugar—"

"You don't have to say it. I shouldn't have called in the first place. I don't want to lead you on."

"Lead me on? Darlin'—"

"I'll just say goodbye now."

"Cherry—"

I hung up before I said something stupid.

More stupid.

Like, "I may love you but our families will never give us their blessing, so what's the point of nekkid fantasies when we're never going to live the real thing?"

TEN

As it turned out, I was not as put off from eating as previously thought. Crackers and Coke weren't nourishment enough for my hummingbird metabolism, nor were they comfort enough for my broken heart. On my search for sustenance, I bumped into the lodge's twenty-four hour security patrol: a Red Bull-swigger named Ty, who manned a diesel-powered golf cart. My stomach's violent growl had reminded Ty of his favorite stock car. After recovering from his shock, he regaled me with a story of similar engine noise he had experienced at his last NASCAR weekend. Then learned he spoke to the gal who had found Abel's fallen body.

"I'd say I was surprised, but I wasn't. Abel was looking for an accident in some ways." Ty blushed. "That's an ugly thing to say about someone who just passed, pardon me. Where'd that come from?"

"I have that problem all the time. Somehow my mouth got wired to my subconscious." I wondered if Ty's subconscious matched the unsaid suspicions of Rookie Holt's. "That sounded like Abel's accident was deliberate. Like someone had it in for him?"

"No, I don't know why I said that." Ty sipped from his Red Bull can, considering. "Abel did like stirring pots, though. You had to watch what you said around him. If you spoke out of turn about someone and Abel happened to overhear, they'd sure learn what you said quick enough. Most folks ignored him, but Abel seemed to enjoy tattling whenever he could. Real spiteful. He probably caused enough divorces and broken friendships 'round here anyway."

"Why do folks love getting up in other people's business?" I said, thinking of my nemesis Shawna Branson, the darling of Forks County who had caused my brother's unfortunate incarceration. Shawna'd had it in for me since the Forks County Courthouse's live nativity when, as one of the Christmas angels, I had stood too close to a mini heater and caught my wing on fire. My dance through the stable accidentally knocked over the manger, exposing Mary secretly holding hands with the donkey and not Joseph. Joseph (Wade Boiken) broke up with Mary (Shawna) and Shawna had hated me ever since.

Shawna had a similar quality for spreading gossip just for the enjoyment of getting others in trouble. I felt saddened by this new information about Abel Spencer. He hadn't struck me as Shawna-like when I met him. Other than he loved animals and she loved to wear animal prints.

"You'd think they'd recognize the pain caused by rumors. You'd think they'd feel ashamed."

Ty nodded.

"Besides, Wade Boiken, that idiot, ended up taking Shawna to prom five years later anyway."

Ty had no answer for that.

I returned to the original subject, internally cussing myself for opening that damn mental box. "If he was so disliked, how did Abel learn the local scandals? I'd think everyone would avoid him."

"He was pretty sly. He mostly did his spying at the Double Wide." Ty smiled at the name. "The liquor makes folks forget to shut their mouths."

"Where's this Double Wide? And do they serve real food?"

Todd and Max had returned to their cottage, but I called to see if they would join me for a drink at the Double Wide. A bar where liquor-loosened tongues seemed like a good place to appease my hunger and revive my downtrodden spirits. And hopefully, quench my curiosity about the mysterious Abel Spencer. Max had planned on spending the evening cleaning his guns, but, as usual, Todd had been amenable for greater amusement. He offered to meet me in their golf cart, the vehicle by which the cottage dwellers traveled around the large bass pond to the main lodge grounds.

Outside in my puffy coat, I admired the Christmas lights reflecting off the pond before turning to watch for Todd's golf cart. A long, low building that looked like a giant chicken coop blocked my view of the dirt drive that led around the pond to the cottages. Decorative lighting shone on the quaint structure, obscuring the inhabitants. It was too far for me to see clearly, but a bird much larger than a chicken strutted along the pen adjoined to the coop. Which made me think of Thanksgiving turkey, the particular fowl I had missed this year.

Had Abel Spencer shared his Thanksgiving dinner with people or just his dogs? Was he only friendly to Swinton outsiders, like me, or had I mistaken the sweet affection with his dog for a general amiability? He had wanted to know about my participation in the hunt and whatever information I had about the contest. I thought he had just been curious. Was there a more malicious intent to his questions that I didn't notice?

A strange scream, high-pitched and piercing, rang out from the giant chicken coop. My hands flew over my mouth as I stifled a scream of my own.

"Get a hold of yourself," I muttered. The screech still rang in my ears and sent tiny aftershocks buzzing through my nerves. "Why is every little thing giving me the jitters today?"

Cherry Tucker did not get the jitters. And to prove it, I jogged up the path to check out the odd building. Twenty yards from the coop, I halted. "What in the hell?"

A heavyset man crept around the edge of the building. A camouflage balaclava covered his face, except for the pair of glasses balanced precariously on his camo nose. Matching coveralls stretched over his full stomach.

As the building was painted Scarlet Lake and spotlighted, his Army Surplus camo did not blend but gave the appearance of skulking vegetation. Vegetation that had just digested an extra-large beach ball.

"Hey," I called. "What are you doing?"

Balaclava Beach Ball froze against the building, but the protruding belly blocked his ability to flatten himself. He stretched his arms and clung to the walls with his fingertips.

"I can see you," I said. "Are you a guest of the lodge?"

He ran with the eagerness of a bat released from hell, but without the necessary wingspan to lift his weight productively.

As he took off, another shriek pierced the night.

Eleven

Like Balaclava Beach Ball, I ran surprisingly slow. Which is really not so surprising, considering my runty size.

The pen was now empty, but another high-pitched scream resonated from inside. I followed the path around the corner and found the far side of the building dark but covered in a fine mesh screen.

Yanking my phone from my pocket, I pressed the lit screen against the mesh. More shrill cries rang out. Inside, turquoise and brilliant blue fans brandished and cascaded.

"I'll be damned. Peacocks."

A large "Keep Out" sign made me wonder if Balaclava Beach Ball had planned to disobey orders. I scanned the pen door and walls for breaking and entering. The padlocked door remained fixed. Curiously though, a section of wooden slats had been replaced and one of the posts had been splinted with two-by-fours. Something had cracked the thick beam. Recently. A can of red paint sat next to the beam, waiting for someone to finish the job.

"What was up with that guy?" I asked the birds. "Just some weirdo playing GI Joe? Or a man with an unnatural love for peacocks?"

A shadowy peacock shape stopped in mid-strut and paraded to the mesh to stare at me.

"I hope the owners aren't raising y'all for some fancy meal. I'd be worried after seeing the gourmet stuff coming out of that kitchen. Can you even eat peacock?"

The male peacocks screeched a decibel short of permanent eardrum damage. I took it as a no.

"Why is everything at this lodge so strange? Or am I just seeing strange because my life is a mess?"

As the peacocks had no answer to that, I turned toward the path. A few minutes later, the whir of a battery-powered motor and the churn of tires on damp clay told me Todd approached.

He stomped the brake on the golf cart, slamming to a stop and flinging mud. "Hey, Cherry. Hop on."

I eyed the cart, caked in more mud than a redneck tailgate party, and turned my attention to the bulky blond driving. "Did you see a fluffy GI Joe running through the trees? I just caught some guy decked in head-to-toe camo about to do who-knows-what to these peacocks."

"Aren't those peacocks something? They scream every time I drive by. About scared the life out of me the first time." Todd turned to glance back at their pen. "I didn't see anybody. Who do you think he was?"

"No clue. But he ran when I confronted him." I climbed into the golf cart. "I tell you what, Todd. This relaxing weekend has turned into some kind of sideshow act. I am looking forward to spending a little time away from this fancy lodge at a real bar."

"Bars suit you better," agreed Todd.

"However, a trailer bar might not get me far from the sideshow act."

"Trailer bar?"

I'd had a similar reaction.

According to Ty, the Double Wide was located on the land next door to Big Rack Lodge. "Can't miss it," Ty had said between swigs of Red Bull. "The neighbor, Guterson, has that little trailer town you passed just before reaching Big Rack's property. The Gutersons wouldn't sell, even when the Woodcocks bought the land around them."

"Right," I had said. "Seemed out of place. A few trailer homes on that narrow strip of land."

"One's a bar. The Double Wide."

"A trailer bar?"

I figured a trailer bar would be easy enough to spot, and as the Gutersons' property wasn't far, Todd and I took the golf cart. Outside the lodge, the dark forest loomed on either side of the road, increasing the shiver factor in both temperature and setting. My eyes swept the dark for wild-eyed hogs and rotund men. Rain began to spit, dotting the plastic windshield and dampening the seats. I burrowed deeper into my insulated coat and wondered if outlining camo vines in puff paint had diminished the waterproof factor.

"I hoped we could talk. At the lodge, it seems we never get a chance." Todd squinted at the road, barely lit by the headlights.

"I know what you mean. Either we can't hear ourselves think with all the hunters' boasting or there's something crazy happening."

"Crazy?"

"Like that cake and then this odd peacock fellow. Plus my hipster lodge neighbor's ranting carried through my walls. He's wanting to kill someone. Not that I don't take that particular phrase as a figure of speech, but those words tend to stick in your craw when you've found a body earlier in the day."

"I guess that's true."

"You know, I really get the feeling that Rookie Holt thinks something happened to Abel Spencer. Not sure what she's suspecting, just that he didn't drunkenly fall into that ditch. I hope the Double Wide folks or their patrons can help me. The news said he was last seen there before his death. At least I'll find out if he had gone three sheets between meeting me and his untimely demise. That'd settle some of my nerves."

"That's why we're going to a trailer bar?" Todd began tapping a jerky rhythm against the steering wheel. "Are you sure you're not trying to make an accident into something worse? To give yourself something else to think about?"

"Possibly." I unfolded my arms, then folded them again to regain my escaped body heat. "But maybe I can help Rookie Holt.

I'm sure if I learn something at this bar, she'd be mighty happy to hear about it." I wanted to make a better impression with Rookie Holt. I hoped to get her to warm to me.

Or at least thaw her a little.

The look Todd gave me reminded me of Abel's coonhound.

Embarrassed, I looked away.

Murky light broke on our path as we passed a bend in the road. "Almost there," I said, looking for a change in subject.

The trees fell away for a collection of ramshackle trailers and sheds. The diffused glow of a telephone pole's security light illuminated several trailer homes surrounded by rusted-out vehicles in various stages of decrepitude.

Behind and inside the homes, dogs snarled and barked. Two pickups, a golf cart, and one tractor had been parked before a single weather-beaten trailer. A large sign made from plywood had been nailed to the building.

The Christmas lights poking through the sign's holes told us the Double Wide was open. I wasn't sure if it was meant as a greeting or warning.

If it weren't for the crazy delicious smell of hot oil and batter emanating from that trailer, I would have run back to the lodge, abandoning Abel's demise to the official police report.

"I've seen worse," I said, trying to stay positive.

"I've played poker in worse," said Todd, parking beside the tractor. "In fact, it looks like this bust-out joint I once visited."

I nodded, my concentration focused on a search for unchained dogs. The barking here had a fierceness I had not heard at Abel's.

"I wonder what they're frying," said Todd. "It smells like heaven. Like funnel cake?"

My stomach cried in anguish. "Let's not get my hopes up. I'd take a cold hushpuppy at this point."

We mounted the cinderblock steps of the Double Wide and opened the door once painted white. Inside, we stood on a welcome mat missing most of its letters.

Three barstools rested before a kitchen counter turned bar.

A beaded curtain separated the back hall from a living room fitted with two picnic tables and a decrepit couch.

A vintage Blow Mold Santa lit one corner. With his off-center eyes and red cheeks, he looked as tipsy as the customers sitting at the picnic tables.

I recognized one woman as the lodge housekeeper. She was deep in conversation with a gentleman in sleeveless flannel with matching beard and ponytail braids. I left them to their date and pointed Todd toward the empty barstools.

Behind the kitchen counter, two women alternately handed out mugs of beer and poured a clear liquid from a glass tea pitcher. A generation separated the women, but both wore self-dyed roots, frown lines, and a hard set to their eyes. They studied us peripherally while hurriedly rearranging items below the counter.

Hiding the illegal stuff, I gathered. But I didn't need to make that my problem, so I kept my gaze elsewhere.

"You here to drink?" asked the older woman.

"And eat, if you're still serving."

Todd slid onto the stool next to me. "Two beers, ma'am."

The woman nodded, but jerked her chin toward the tapper in the back corner. A hole had been cut out of the counter for the nozzle. "We've only got one kind."

"That's fine. And we'll take whatever I smell in your fryer." I arched my neck, searching the tiny kitchen for a deep fryer. "What's your name?"

"I'm Desiree Guterson. My daughter-in-law, Sheri, made up a batch of okra tonight. And I've got wild turkey patties and deer sausage."

Sheri tipped a plastic cup beneath the keg spout. She placed the beers on the yellowing Formica counter. "Two bucks each."

While Todd fished out a five, I leaned my elbows on the sticky counter. "We'll take the okra and turkey too."

Sheri grabbed a tray from the fridge and disappeared through the back door.

"You got a kitchen elsewhere?" I asked.

"We keep the turkey fryer on the back porch." Desiree's thin lips quivered. "Safety, you know."

"Of course." I left off my wonderment about the health inspector's feelings about porch turkey fryers. At least I was finally getting some turkey.

Todd leaned into me and placed his lips next to my ear. "You sure about the turkey?"

"Seemed safer than the sausage," I muttered, then turned back to Desiree. "I heard about your recent troubles. Sorry about the passing of Mr. Abel. Actually, I'm the one who found him. Met his dogs too. They nearly broke my heart with their grieving."

Desiree clucked her tongue and folded her arms. "Real shame. He didn't even have his usual. Poor guy."

"Usual?"

"Home brew. You want to try some?" Beneath the counter, Desiree drew out the glass pitcher.

Todd poked me in the ribs, but I ignored his worry. "Sure, why not?"

Desiree set two new cups on the counter and poured a tablespoon in each. "That's free. You want more, I charge five a cup."

"Thank you, ma'am," said Todd, accepting his cup. He sniffed and jerked his head back. "I think I'll stick to the beer."

I took a careful sip and felt the slow burn start at my lips and travel over my tongue, down my throat, and into my stomach. I tried to cover my cough and reached for the beer cup to put out the flames.

Desiree barked a laugh. "Can't handle your liquor, hon?"

"Not when it's jet fuel," I panted. "This was Abel's drink of choice?"

"Usually. That's why most show up. Not for the fryer."

Todd and I exchanged a wary glance.

In the back of the room, a shout preceded a boisterous scuffling. Desiree stomped to the back of the room and hollered a string of curses, ending in a mangled Bible verse.

"If Abel didn't have his usual and I didn't smell anything on him, there goes the town's theory of him falling drunk into a ditch. I'm going to see what else I can learn about his last visit."

"At least you're cleared as a suspect," said Todd.

I lowered my voice. "Witness, Todd. Witnesses are not suspects. Usually."

The picnic table argument quieted and Desiree returned. "So how's the big hunt? Are the police going to make them cancel?"

"The hunt's still on. The location of Abel's fall wasn't in the preserve anyway."

"Bet the Woodcocks loved the news about Abel." Her snarky tone struck one of my already shortened nerves.

"I'm sure the owners are upset a local man died."

"Pissed at a dead man for ruining their big event, you mean." Desiree pursed her lips. "I hope it puts those Atlanta snobs out of business. Stealing folks' land and keeping honest people from hunting in spots where they've always hunted. The Woodcocks probably fixed things with the police to quiet it all down. They sure wouldn't want it in the news."

Before I could remark on that interesting tidbit, the back door banged open. A heavily bearded and tattooed man held the door for Sheri, then folded his arms to stand sentry. She stepped into the small kitchen and shoved paper towel-lined paper plates of okra and turkey patties on the counter. The heap of crispy, golden okra still sizzled. The patties steamed, giving off an herbal fragrance of thyme and sage. A droplet of drool rolled off my lip and I quickly wiped it with my hand.

Todd snatched a plastic spork from the coffee can holder.

"I guess you don't care for the Woodcocks," I said to Desiree.

"They tried to buy out our land. No one takes property away from the Gutersons. Accused us of poaching too. We're hunting where we've always hunted."

Sheri laughed. "We opened this bar just to tick them off. Their lawyer sent a letter asking us to clean up our property. We cleaned up all right. Cleaned out this old trailer and made it a bar."

"That's very enterprising of you," said Todd.

As I dug into the okra, the front door smacked the flimsy trailer wall. Our gazes fell upon the newcomer, Rick Miller, the lodge's vanishing dinner guest. Rick gave the bar a quick glance, ducked his head before we could catch his eye, and shuffled to the mangy couch. Sheri scurried to bring him the house pour.

I lowered my voice. "We met Rick tonight at the lodge. He won the raffle to enter the hunt."

"Heard about that. He's here all the time, just like Abel was," muttered Desiree.

"Friendly guy?" asked Todd, popping a bite of okra into his mouth.

"I wouldn't say that." Desiree curled her lip. "If people pay and don't cause trouble in here, I'll serve 'em. Men like Abel and Rick keep us in business. They're here just about every night."

"Rick wasn't here last night," piped Sheri, waving the five ones.

Desiree snatched the money and shoved it in her back pocket. "Well, he's here tonight, ain't he? So stop shouting his name for everybody to hear. They've all got eyes and ears."

I noted Rick's absence in my mental "Abel Spencer's Suspicious Death" file. "I'm glad Abel didn't spend his last night alone. Did he hang out with anyone last night?"

"That stranger was here," said Sheri.

I nudged Todd, who seemed too busy consuming our fried okra to mentally file anything.

"That's right. Guests from the lodge. That singer, Bob Bass, and his group came in for a drink." Desiree's tone revealed Bob Bass's charm had not won him any favors at the Double Wide. "They couldn't fool me. Stopped in to look down their noses at us."

"That's not who I meant," said Sheri. "Another lodge guest. The fat one. He was asking questions about Hogzilla. Talking a lot of weird stuff. I think he said he was a writer."

"Weird stuff?" My voice rose with my interest. "Was Abel interested in this weird stuff?"

"I don't think so," said Sheri. "He's not into that sort of thing."

"Abel'd rather talk about local doings," said Desiree.

"I heard that about him." I kicked my heels against the stool rungs. The Bob Bass party might have met Abel. Although it didn't seem likely that their visit would have anything to do with his death.

"Abel didn't really talk to anyone. I think he was waiting for someone," said Sheri. "And he was kind of agitated. Like Ma said, he didn't even drink his regular. Cut out early."

"It's not our business, Sheri," said the lone male Guterson. "You're stirring things up."

"I'm not," said Sheri. "It's not like I talked to the cops when they came by, Caleb."

"We don't talk to cops." Caleb Guterson pierced Sheri with a hard stare.

"Nothing to tell, anyway. Just Abel all riled up. Like he gets when he's got news to tell."

"Sheri didn't say nothing to 'em, Caleb," said Desiree. "I did. They just wanted to know when he left so as to get a time of death. But I also told 'em Abel knows those woods well enough not to get his neck broke."

"You sound like you don't think Abel's death was an accident."

Desiree shrugged. "Don't know if it was or wasn't. All I know is Abel's been walking that path his whole life. And that ditch ain't even on the path. I can't believe they found him there."

"He left the path? I didn't think that looked like a path." I pushed my beer away. "Was Abel even drunk? You said he didn't drink his regular. He hadn't been drinking when I met him either."

Desiree and Sheri looked to one another to jog their memories.

"Maybe not," said Desiree. "The man's been stewing in liquor for so long, it's hard to remember."

"So, Abel wandered off his path and fell into a ditch sober?" I muttered. "I wonder how long it'll take to get the blood alcohol report back from the state lab?"

Todd coughed. Desiree was exchanging a look with her son and daughter-in-law. Their eyes slid back to me.

Realizing my social gaffe, I scooted off my stool. “Can I use your facilities?”

I needed to think about how to extract more information from this group without ticking them off. And I really wanted to know if they spoke to Rookie Holt or someone else. Maybe this very information is what made Rookie Holt doubt Abel’s fall as an accident.

Desiree jerked her chin toward the back of the trailer.

I squeezed between picnic table revelers and flung back the beaded curtain.

Upon entering the tiny bathroom and closing the door, I decided the forest would be a lot cleaner. I undid the dubious hook and eye lock and pushed open the door. And found Rick Miller waiting.

“You can have it.” The open bathroom door blocked my view of the main room. I took a step toward Rick.

Moonshine wafted from his pores. His dull eyes glinted with the transmuting spark of alcohol. “You’re the girl from earlier tonight. At the lodge.”

“Yep, the artist.” I scooted sideways into the tiny hall, but Rick and the open bathroom door blocked my escape. “If I can just get around you, maybe we can talk when you’re all...finished with your business.”

Rick shoved his hands in his pockets, but otherwise didn’t move. “Are you a cop?”

“No,” I said. “Why?”

“I heard you asking questions about Abel.”

“I’m sorry about Abel Spencer. I didn’t introduce myself properly earlier. Cherry Tucker.” I stuck out my hand.

His handshake was akin to holding an angler worm. He also smelled like Guterson homebrew. Which meant Rick had downed quite a bit in the short time he had graced the Double Wide.

“I found him,” I said. “I wanted to talk to you about him too.”

His shoulders twitched. “Talk?”

“I thought you might know Abel.”

"We hung out some." His eyes shifted to a point next to my left boot. "I tolerated him where others didn't. At least since I moved back."

"How long were you gone?"

"About ten years. But I'm leaving again. I don't like it here. Actually, I was getting ready to move when I heard about this contest. Winning that twenty grand would make for an easier relocation, that's for sure."

"I moved back home too. After college. And like for you, it was difficult for me. But I like Halo, despite some of its residents, so I'll stick it out. My friend Red said that's to do with unresolved mother issues. He claims I'm subconsciously afraid she'll return and not find me. Red's kind of a daytime TV junkie."

My face heated, realizing my interior issues were slipping into off-topic tangents. "Anyway, I'm glad I got to talk to you. I realize the impropriety of speaking about a man so recently deceased, but I'd like to know more about Abel."

"What do you mean?"

"I just found his fall kind of peculiar."

"Peculiar?" His gaze rose to my shoulder before moving behind me.

"Yes. Peculiar. It didn't look right."

"Abel hit his head on a rock. Don't know how that's going to look right."

"Did you see Abel the night he died?"

His eyes narrowed and honed in on me. "Who said?"

"Nobody. The Gutersons thought something was bothering Abel before he died. Maybe that's connected to his accident. Some of the lodge guests were here last night. Do you think something about the hunt bugged him? It could be important."

"I don't know anything."

"I ask because there's a deputy who may be investigating on her own and if she doesn't find any evidence quickly, she'll probably be forced to stop."

Rick moved forward a step. "You're some kind of snitch?"

"No, you're misunderstanding me." I backed into the door frame. "You see, I met him the night he died. Abel asked me a lot of questions about the hunt."

"That's nothing to do with me."

"Listen, I saw you at Abel's. I was there checking on his dogs. Rookie Holt pointed you out to me. Did you follow me there? Maybe you're worried about what happened to Abel too?"

"You leave me out of this." Rick's hands ripped from his pockets and he lunged drunkenly towards me. "Stop talking about Abel Spencer."

I pushed forward, knocking him into the open door and scooted around him. Plastic beads swung and clicked, licking my shoulders and back. Beyond the picnic table crowd, Todd turned, caught my expression, and a moment later, he hustled me out the door. A cold gust blew rain off the roof of the trailer and sprinkled our heads.

"The Gutersons said you were sounding like the cops. I thought we better get before they kicked us out." Todd handed me my coat and we slipped into the golf cart. "What happened back there?"

"Rick Miller. He knows something. Unfortunately, my interview techniques haven't improved much."

"Are you worried? He's going to be on the hunt with us." Todd's fingers rapped a breakneck rhythm against the golf cart steering wheel.

"Rick was full of shine. Maybe out in the woods, I can make amends. He'll be sober and hopefully calmer."

"Cherry," said Todd, "in the woods, Rick will have a gun."

Twelve

If I had been in my hometown, I would have marched myself to Uncle Will's office at the Forks County Sheriff's Department and reported the hearsay pointing toward Abel Spencer's suspicious death. Uncle Will would have leaned back in his desk chair, making it groan in protest under his considerable weight, and steepled his hands over his belly to consider my information. More often than not, he would have told me I was jumping to conclusions—something he didn't favor—but he would file the scuttlebutt into his cranial bank to use later as needed.

Uncle Will never trusted rumors, but always said, "A good officer could use the right rumor to point toward the location of facts." It pleased me to feed him those rumors.

I wanted to help Rookie Holt in the same way. I imagined her arguing with her commanding officer, pleading with him to ignore her rookie status and to let her follow her instincts.

He wanted hard evidence that Abel's death hadn't been an accident.

She didn't have any. Yet.

The scene ended with Deborah tossing her badge and gun on his desk, storming out of his office, and driving like a bat out of hell to Big Rack Lodge. I would jump into her '66 Thunderbird—in my imagination, not only did she have that sweet car, but the Georgia sun had returned—and together we would investigate Abel's death.

Following our success, we'd share a round of beers back in Halo at Red's. Shawna Branson would walk in and see everyone congratulating us. After Shawna's hissy fit of immeasurable magnitude, the scales would fall from Halo's eyes, calling her out on her snobbish and unjust attitude toward my family. Humbled, Shawna would testify she had lied about her alleged forced abduction by my brother. My family would forgive the Bransons.

Luke would walk in, see me, and fall on one knee and...

"You're awfully quiet again, Cherry," said Todd.

"Making out my Christmas wish list," I jabbered. "Also I think I'm long overdue for a GNO. Do you think Rookie Holt does Girls' Night Out?"

Todd's doubtful grunt was lost in the wail of the golf cart engine as he accelerated through Big Rack's gates. The lodge grounds were quiet, but music and laughter drifted from across the fishing pond. In the largest cabin, an open porch door and brightly lit windows displayed the profiles of hunters partying in Bob's cottage. The pond Christmas lights bathed the surrounding darkness in a soft, enchanting glow. A world removed from the gritty realism of the Gutersons' trailer town.

"We better keep an eye on Rick," I said. "Maybe he's just a mean drunk and he'll be calmer tomorrow. He was pretty quiet earlier today."

"Maybe." Todd kept his eyes off me and on the enchanting glow. "Or maybe put this Abel Spencer business to the side and just focus your energies on your family's problems. I know you'll feel better if you do."

"Todd, my purpose for this weekend was not to think about home. Anyway, you know I'm not a good peacekeeper. I get riled up and shoot off my mouth before my brain warns me of the consequences. Especially when it comes to Shawna Branson. I don't fear much, but I am afraid if I get involved, I'll just make everything worse. I need another solution."

"I know you don't want me to bring it up, but you have to think about Luke Harper's part in this. Everyone in Halo suspects you two are sneaking around. As the arresting officer, Harper shouldn't be involved with you at all. Cody's trial could get real ugly."

I liked to give Todd his due, but when it came to this subject, I really hated to admit he was right.

Instead I gave him a half-hearted hug, leapt from the golf cart, and turned toward the brightly lit lodge. My comfortable bed beckoned as an escape from the seediness of the Double Wide, but I felt keyed up. Strolling down to the edge of the fishing pond, I watched the shadowy revelers. But instead of celebrity hunters, Abel Spencer, or even Rick Miller, my thoughts still stole toward home.

Exactly where I didn't want them, thanks to Todd's badgering.

But I did need another solution.

I should've been celebrating this mini-vacation like those hunters. But Shawna Branson had ruined this holiday season and now threatened to ruin my future Christmases. Just like her father, Billy Branson, had ruined all my past Christmases by stealing my momma. But then, I guess Billy had also ruined Shawna's Christmases in the same way.

I sucked in a breath. That meant Shawna and I had something in common. Besides an unhealthy attraction for her step-cousin.

A step-cousin trained to solve particular problems.

I turned my back on the holiday lights and my hand fumbled for the phone in my coat pocket. So much for being on the wagon.

Calling Luke made everything worse. And calling Luke made everything better.

There's a rub for you.

I hit his direct dial number and counted off the rings.

"Sugar," said the sleepy drawl. "I know you don't sleep, but some of us have early shifts."

"I probably won't get any signal out in the forest primeval. I wanted to say good night."

"Then I'm glad you woke me. Does this mean what I think it does?"

As much as Luke's voice settled my nerves, I couldn't go there with him. "If you mean a professional consultation, then yes. I visited the Double Wide tonight." I explained what I had learned about Abel, but left off Rick's bumbling attack. No need to worry a man one hundred miles away. "I bet you anything Abel's blood alcohol comes back low. He did not fall into that ditch drunk."

"You won't be at Big Rack long enough to find out what his BAC report says."

"I know."

"You think someone pushed him."

"I don't know. Maybe. Yes. But I don't have a real motive. Just some guesses. Probably the same as Rookie Holt."

"What you've learned is circumstantial. Holt's probably learned the same. She may not find any evidence. The BAC report won't be enough."

"Desiree Guterson also mentioned the lodge owners have enough weight to influence the police not to look too hard at Abel's death before the big hunt. The lodge employs a lot of locals. That might be why Rookie Holt is alone in her theories."

"I guess it could happen, but without evidence she can't do much. If you're really worried, talk to the friend, Rick. He might give you something that he won't tell the police. Maybe he knows why Abel was agitated. If you can learn what worried Abel, you might have a motive. Point the rookie in that direction."

I chewed my lip, considering Rick's drunken warning. "Rick's not so hot on social skills, but I'll give it another shot."

A long sigh carried from one side of Georgia to the other via the airwaves. "I've a feeling you're getting your nose stuck in business where it doesn't belong."

"The only issue I've had with my nose is detecting the foul order of death and the even fouler odor of the Double Wide." I shivered and ambled toward the lodge doors.

"Just don't let your suspicions bend someone else's nose out of joint."

"Is this your way of telling me to be careful?"

"Would it matter?" He yawned. "You'll do what you want."

I smiled. "That's the first time I've ever heard you recognize that fact. You've come a long way, baby."

"I'm half-asleep here. Don't even know what I'm saying." He paused. "Sometimes it feels like this isn't going to get any better. Late night calls spent discussing a vagrant's death instead of making breakfast plans in bed."

Hope took a nosedive and I struggled to swallow my misery. "Abel Spencer wasn't a vagrant, just an alcoholic."

"You're avoiding the subject of us again."

"I had an idea that might help our situation. It could resolve some of the issues between our families." Or make them worse. But he didn't need me to spell out that possibility.

"What's that?"

My voice thickened, letting sugar dissolve the words he wouldn't want to swallow. "Find Billy Branson."

"Billy Branson?" The sleepy voice sharpened. "The man's been missing for twenty years. What would that accomplish?"

"A kind of trade-off for Shawna," I said. "Her daddy for my brother."

"Cherry." His voice held that awful pitying tone, similar to the one the church ladies used on my younger self when they'd find out my lineage. "What makes you think Shawna even wants to know her father?"

"She had those pictures of him and my momma."

"That doesn't mean anything."

"Why else would she resort to these tactics? Shawna's not just hitting below the belt, Luke. We're talking full body blows. Knockout punches for my family. All starting when those pictures went missing."

"Cherry. It's not like you've ever been sweet to Shawna. Your sister can be downright mean. And your brother did try to forcibly abduct her in order to perform a flippin' DNA test."

"Allegedly." My jaw ached from my teeth clench. "You just wouldn't understand about missing parents. Shawna wants to know what happened to her father more than she wants to hate on the Tucker kids. She thinks our momma took him from her. It's basic psychology."

"Sounds like basic horseshit to me. I know something about not having a father, or have you forgotten?"

"Burying a parent is different from one gone missing. I should know something about that, or have *you* forgotten?"

"Sugar," he said without a lick of sweetness. "How can I forget when you constantly remind me? Did you ever think you might be transferring your feelings about your mom to Shawna? That's basic psychology too."

I never did care for Freud.

Halting on the steps of the lodge, I considered a sharp retort when movement caught my eye. Between the lodge and the gift shop, a dark shape lurked. I sucked in a slow breath.

Had Rick returned from the Double Wide without my noticing?

"Luke, hon, I'm sorry," I whispered. "We'll talk about this later. I've got to go."

"Sugar, wait. I'm sorry too."

The lurker slipped to the corner of the building. Red and green lights in the gift shop window outlined the shadowy form. The man hesitated, then darted toward the open drive, heading toward Big Rack's gates.

THIRTEEN

I expelled the breath I hadn't realized I held. There was no mistaking that silhouette. Or that awkward gait.

"Cherry?" Luke's voice called from the phone I still clasped against my ear.

"Dangit if that's not Balaclava Beach Ball," I exclaimed. "What is he doing now?"

Fed up with the mysteries of Big Rack Lodge, I charged toward the man.

"What's going on?" hollered Luke.

"Everything's fine. I just saw someone who needs to bend my ear a bit. Later." Shoving my phone back in my pocket, I chugged my legs and felt the ice melt from my veins with the heat of the chase.

Balaclava had traded army greens for black. On his back, he carried a bulging pack that almost matched his midsection. He looked like an overripe plum. Glancing over his shoulder, he spied me and hurried out the gates onto the main road dividing the lodge grounds from the preserve.

"Hey," I called. "Stop running from me. I need to ask you something. Were you at the Double Wide last night asking questions?"

How many other lodge guests could be described as big and weird?

The man jerked to a stop, teetered, then spun in a sloppy pivot. "Shush," he hissed. "Why do you keep stalking me?"

"Because you're sneaking around on private property." Panting, I jogged to a stop before him. "Why did you run last time?"

"I don't know you. Why shouldn't I run?" Mr. Plum had a slight lisp. And halitosis. And that creepy air of those who wrapped themselves in the cloak of geekdom to stifle any glimmer of reality.

"I am Cherry Tucker, a portraitist. I'm the official artist for the hunt." A horseshoe and hand grenades sort of lie. "I heard you were a novelist."

"Lesley Vaughn. Not a novelist. I write nonfiction." He adjusted his glasses, the thick variety that were probably often duct taped as a kid.

"Anyway, I'd like to know what you're doing." I waved a hand at his ninja hiker outfit. "Where are you headed? I hope not back to the Double Wide, because I don't like the thought of what might happen to you there. They're a bit nervy tonight."

"Of course not," he sneered. "Do I look like I'm dressed for a bar?"

"I don't know what you're into."

"What I am into is cryptid animals. The Wendigo. Yeti. Pukwidgie. Sheepsquatch. Et cetera."

"Sheepsquatch?"

He resettled his glasses on his nose. "This creature you so callously hunt is one of many found in history. Perhaps you've heard of the Calydonian Boar?" At my headshake, he continued, "The Crommyonian Sow? The Erymanthian Boar? Surely you know that story. Hercules captured that giant wild boar."

"I'm no historian, but I'm pretty sure Hercules wasn't real," I said.

"Please," lisped Lesley. "The point is not whether Hercules captured the boar. The point is there have been stories about super swine since the dawn of history. Ten years ago, a man named Larry Earley killed an eleven-hundred-pound hog in Florida. Hog Kong. Surely Larry Earley is not mythical."

"I don't know Larry Earley, but his name doesn't sound mythical, I'll give you that."

"These are feral hogs. You can tell by their foreheads which are concave and not flat. The media likes to call them Hogzilla." Lesley wheezed a laugh.

"And you're writing a book about Hogzillas?"

Lesley cut the laugh. "I am researching the reality of such mythical beasts for my book. The world needs to see that these creatures do exist. The word on the street is Big Rack's particular swine exceeds Hog Kong in size."

"The housekeeper told me it ate one of Big Rack's calves. Looked like something large tried to get in the peacock pen too." I didn't mention I had thought the something large had been Lesley.

"Aha. The wild boars caused widespread havoc and death in ancient Greece as well. I must write this down. Hogzilla eats small cow and attacks peacocks. I thought those peacocks looked suspicious."

He reached to pull off his backpack.

"Did the Greeks hunt those boars too?"

Lesley jerked his head from his pack. "Have you forgotten? Theseus killed Phaea, the sow. And most likely Tydeus killed—"

I interrupted. "Lesley, if you know how dangerous these hogs are, why are you skulking around in the dark? Don't you know they're semi-nocturnal? This is dangerous. Let the hunters do their job and you can take a picture when they're done."

"No. No!" screamed Lesley. He dropped his pack to jab a finger at me. "You cannot let them kill Hogzilla. Who knows when the next super swine will turn up? They're crafty and superb predators. Larry Earley got lucky. This is an organized hunt. I know Jeff Digby's using special feeders to trap Hogzilla. The man is a menace."

"Calm down," I snapped. "What's going on? Are you trying to stop the hunt?"

"I'm going into those woods to find Hogzilla and get footage before he hides for good."

"It's a hunting preserve, Lesley. It can't hide forever. Besides that, the hog's tearing up the local farms. They need it gone."

"I'm sure they said the same of the mastodon." Lesley grabbed his pack and shoved his glasses up his nose. "Farewell, Miss Tucker."

"Sorry, Lesley, but I can't let you endanger yourself. And I still have some questions for you."

He made a move to leave and I launched myself at him, knocking his pack to the ground and skewing his glasses.

"Now, tell me about the Double Wide. Did you speak to Abel Spencer?"

He let out a shrill shriek. "Control yourself, Miss Tucker."

"I've got this." Jeff Digby's deep voice called from the lodge gates. "Mr. Vaughn, I've warned you. Do not go hiking into the forest at night alone. It's too dangerous. I don't care if you've paid for a room, I'll get you kicked out."

"You are no Theseus, Jeff Digby," squawked Lesley. "I will not let you kill the Georgiana Boar before I can study it."

"Miss Tucker?" Jeff stopped in the road, surveying us. "What are you doing out here? Maybe you should go on back to your room."

I had wrapped my arms around Lesley's belly. My head butted against his beach ball protuberance and my feet dug into the road. Lesley waved his arms above my body, afraid to touch me. Rain had begun to drizzle again, slicking Lesley's coat.

It was like trying to cling to a tubing raft.

"I'm protecting him from endangering himself," I exclaimed. "Plus he met Abel Spencer. Rookie Holt needs to talk to this man."

Like a tick on a pug, Jeff Digby grabbed my hips and pulled me off Lesley Vaughn. Setting me down, Jeff cast an uneasy eye on me, and then on Lesley. "Mr. Vaughn, no one but the hunt party is allowed in those woods. You have a good chance of getting lost and hurt. Possibly shot."

"Shot?" exclaimed Lesley. "Ridiculous."

"Look at you," said Jeff. "Dressed head to toe in black. What if we went out tomorrow, not knowing you were in the woods? That's why we wear safety colors, man."

"You insult me," lisped Lesley.

One of God's lightbulbs cut on in my brain. "Lesley, did you send the hunt party a themed cake?"

"Themed cake?" Lesley snorted. "This woman is a nuisance."

Jeff pointed toward the lodge. "Let's go, Mr. Vaughn. I'm personally going to see you to your room. Miss Tucker, next time there's a problem, just let our staff know."

"I was just trying to help." I raised my chin. Frigid raindrops splattered my face. I dropped my head.

"Let's get moving, you two." Jeff jerked his chin toward the lodge. "I'm seeing you both back to your rooms."

It was a good thing I was used to public humiliation or the idea of Hunter McHottie lumping me in with Lesley Vaughn would have burned the rain right off my cheeks.

Under escort from Jeff Digby, I trudged through the antler chandelier-lit foyer and rode up the elevator to the symphonic rendition of the Ramone's Christmas hit, "Fight Tonight." Alone at my door, I paused to listen for stirrings from 206, but No-Mustache was either asleep or out.

With my keycard, I slipped through the door and trod on paper. Below my wet boots lay one of my drenched and dried watercolors. I picked it up and examined the streaky woodland scene, now looking more Jackson Pollack than Claude Monet.

"What a mess," I told the painting. "Did housekeeping stop in and drop you?"

I tossed my wet coat on a chair and walked into the bathroom. My easel and supplies still stood in the tub and the watercolor pad still in the garbage. Feeling relieved the maid hadn't trashed my supplies, I retrieved the watercolor book. I grabbed the last dry towel, wrapped it around my head, then flipped through the pages until I reached the blue hat scene, hoping I could pick out something I might have painted unawares.

Then it hit me.

My eyes darted around the bathroom. Towels still lay under the sink and the toilet paper had not been refolded into an origami arrow. Also, the shampoo and conditioner I had pilfered had not been replaced.

No maid had entered this room.

I spun from the bathroom and quickly searched my small living quarters. It was difficult to tell if my suitcase had been rifled through since I had torn through it to find my reindeer sweater. My drawing pad still lay on the bed. I pawed through it, but nothing was missing. Not even the deer and bunny drawing.

"Maybe I'm going crazy," I said to the soul-patched deer. "Or maybe I forgot I had picked up that painting, then dropped it on my way out to meet Todd. Clearly, the day has taken its toll."

That seemed a better explanation. I blew off the willies, grabbed my Talladega sleeping t-shirt, and headed for the bathroom. The scrunched landscape lay on the counter and I flicked it away from the sink. The paper fluttered to the floor, landing backside up.

I snatched the drawing and stifled a gasp.

Scrawled, most likely with one of my Berols, was a message.

"Accidents happen."

FOURTEEN

I paced the room. Did the note mean that Abel's fall was nothing but an accident and I should leave local tragedies alone? Was it aggressive or plain-spoken? The scrawl looked neither angry nor peaceful, just rushed.

Knowing small towns, my curiosity probably shared a grapevine byline with Abel's fall. And knowing small towns, my curiosity was unappreciated. The Cutersons didn't like it. Rick didn't like it. And here at the lodge, the hunters wouldn't like me calling more attention to the drama and possibly further delaying or ending the hunt. Someone snarky like Bob Bass or the Sparks could have paid off one of the staff to leave me a note.

Jeff Digby had popped up out of nowhere tonight. No issue for him to get a key to my room. On the other hand, Lesley Vaughn had been sneaking away from the lodge building when I caught him. Maybe he had left notes on paintings and cakes to scare us into stopping the hunt.

Leaving the message on my own paper would keep the accuser more anonymous. And it made no bones about the intended recipient of the message.

Was it a threat? Could my poking lead to an intentional accident?

I debated what to do. Luke would want me to pull up stakes and come home. Or he'd drive out and draw attention to the relationship we weren't having. Uncle Will would have my hide if he thought I was interfering in an investigation. If he thought me threatened, he'd raise some hell with Swinton PD, which would cause that hell to rain down on me.

I called Rookie Holt instead. Better to do my own rain dance.

"Did you find someone to take care of the dogs?" This had been in my thoughts, but it also eased us into a conversation instead of jumping into, "I've been asking around about Abel and received a questionable note for my efforts."

"I took them in temporarily," said Deborah.

"Lord bless you, Deputy Holt. I've been worried about the dogs. Particularly the Bluetick. I can't get her cries out of my head."

"She's still howling." She held the phone away to give proof to the mournful lament. "The neighbors aren't happy. Neither are the other dogs. I'm hoping they'll settle in soon. It's only the first night. And one's still at the lodge, the Mountain Cur. Maybe she's some kind of alpha for them."

"I need to visit her. Can't believe I didn't think of it until now," I said. "Speaking of Abel Spencer, I heard the police were asking questions at the Double Wide. Was that you?"

"Where'd you hear that?"

"At the Double Wide. Do you think Abel heard or saw something that afternoon that might have caused some sort of retaliation towards him? Sheri Guterson thought he seemed excitable and like he was waiting for someone. Desiree said he didn't have his usual."

"Abel Spencer was a nosy old coot, but he's been a nosy old coot his whole life. If someone around here wanted to retaliate against him, I'd expect to find a few slugs, not blunt force trauma. It's an unfortunate thing to say, but it's true."

A long, insistent howl accompanied the deputy's words. I pulled my ear from the receiver to separate myself from the painful wail and search my brain for something useful. "What about footprints? There must've been some footprints around the ravine."

"Sure, lots of footprints," she snapped. "Abel's. Yours. Your friend Todd's. Also a nice cushion of pine straw and leaves that prevents footprints from showing up."

"You sound frustrated. I know you need physical evidence, but it doesn't always tell the whole story. I can help you by relaying anything useful I might hear."

"I hope you're not telling me how to do my job." After a long, weighted pause, she adopted a more businesslike tone. "I made a few calls. It seems you have a habit of getting involved in criminal investigations. This is not Forks County. I'm here to uphold the law, not entertain you. I don't know if you just have a morbid curiosity or are some kind of instigator, but I am warning you to cool your jets. If we feel you're causing problems, we'll serve you with a warrant quicker than a flea can bite."

Shinola. I guess now would not be a good time to bring up the semi-threatening message. I also guessed our *Thelma and Louise* adventures wouldn't be starting anytime soon. "Yes, ma'am."

"Enjoy your stay at the lodge."

That possibility ended with the dead man in the woods.

The next morning, I ducked out of the room just as No-Mustache stepped into the shower (he had a pretty good falsetto). Instead of rooster crow o'clock, the hunters wouldn't leave until the afternoon, which suited me fine. I was up and raring for answers. The heebie-jeebies and a gusty storm had kept me awake most of the night but had given me plenty of time to doodle in my sketchpad. As I made quick caricatures of my list of possible suspects—the hunt party, staff, Lesley Vaughn, and the Gutersons—I noted each of their connections to recent events. If Abel Spencer's fall had been a simple accident, why did I receive this vaguely insidious message? I'd bet my best sable brush he hadn't taken a spill on his own accord.

Lesley Vaughn and Bob Bass had been at the Double Wide that fateful night.

If Abel had learned something dirty on either of them while dropping off his dog, their appearance at the Double Wide might explain his edginess and inability to drink. They could easily have followed Abel. Then an accident had occurred. An accident otherwise known as manslaughter.

All the more reason to investigate before getting trapped in the woods with a homicidal maniac. Or, as it might be, I thought, a maniacal manslaughterer.

Through a spattering of drops, I rushed up a brick path winding through a garden speckled with fall flowers and metal animal sculptures to the tin-roofed cabin housing the lodge's nerve center. Each raindrop smacked the sculptures with a brittle ping.

The lodge office could help me. Security footage of the hall could tell me who had snuck in my room. And shut the door, I would've solved a case for my new BFF, Rookie Holt, and a pack of lonesome hunting dogs.

I found manager Mike Neeley behind the counter, tapping on Big Rack's laptop. Closing the computer, he swept his Big Rack cap off with a good morning.

"Sleep well?" he asked. "Hope you caught breakfast before heading over."

"Not yet. Best meal of the day in my opinion. Particularly if it starts with biscuits," I said with a voice full of hopeful persuasion. "Jeff Digby mentioned one of your cooks, Jessica, was particularly talented with Southern fare."

Mike grinned with managerial pride. "Jess's cooking has consistently drawn in weekend diners from surrounding counties, which is great for the lodge. People around here have family land to hunt on, they don't need to pay to hunt. But we like having them for dinner."

"Can I get counted as a local instead of a lodge guest for the rest of my meals?" I fluttered my eyelashes and flashed him my sweetest smile.

He laughed. "Viktor's cooking at the bunkhouse. We need Jessica here for the weekend."

Viktor. I had almost forgotten about his veiled stalking promises. Maybe he had left the note. "Sounds like Jessica's doing well for you. Why did you bring in Viktor?"

"The owners want to provide the lodge guests with fine dining."

"Where's he from?"

"Canada. He was a chef at a five-star inn. The Woodcocks were impressed with his awards and they enticed him down here with a chance at head gourmet chef at the lodge."

"Are you sure he's from Canada?"

"I flew out to meet him there." Mike's eyes widened. "Is there a problem?"

"His accent didn't sound Canadian, that's all." I eyed the computer, thinking about segues to security footage when another thought struck me. "Did you contact the bakery to find out who sent the cake?"

"There was some confusion about that. An online order, but paid in cash. No one can remember who dropped off the cash."

"Dang," I said. "And no activist group taking credit for it?"

He shook his head.

"Seems strange to go to all that trouble and not publicize your protest. I met Lesley Vaughn last night. Strange would be a good way to describe his obsession with giant hogs."

"That's Lesley." Mike gave me a quick smile and popped open his computer. "Enjoy your breakfast."

"By the way, I got locked out last night. Your security guy gave me a new key." I crossed my fingers behind my back. "I'm worried that someone could have gotten in my room using my old keycard."

He shut his computer. "If you lost a key, Ty should have recoded your door for the new key."

"Maybe you could check your security footage of the hall to see if anyone tried to get in my room."

"Was anything stolen?"

"I don't think anything's missing." His stricken look caused pangs of guilt to shoot through me. I hated lying. Although the secret romance I wasn't having made me more proficient.

"That's good." He opened his computer. "I understand if it makes you nervous, what with everything that's happened, but our key system is very good. Our cameras only watch the entrances and exits. So I wouldn't be able to tell if someone went into your room. As a small hotel, we don't have hall cameras."

"I thought I saw one in my hall."

Mike's face reddened. "Decoys. The Woodcocks invested in a state of the art key system and felt it would be sufficient with the exit cameras. We've not had issues with our security before, so we haven't felt the need to pay for CCTV in the halls. Plus we have Ty roaming the grounds at night."

"I don't suppose I could take a look at last night's footage anyway?" It was worth a try, although I hated how it made me sound pushy. And paranoid.

"I'm afraid as a guest, I can't let you do that." He raised an eyebrow.

"Don't worry about it. Like I said, nothing's really missing."

"Of course. I'll look to see if anyone who isn't a guest or staff entered the building." Mike glanced at the clock. "I'll check on that and let you know what I find. We've scheduled target practice this morning. You're welcome to join the hunters for lunch there. We'll be headed into the preserve just after."

I had until lunch to find the culprit. "See you then, Mike."

Defeated, I slunk out the office door. No way to tell who entered my room, and unless the perpetrator was an outsider to the lodge, Mike wouldn't alert me. I pulled in a deep breath, relishing the wet pine and woodsmoke-scented air, but shoved my hands into the pocket of my fleece fuchsia and lime green hoodie to stave off the cold.

I guess some people would give up or go home.

But no way in hell could someone break into my room, vandalize my own art—even trashed art—and think I'd slink away from asking questions about Abel now.

FIFTEEN

Seeking expert consultation on threats, I found Todd and the Bear in his new den. The picturesque cabins circling the far side of the fishing pond were built from roughhewn pine, painted Scarlet Lake with white trim, and had a covered fishing porch built over the big pond. Max's had two bedrooms, two bathrooms, and a living area with a small bar. His also had a squirrel painted on the door, with more stuffed squirrels cavorting in his rafters. I eyed the squirrels and then Max, who glared at the frolicking creatures.

"This insults me," he said, waving a hand at the squirrels.

"I don't reckon you feel bad for their death," I said, "but I thought taxidermy was universal. Don't they hang trophies in your country?"

"Of course."

"Then what's the problem?"

"The laugh at my expense. I know this joke."

I reexamined the squirrels, who although happy, did not seem mocking.

Todd caught my eye and shrugged. He didn't get the joke either.

Max scowled and folded his brawny arms over his black flannel-covered chest. "The American television show with moose and squirrel that attempts to teach children Cold War ideology."

Todd's brain chugged. "*Rocky and Bullwinkle.*"

"You think someone is making fun of your accent? How did you put that together?"

"A man such as me should have the cabin with the large game animal. Not the tiny creature for the young boy to trap." Max pointed his gaze out the window at the next cabin. "I was known as the Bear. I should have that cabin."

"Who has the bear cabin?"

"Bob Bass," said Todd.

"Oh my stars, is Bob Bass making fun of you for having the squirrel cabin?"

Max shifted to glare at a dancing squirrel on the rafter beam.

"We've got more important issues than you getting teased by Bob Bass." I explained what we had learned at the Double Wide, my meeting with Lesley, and the discovery of my painting-turned-secret-memo.

"I told you to leave this alone," growled Max.

"Now you believe me?"

"But this 'accidents happen' message. I do not find so threatening."

"You don't?" asked Todd.

"If I send the threatening note, it is explicit," explained Max. "I describe in detail the consequences of the action. For example—"

"I prefer not to have examples," I said. "You see the note as someone telling me that Abel had an accident."

"Yes. But this means it was no accident."

"Come again?" said Todd.

"Why else would they leave the note?" Max steepled his hands under his chin. "You must take into account the timing."

"I agree," I said. "A man dies on the eve of the lodge's biggest event."

"Perhaps there are peoples who would wish this to not be an event."

"Peoples like Lesley Vaughn?" I shook my head. "I mean, people?"

"Perhaps. But in the sport hunting, you must be responsible, paying attention to sex and age of the animal for the conservation. Some say Bob Bass does not follow these rules."

"That'd bring him some enemies. Anti-hunters and hunters alike."

A scowl curled the Bear's lips. "And I think Bob Bass cheats to win. He's won too many times in my presence. But he is like fox."

"You're talking about gambling," I said. "How can he cheat in a hunt?"

"I tell you, this Bob Bass is sly. Maybe he sends this cake to himself. To spook other contestants and make himself look more important."

"I thought we were talking about Abel Spencer's death. And it was just a cake. These are separate incidents." I stopped and circled back to an earlier thought. "Or are they? Lesley Vaughn wants to protect his mythical Georgiana Boar. He's crazier than a sprayed roach."

"You said Lesley didn't know about the cake," said Todd.

"Lesley could have been lying. Abel provided the hunting dog. Maybe he tried to scare Abel too, and that's what caused Abel's fall." I lowered the finger that had shot in the air. "But if he did and Abel died, Abel's death should have frightened Lesley into hightailing it out of town before he's caught."

Max raised a heavy brow. "If the perpetrator thought this Abel's death served some purpose and they are not afraid of being caught by police, they would continue their plan."

"That means they have no problem with murder," I exclaimed. "I figured Abel's death as manslaughter."

"Cherry." Todd's fingers drilled the wooden chair arms in a rapid-fire rhythm. "They're not afraid of getting caught by the police, but they were worried enough to warn you."

"Then we're back to my note being menacing." I scowled.

"Maybe Mike should call off the hunt," said Todd. "You could be in danger."

"I don't want to get Mike in trouble if it's nothing," I said. "He hasn't worked at Big Rack long, and I get the feeling the lodge may be in trouble. Let me do a little more digging first. It takes more than a vague note to scare me."

No protest issued from Max. The Bear wanted the hunt to continue. It hurt a teeny bit that he never tried to climb on a white horse for me, but I was glad Max trusted my intuition. I had meant what I said. I needed more information before I'd pull up stakes. We were back to square one.

The discussion had felt like a dog chasing his tail.

And I feared it was my hindquarters that would get bit.

I needed to clear my head to think, but my sketchpad was at the lodge. As it was not raining, I chose to walk back. Max, Todd, and I had agreed to meet at the skeet range for the scheduled target practice, an opportunity which would bring all the contestants together again. Without mentioning it, we acknowledged if someone wanted to stop the hunt, the shoot was also an opportunity for another incident. We had debated whether to warn Mike and decided to wait. Mike had enough on his plate.

At this point, we, like the police, were without any real evidence to prove foul play was at hand.

A golf cart whizzed past me, and I jumped to avoid a splash from the water-filled ruts. Jenny and Clinton zipped by in matching gear and Big Rack ball caps. Jenny waved.

A high-decibel shriek had me clutching my chest. Switching my hands from heart to ears, I hurried around the peacock pen and spied the Twenty Point.

I hadn't explored another obvious motive. Max didn't know Viktor, but Viktor thought he knew Max enough to wave a knife at my reindeer buttons. Viktor might have planned the squirrel cabin as a Boris and Natasha message for Max. Maybe Viktor killed Abel because he had learned Viktor was a communist spy from the Bear's homeland. However, Max's homeland politics were more criminal than philosophical.

But what did we know about Viktor, other than he snuck over the border from Canada? Why would a chef leave a five-star inn for Swinton, Georgia?

A sudden gust swept icy droplets off the peacock's roof.

Canada for Georgia? Probably for the weather.

I still had yet to spy the lauded cook, Jessica. I also failed to have breakfast. I figured two birds with one stone might land me a leftover biscuit and some information about Viktor. Because I'd met most of the other staff, I had this crazy feeling she hid from me. And why would someone who's heralded for their chicken fried steak hide from me, of all people? Maybe Viktor kept her hostage. Chained to the fryer, so he was free to serve VIPs his gooey superfoods.

I circled round to the back of the Twenty Point and knocked on the kitchen screen door, hoping my friendly assertiveness might grant me a stray piece of ham. The enticing aroma of grill grease spilled out as a woman cracked the door, then pushed it open. Her Big Rack hat covered her blonde curly hair except for the ponytail poking through the back. Beneath the brim of her hat, dark circles lined her eyes. I supposed most cooks serving three meals a day often wore weary.

"What can I do for you?" Her words were curt and her eyes wary.

"Are you Jessica?" I asked.

She searched the gloom behind me, then studied my face. "Who are you?"

"Cherry Tucker. I just wanted to meet the cook famous for her chicken fried steak." I extended a hand to shake.

"Are you one of the hunters in the contest?"

"Not a hunter, but I am in the entourage. I'm a painter and am supposed to do the winner's portrait with the prize pig."

She hesitated, glanced at my extended hand, then began to pull the door shut. "I can't talk. I'm busy."

"Wait." I'd had enough of Big Rack oddities and shoved my foot into the crack of the door. "You are Jessica?"

She peered beyond me. I glanced over my shoulder to see what could possibly have her so spooked. I may be a lot of things, but spooky was not one of them.

"Are you afraid of someone?" I covered her hand gripping the door frame. "What's going on at Big Rack?"

"Nothing's going on." She jerked her hand out from under mine.

"Then what's scaring you? Does this have to do with Abel Spencer?"

"Abel Spencer?" she said. "What about Abel?"

"You must have heard he died on Big Rack property two nights ago. Strange doings are going on here. What do you know about Abel?"

"Nothin'. Abel had one too many and should've asked for a lift instead of cutting through the property." Her eyes narrowed beneath her cap. "Now, leave me be. I've got no more to say to you."

Jessica slammed the door, leaving my foot sore, my stomach empty, and my skin crawling with the willies.

SIXTEEN

Something scared Jessica, and my suspicion meter had shot to the top of the charts, just like Bob Bass's Christmas hit, "I'd Rather Be Downtrodden Down Home Than Uptight And Uptown." I didn't know if Jessica's heebies were connected to the jeebies jumping around Big Rack, but I'd bet my best boots she was hiding from someone on the premises.

With an eye toward mysterious skulkers, I circled to the front of the Twenty Point, deliberating on my next move. Would Rookie Holt be interested in the caginess of a cook? Likely not. I'd best find other staff who might enlighten me on the reason for Jessica's paranoia before calling.

As I stood in front of the restaurant, scanning the grounds, the angry screech of the peacocks caught my attention. I hurried to see why the peacocks had halted golf cart traffic, half expecting to find Lesley playing Spiderman against their pen. A small crowd had gathered in front of the coop.

I sped my hurry to a trot.

I had questions for Lesley that had nothing to do with magical pig quests and everything to do with meeting Abel Spencer at the Double Wide Wednesday night.

"What's going on?" I shouted.

A light rain began to sprinkle. I flipped my hood up, lost my peripheral vision, and shuddered. Yanking my hood off, I let the rain style my frizzy hair and cursed my silly nerves for furthering my bad hair day.

The Sparks sat in their golf cart, parked in the middle of the path. They turned at my shout, almost drowned by the ear-splitting peacock screams.

"Another demonstrator," said Jenny. A breeze whipped her hair and her eyes gleamed with excitement. "I wonder if it'll make the news?"

"Is the demonstrator named Lesley?" I tried to see beyond their cart, but the angle only revealed Peach and Bob, not the front of the peacock cage. "Did he get in there with the peacocks?"

"Nobody's inside, they just left another message on the front of the cage," said Clinton. "Jenny, we don't want the media here. Better to ignore this."

"It might be good publicity for the hunt." Her voice rose.

"Not all publicity is good publicity."

Disappointed, I left them to their argument and ambled past their golf cart. I wanted Lesley, not another scary pig cake. Reaching the corner of the coop, I halted. A banner flapped against the wire mesh while Bob bent over an object resting against the coop. Each time he tried to get his hands around the pumpkin-sized orb, the peacocks screeched and pecked at the mesh.

Bob's hands flew from the flesh-colored object and jogged backward. "Damn birds."

"What is that?" I said to Peach as she filmed Bob's struggle.

"Hog head."

Bob took a run at the cage. A peacock brandished its fan with a screech, Bob backed off, and the bird strutted away.

"Still cold," said Bob. "Probably butchered around here. Damn activists."

The breeze stilled and the sign left off flapping to recline against the wire mesh. I sucked in my breath. In dripping red letters, someone had written, "Squeal like a Pig." Below the sign, the empty eyes of the hog stared at us, an almost ghoulish smile frozen beneath its snout.

I shuddered. Instead of a horse head in bed, the hunters had been left a severed pig.

"Get rid of it," called Clinton Sparks.

"I'm trying," said Bob. "Damn birds peck me if I get close."

"They can't peck you through the screen," said Peach.

Another golf cart whirred to a stop before the peacock coop. I glanced behind me and caught Rick's blanch as he read the sign.

"Who put that there?" He pointed a shaky finger to the sign.

"We don't know." I strode toward him, gathering courage. "I need to talk to you about last night."

Before I could reach him, he accelerated toward the Sparks, careening around their cart and through a flower bed.

"Hey," I shouted, but a peacock cut off my holler.

Bob made another run and swipe at the head.

I abandoned Rick for the sake of the peacocks. "Mr. Bass, leave that hog's head alone. It's evidence."

"Don't be an idjit. It's just some flaky treehugger ticked off because there's no TV crew. Best thing to do is ignore it."

"But we don't know if it's a treehugger. I mean, activist." I wasn't sure if Lesley could be called an activist. Maybe just screwball. "I just walked by here not fifteen minutes ago and the sign wasn't here. That means whoever left it is still on the grounds."

That thought left me cold. I could have passed the culprit and not even noticed. Was that who scared Jessica? I spun toward the tree line, searching for movement.

"It's a hunt hater message if I've ever seen one." Bob pounded a fist against the mesh, causing the birds to scatter. "Serves you right for pecking at me, peckerheads."

My hands landed on my hips. "If the activist trespassed leaving this sign, you need to let the police document it as evidence. That's how to legally deal with their shenanigans."

"Believe me, it's not worth it. It'll attract attention, which is exactly what the treehuggers want." Bob tapped his head. "Publicity. Don't give it to them."

"Mike needs to see this either way. Someone staying at the lodge could have done this. That person could be planning more stunts to disrupt the hunt. The police should deal with them."

Clinton Sparks hopped from his golf cart and strode toward us. "Bob's right. We don't need the publicity."

"Or we could document it like she said, to use later. After the hunt," said Jenny. "To show how this event attracted protestors."

"Peach's getting footage," said Bob. "Great idea to use the demonstration after the hunt. Use their publicity to make us look good. I like it."

These people boggled my mind.

"There aren't protestors. This has to be the act of a single person," I said. "That's how they got the sign up undetected. You're not dealing with a demonstration."

"One or many, it's the same thing." Bob smacked the mesh and made a grab for the hog head. "Ow. Stupid birds."

"Get 'em, Bob," said Peach.

Clinton snagged the sign and wrenched. The paper tore, leaving the ragged word "Squeal" to flap against the mesh.

"Don't you see?" I cried. "In this case, a group of protestors is a whole lot more benign than one nutjob sneaking around, leaving threatening messages."

"You don't know activists," said Bob, diving once more for the hog head. "They can get out of hand."

"Maybe this wasn't even meant as an anti-hunt sign." I stared at the dripping "Squeal." Had the culprit seen my interest in the peacocks and left the message for me? Warning me publicly not to squeal about Abel? Was this *my* horse head?

"Of course it is. What else could it be? An ode to *Deliverance*?" Clinton fisted the paper and ripped it from the cage. Shrieks rose behind the wire.

"This'll make a nice snack for something higher on the food chain." Bob staggered toward the woods, carrying the large head.

I gave up the battle, too worried about what to do without knowing for sure what I should worry about.

* * *

I headed to the lodge rooms to change out of my wet hoodie, hoping to still get some information about the mysterious Jessica. Maybe she knew something about the supposed protestors with their quasi-threatening notes and love of severed pig heads. Which, I felt, would offend Lesley, the mythical pig lover, but what did I know about defending legendary hogs?

Because I'm a naturally curious person, I couldn't help but glance into room 206 while the housekeeper cleaned the bathroom. Either No-Mustache was a last-minute packer or he was staying another night.

Two laptops blinked from the desk and a weekend's worth of flannels had been strewn about the room along with an odd assortment of camera equipment.

As the industrious housekeeper continued to swish blue stuff in the toilet, I checked the room list on her cart. No-Mustache carried the name J. Deed. Bob Bass's entourage had been on the first floor, but was checking out today. L. Vaughn also had a first-floor room, number 103.

Could one of these guests have swiped a card from housekeeping to get into my room? I dug around in her cart, looking for an extra key or some clue as to how someone could have left me that note.

The door to the bathroom closed and I jumped from the cart.

"Can I help you?" asked the housekeeper.

"Yes, ma'am," I said. "Do you know the cook, Jessica? I saw her earlier and she seemed upset. Is she doing okay?"

"I'm not sure. But you know, she hasn't been the same since...well, you know."

"Yeah," I said slowly. "How long's that been?"

The housekeeper tapped her chin. "A year, maybe? Can't believe it's been that long."

"Right, a year since..." I paused, hoping she'd fill in the hole I had just dug for myself.

"Poor Jessica," sighed the housekeeper. "Maybe it's the anniversary of Ruby's death. I can't quite remember when it happened."

"Such a shame."

"You never want to outlive your kids." The housekeeper shook her head. "Jessica's been a walking ghost ever since. I'm glad family moved here to be near her."

I tried to shake off the punch to my gut. "Poor Jessica."

Unable to bring myself to ask any more questions, I thanked the housekeeper and slipped into my room. I felt horrible about hassling Jessica, when grief had most likely forced her into the life of a kitchen recluse. My nosing around didn't seem to be getting me anything but trouble.

But then what else was new?

After packing for the bunkhouse, I changed into a cyan blue sweatshirt bedazzled into a work of art featuring a retriever carrying a dead pheasant in his mouth. I liked to match my clothing to my environment and my mood. Like the retriever, I hoped to carry the truth home from this hunt.

Although not so much in my mouth as with my mouth. By reporting helpful information to Rookie Holt so she could settle Abel Spencer's suspicious death with justice.

Maybe I should have rethought the sweatshirt.

I glanced at my phone, still plugged into its charger. Useless out in the woods. The thing was so old I could barely get a signal next to a tower. I had a mission in the next hour—to learn more about Abel's death, or at least the writer of my note—but this moment might give me one last chance to call Luke. And no one would overhear me next door.

Guilt restrained my fingers from dialing his number. Each call reminded me from what family tree Luke Harper's acorn currently dangled. But I really wanted to hear his voice. Especially after last night's abrupt ending.

Generational family feuds have no business in small towns. Statistically, someone will eventually fall in love with the wrong family member. Better to keep vendettas in the cities where a bigger population offers more choices for romance.

Too bad I hated cities.

I dialed quickly, before the most reasonable part of my brain—and as I acknowledge, the tiniest—told me to stop.

If the call wasn't meant to be, Luke would be busy patrolling or in court or doing paperwork.

Although, if he was doing paperwork, he'd probably pick up. He hated paperwork.

"Hey, darlin'." The smooth baritone caused my toes to curl inside my boots and a jolt of electricity zipped through my veins. "Caught me at a good time."

"Typing a report?"

I heard his smile. "Sitting behind Shorty's Barbecue looking up incident numbers."

"See the benefits of working in the country? You think Atlanta crime slows enough to let officers take breaks from writing reports to talk to their girl?"

"Is that what you are? My girl? Funny, since I'm not allowed to date you."

"Actually," I stammered, "the reason I called is a criminal matter. I think."

A sigh gusted from the other side. "More crime reports? What happened now? Somebody tip a cow? Or you overheard a plan to tip a cow?"

"The cows I have seen are entirely upright. It's really the mythical pig lovers that have me worried."

"You lost me."

"There's a guest who aims to save Hogzilla from his horrible fate. He thinks giant pigs descended from Greek gods or something." I explained Lesley Vaughn and the latest hog head. I'd save personal threatening notes for the dessert course. After I sweetened him up.

"You think this Lesley sent that cake and left the sign on the peacock cage?" asked Luke.

"Possibly," I said. "The hunters think it's from some kind of activist. Lesley wants to save the hog. He wouldn't admit to it, but wacky pranks seem his style. Probably cooks them up in his mother's basement."

"Then what's the big deal? It's not bothering the hunters."

"I don't know." I paused. "It's just that the intention isn't clear. Although Bob Bass is sure some kind of protestor is trying to make a statement, no group has laid claim to the disruptions. That doesn't make sense to me."

"If you had some of those gals who show up nekkid to demonstrate, I'll be sure to come on down."

I laughed. "You think I'd tell you if there were? I'll call for you when a portly pig lover decides to strip."

"This hunt is going to get a lot of exposure, what with Bob Bass's show. It would make sense for activists to draw negative attention toward the event." Luke's tone deepened into his cop voice. "However, I don't like the timing. A man falls to his death on property the night before the event begins? That concerns me."

"I know," I exclaimed. "But spooky pig heads are not murder, so it's hard to take this seriously. Unless Lesley or whoever's making the statement scared the life out of Abel Spencer."

"If this Lesley did have a run-in with Abel, then why's the perp still hanging around?"

"Exactly what I thought." My heart overflowed with pride and joy. Luke and I were on the same page for once. We couldn't dismiss the pig protestor with a suspicious death still hanging around. If we were in the same room, I'd likely attack his lips with gusto.

I offered Luke that description as a reward for his service.

"Lord have mercy, girl. I'm on duty. Where was this last night?" Luke cleared his throat. "What's the lodge say about all this?"

"Nothing. I get the feeling Big Rack is facing budget issues, due to an unreasonable amount of discretionary spending by the owners. If the lodge has to pull the plug on the hunt and pay back the ridiculous contest fees, that and the PR blight from Bob Bass's big mouth might put them out of business."

"Bob Bass's big mouth?"

"That guy is as fake as his teeth. I almost wonder if he's behind the pranks just to give himself an out for not winning. I heard he doesn't even make the kills on his own TV show."

"Who told you that?"

"Max Avtaikin. Bob spends time in the Bear's gambling cave. That's where this portrait bet came about."

"I don't trust that guy."

"Bob Bass?"

"Him too."

I let that go. Max felt similar about Luke. "Thank you."

"For what?"

"Believing me."

"Sugar, I don't think you're delusional. I think you wrap yourself in other people's business just a mite too easily. Especially when you've got other issues more pressing."

I opened my mouth to respond, then decided I needed help more than I needed to be right.

My deceased Grandma Jo would be so proud.

"Can we talk about something else for a minute?" The exhale from Luke's breath whistled in the phone. "I miss you."

"I miss you too," I whispered.

"I miss your smile and your pretty eyes and your legs when you wear that skirt. The way your hair smells like flowers and sunshine. The funny things you say." His voice dropped to a caress. "And the way my hands feel on your skin. I miss that a lot."

"Keep talking."

"I miss the way your little chin sticks out when you're feeling tough. And how you like helping folks." His purr deepened to a growl. "Even when they don't ask for it. Like a dead man. Or a rookie cop."

Now would *not* be a good time to mention notes stating "Accidents happen." Or how one of the contestants had threatened me in a bathroom. Or that "Squeal Like a Pig" might've been aimed at me.

It was a good thing we weren't having a relationship because that would mean I had issues with honesty.

"And how your need to help often gets you in a heap of trouble," continued Luke, with his uncanny ability to suss out when my personal shit-fan blew. "Trouble that gives me heartburn. I started popping Tums after our conversation last night."

"Tums are not sexy, Luke."

"So stop giving me heartburn." In the background the radio squawked and Luke paused to listen. "Cherry, we can't keep doing this. I could get suspended for having a secret relationship with the defendant's sister. It won't look good in court. Listen, I don't give a damn about our families or this archaic feud."

I chewed a thumbnail. "That's a big word, archaic."

"The whole thing is ridiculous. Finding Billy Branson won't make a bit of a difference. So the Bransons and Ballards have hated each other since Reconstruction. It's the twenty-first century. You and I need to make a stand."

"It's easier for you to turn your back on your stepfamily than it is for me to ignore my blood. I couldn't do that to Cody, not while he's sitting in jail."

"Sugar, I'm tired of relegating our relationship to phone calls. Lord knows I wouldn't have done it for anyone else."

I caught a lock of hair and twisted it around my finger. "Why's that?"

"I guess it's just that other girls are so..." He hesitated.

I held my breath, waiting to hear his verdict. Other girls are so boring? Uncreative? Silly? Intellectually inferior? High maintenance?

"Normal."

"I'm not normal?"

"Yep."

I held out the phone, throttled it, and put it back to my ear. "That's real sweet of you. I've got to go."

"Again?" He drew in his breath. "Now where are you going?"

"Target practice."

I felt the need to blast a few holes in a hay bale I'd imagine as Shawna Branson. Or Luke's hind end.

Though I'd hate to do anything to damage that delectable bit of art. It'd make the Greek gods weep.

SEVENTEEN

The overcast skies hid the time of day, but I knew skeet practice was imminent. A hunt party gathering may attract our instigator, and I wanted to be on the lookout for party poopers, particularly ones who believed in supernatural swine.

The clay shoot arena was on the far east side of the lodge grounds, beyond a strip of forest that safely separated the guest area from any stray skeet. Which meant I had to walk through the lodge gates and follow the road in the opposite direction of the Gutersons' Trailer Town, a half-mile hike.

I confiscated a stray golf cart and drove.

The skeet range was a wonder. The baseball diamond-shaped clearing had four wooden towers at each base and a shorter box for teals at the pitcher's mound.

Behind home plate, the shooters lined up in a semicircle waiting for the clay birds to fly from various towers. The control tower stood behind home plate and a long covered pavilion anchored the parking lot.

All buildings had been painted a cheery Cadmium Red. Cute as the dickens.

I found the contestants and Chef Viktor huddled against threatening precipitation in the pavilion. Viktor stood behind a ceramic-topped bar, his arms folded over his chef's jacket, studying the crowd. Smoke rose from the grill behind him and wrapped trays of food waited on the cooking space next to the grill. According to the updated schedule, an early lunch was available during the practice shoot, after which everyone would reconvene to drive to the preserve for the hunt.

Bob's entourage had circled their chuck wagons around Bob while he winged jokes, braying at his own punchlines. His eyes worked as vigorously as his mouth, darting glances about the pavilion. Was he hoping for a bigger audience or acting skittish?

Next to him, Peach's gaze remained fixed in space. At each burst of laughter, she'd flinch, then titter before resuming her dust mote observation.

Bob's manager and Risa the publicist laughed on cue while focusing on a war of thumbs, pounding on their phones.

Rick alone stood studying the targets set up on the skeet shoot grounds. A burning cigarette hung from his mouth and he appeared paler than usual. Did he suffer a hangover from the Gutersons' venomous home brew, or did something more noxious dwell beneath the morning's detachment?

Spotting Max and Todd, I headed toward their group. With the Sparks and LaToya, they stood around a stone pit where a cheery fire blazed. Max chatted with the Sparks, so I sidled between LaToya and Todd.

"What's going on?" I squinted at the targets set up on the far side of the range, then positioned myself to watch Rick and Viktor. "Guess y'all aren't shooting skeet."

"No ma'am," said LaToya. "Skeet is for birds. We're doing long range rifle practice. Just waiting for instructions."

"Although there's already been an argument about who's shooting first," said Todd.

"Let me guess who wants to be first at bat," I said.

"Jackass," muttered LaToya. "We should draw numbers or something. Everyone wants to go first."

"It does seem unfair." I eased against Todd.

He threw an arm around my shoulder and grinned down at me. "Hey."

"Hey, yourself." I stood on my toes to get closer to his ear. He inclined to meet me halfway. "I met the cook in hiding, Jessica."

"Yeah?" His words were muffled in my hair. "Did you talk her into a sausage biscuit?"

"I wish. She refused to talk, let alone feed me. I think she's afraid of something or someone. She kept looking over my shoulder until she shut the door on my face."

"What a dis."

"Peculiar is a better word for it," I whispered. "Everything's looking peculiar these days. Did you hear about the new message on the peacock shed?"

Todd nodded.

Raucous laughter, more nervous than amused, burst from the Bob Bass circle.

I drew away from Todd. "LaToya, how are you feeling about the hunt? Did that ugly cake or the sign on the peacock cage unsettle you?"

She shook her head. "Just someone acting stupid. That happens. Like I said before, sometimes we get protesters. At a marksmanship contest, they're usually crackpots who don't know anything about guns. Bob Bass has a lot more enemies, though. He's a better one to ask."

"Enemies?"

I switched my gaze from LaToya to Bob and was caught by the rocker's restless eyes. Bob tipped his hat and winked.

"If that man lays a hand on my butt, I'm going to borrow a rifle. Peach may put up with it, but I sure as hell ain't."

"Who?" Todd checked my rear, still safely hidden in my jeans.

"Bob Bass," I hissed.

"Usually when I hunt with men, they are gentlemen and good sportsmen." LaToya kept her eyes on the fire. "My dad wanted to come with me, but I told him no. I'm eighteen. I wanted to do this hunt on my own, without any coaching. I felt safe with a group of adults. Now I wished I had taken him up on his offer."

"You could call your daddy. It's not too late," I said.

She shook her head. "It'll be all right once we get into the woods. Everyone will stop focusing on themselves and get their head in the game. It's like we feel trapped here at the lodge, waiting to leave."

I studied LaToya's profile. "Is anyone bothering you, hon?"

"I'm fine." She dropped her gaze to her boots. "I just want to get this show on the road. They don't believe I'm good enough to be here because of my age. I've got something to prove."

I spied Mike hurrying from the parking lot. "I guess you'll get your chance here in a minute."

Mike walked into the pavilion and swept off his cap. Jeff Digby stood behind him, legs spread, feet planted, a rifle held against his shoulder.

"Good morning," said Mike. "Hope y'all are ready for another meal prepared by our top-rated chef. I'm sure Viktor's got something special planned for an early lunch."

"Viktor makes a superb grilled root salad with scorzonera, rampion, and skirret," squealed Jenny Sparks. "We are so lucky. Not everyone uses vegetables once lost to history."

"Historic vegetables?" I moaned beneath my breath.

Todd patted my shoulder.

Mike smiled at Jenny. "Grab a bite after target practice. I think the heavier rain is going to hold until this afternoon. We can leave at high noon, but be prepared for a wet ride."

A frisson of excitement zipped through the small crowd.

"It'll take a bit to get out to the area where Jeff tracked the hog's recent activity, especially in the weather we're expecting. The feeders are set up with green night lights and that big boy's been attacking each in turn. We've been watching him on video. We'll set up in the bunkhouse and break into our positions. Sun goes down at 5:29. You'll climb into our stands before then. Because of the weather, he might be out early."

The idea of sitting in a cold and soggy deer stand into the wee hours of the morning made my eye twitch, but the hunters looked akin to a pack of Jack Russells eyeing a treed raccoon.

"Hey, you hear any more about our protestor?" asked Bob.

Mike shook his head. "I hope it's not upsetting you."

"Naw, don't bother me. You'd just think they'd have the balls to come out and say what's on their mind," Bob spat. "Damn activists. Probably waiting on a camera crew. They don't know we're only using the GoPro. I didn't want a crew scaring a hog of this size."

"I don't want anybody out there who doesn't feel safe," said Jeff Digby. "Nervous people make mistakes. They'd be a danger to others and to themselves. Anyone who wants out will get a full refund."

Mike blanched, but his smile remained fixed.

"Of course I'm in," said Bob. "I've always planned on bagging that pig. Peach is in too."

Peach squeaked and jerked upright.

"Besides," Bob pulled his hand from Peach's backside, "we're filming and you know what they say about shows. They've gotta go on."

"I too will continue," said Max. "We have some reassurances, yes? The party is separated, but each has the guide."

"Yes, sir," said Jeff. "Each outfitter has basic medical training and is tacked out with equipment, including their own rifle."

"Very good," said Max. "But I am thinking of the witness to be certain the cheating does not take place."

"What are you implying?" Bob stepped out of his group.

"Maybe there is reason no protestor has claimed the joke." Max's eyebrow lifted. "Maybe it is not the protestor who protests too much."

The publicist Risa and Bob's manager glanced up from their phones.

Mike held his hands up. "Let's just simmer down. I'm sure no one's planning on cheating. Now does anyone want out because of the weather or otherwise?"

"We still want to go," said Clinton Sparks.

"LaToya and Rick, are you okay?" asked Jeff.

Rick had turned to face the group. After LaToya's nod, he added his own. The temper I had witnessed the previous night had been replaced with a lackadaisical deference. Maybe the alcohol did turn his personality.

“I’m going to talk to Rick again during target practice,” I whispered to Todd. “He was acting really weird this morning. I still think he knows something about Abel.”

“Just remember what I said about catching him without a gun.”

EIGHTEEN

I waited to approach Rick until Jeff had finished the safety rules for target practice. As the group headed toward the shooting boxes, I intercepted Rick with a "Morning."

He ducked his head to fix his attention on his boots, but shared my greeting and an apology. "I get a little worked up when I'm drinking."

"Why don't you want me talking about Abel?"

"Can't see how it helps."

"But it sounded like Abel was worried about something the night he died. Do you know what it was?"

"No. Abel worried himself about lots of things that weren't his problem."

"Do you think Abel would have blackmailed anyone? Like listened in on a private conversation and used it against them to make some money? I heard he tended to pry in others' affairs."

"I don't know." Rick's hands clenched and unclenched. "Just keep me out of this. You're drawing a lot of attention. The wrong kind of attention."

"What's that supposed to mean?"

"Nothing." His gaze wandered from his boots to a table leg.

"Are you threatening me?" I lowered my voice. "Did you leave me a note?"

Rick jerked his head up. "Another note?"

"Did you get a note too?"

"There was that cake. And the sign on the peacock house."

"Are you worried about protestors?"

His gaze fell upon my chin. "Have you seen any protestors?" When I shook my head, his eyes flicked to mine. "Those signs aren't from any protestors and you know it."

A large hand clamped on my shoulder. I flinched, then glanced behind me and relaxed.

"Artist," said Max. "Mr. Miller, we are waiting. Mr. Bass would like to change the position with you."

I peered around Max. Behind the row of firing stands, Bob stood with hands on his hips, tapping his boot. At my glance, he threw his hands in the air. "We ain't got all day. You can chitchat later, Blondie."

"We're going to chitchat all right," I muttered, narrowing my eyes at Bob.

Rick used my break in concentration to escape. He scuttled toward the firing point line, meekly agreeing to the stall Bob had chosen for him.

I looked up at Max. "Did you hear about the sign on the peacock pen?"

Max ignored my question, his eyes on Viktor, who had bent over the grill, artfully maneuvering food that was neither burgers nor hotdogs.

"Are you sure you don't know Viktor? He's been staring daggers at you all morning."

"No."

"You aren't sure or you don't know him?"

"I do not know of this peacock sign."

"Another warning." I shivered. "Rick doesn't think they're made by an activist either."

"He is correct. I'm sure it is nothing more than bad sportsmanship on Bob Bass's part. When do you become so nervous, Artist? Usually, you have the bravado." Max shook his head. "Do your problems at home divert your thoughts?"

"If only I could divert your thoughts," I muttered, thinking of his obsession with beating Bob Bass.

"You do so on more occasions than I would like." A thick eyebrow rose, elevating a small scar. He raised a hand as I opened my mouth. "I do not want your theories now. I must prove my skill on this gun range."

"Then I want a word with your competitor to sort out my theories. Bob Bass may be pretending to act as a demonstrator, but he is guilty of visiting the Double Wide the night Abel died. I'd like to talk about that before we're stuck in the preserve with him."

The Bear growled a foreign phrase that needed no translation to understand.

"I won't disrupt the target practice." I gave him my "don't worry, I've got this" smile and marched over to the firing line, where contestants still played musical range positions. Behind the row of firing stands, Todd lounged against a support beam of the control tower, tapping his drumsticks against his thighs. He wore safety glasses, although I suspected his headphones piped in music rather than silence.

"Where are Mike and Jeff?" I asked, then waited for Todd to pull off the headphones before asking him the question again.

Todd hiked his thumb at the parking lot. "Mike ran back to get Rick a new rifle. Rick brought an old shotgun. Jeff followed Mike."

"Good. I've got a minute." I trotted over to Bob Bass, who had switched positions with Rick to take the first stand. He stood with his rifle mounted against his shoulder, fixing his sight on the targets. "Hey, Mr. Bass. Can I talk to you about a man you might have met the other night?"

"I don't sign autographs. It's my policy." He made a popping sound and jerked the gun, pretending to fire.

"No, someone you met at the trailer bar, the Double Wide. Abel Spencer. He's the man who died recently."

Peach turned to face us in the next stall. Instead of a rifle on her shoulder, Peach had a camera before her face. "Say hi to the camera."

"Hey, camera." I turned back to Bob. "Would you mind putting the gun down for a minute?"

He sighed with the impatience of a child deprived of a toy, but laid the rifle on the ledge before him. “Didn’t meet him. We were only there for a minute or two. I offered to sing ‘Santa Got Drunk on Moonshine.’ Can you believe they’d never heard of it?”

“Actually, no. That’s pretty popular in Halo.”

“I know.” He beamed beneath his cowboy hat. “Beat ‘Grandma Got Run Over By A Reindeer’ last year on the holiday charts. Anyway, I didn’t meet anyone named Abel Spencer.”

“Did you, Peach?” I turned to find the camera aimed at me again.

“Nope. Sure didn’t. I try not to talk to Bob’s fans.”

I wasn’t sure if Abel was actually a fan, but I guess at this point it didn’t matter. “What about your publicist, Risa? Or your manager?”

“They didn’t go inside.” Bob shrugged. “City folk.”

I ignored the pot and kettle comment. “I don’t suppose you saw anybody talking to an older man? Kind of wiry and stooped. Had on a blue Braves cap.”

At their indifferent headshakes, I pointed at her camera. “Did you take any footage at the Double Wide? Maybe you caught Abel on screen.”

Bob rolled his eyes. “Did you, Peach? It’s not like I was doing anything interesting.”

“I think I got a minute or two of you trying the moonshine.” She touched buttons on the back of the camera, then held the camera out for us to see.

There was no mistaking the kitchen counter and the surly Gutersons who had handed Bob a plastic cup of white lightning.

We couldn’t hear his comment, but the women had exchanged a look just before Bob swallowed, then spit the liquid on the counter.

“Hey now, Peach. You need to edit that out,” Bob whined.

“Sorry, babe.” Her thumb moved over the delete button.

“Wait,” I said, spying Abel Spencer in the background. He stood by the front window, peering into the darkened glass.

His gaze shifted from the window to Bob's sputtering and the scene disappeared.

"Dammit," I said. "That could be evidence for the police. You shouldn't have erased it."

"There's nothing there but me trying stuff that didn't pass the FDA standard. Don't worry about it, honey." Bob smirked. "Like I always say, hakuna matata."

"Bob," said Peach. "I think animals say that. Vegetarian animals."

"That can't be right."

I had a feeling Bob and Peach were one taco short of a combo plate. Each.

My hair whooshed around my face. A scream sent me spinning.

A small orange saucer flew toward the parking lot. Jeff and Mike halted their hike from the lot and followed the skeet's trajectory before twisting back toward us.

The air whistled. I dropped to the soggy mat.

This time, a heavy thud smacked the control tower and bits of clay rained onto the cement beneath.

"Todd," I screamed. "Get down."

"Drop," yelled Jeff, running forward with his rifle. "Everyone, get on the ground."

I flattened myself. Above me, another orange disc whizzed through the air and flew toward the pavilion, crashing into a pillar.

If I hadn't ducked, that pillar would have been my head.

NINETEEN

"Holy shit," wheezed Bob. He had rolled into a ball on the stall's mat. "We're not supposed to be shooting clay. What the hell is going on?"

I jerked up my chin and watched another teal fly from the low trap house. It zinged like a fastball pitch, flying through Bob's stall and smashing into the control tower behind us. I glanced at Peach in the next stand. The camera lay next to her, still pointed at us, while Peach had covered her head with her hands.

"Peach, it'll be okay," I said. "The traps can only hold so many teals."

"I'm getting soaked," she complained.

Getting wet seemed the least of our worries. But she hadn't been the one almost decapitated by a chunk of china.

A crack broke the air and more clay rained, this time before it reached the firing stands. I turned my head and saw Jeff Digby kneeling behind the stalls. With his rifle wedged into his shoulder and his cheek against the stock, he readied to blow another target out of the sky.

"Jeff, what's going on?" I hollered.

Another disc whizzed from a tower. Jeff's rifle tracked the orange disc and blew it to bits over the range.

"No idea. We didn't even turn on the skeet software." The rifle barrel trained on the next tower. "Mike, get to the breaker panel and shut this down."

"Already on it."

I craned my head and saw Mike running in a crouch toward the tower. I glanced over my other shoulder and saw the contestants flattened on their stall mats. Max's cane had fallen next to his body and he was holding his knee.

Jeff's rifle cracked.

I flinched.

The pungent smell of sulfur and hot metal mixed with the grill smoke pluming from the pavilion.

"Bear," I hollered. "Are you okay? Did you hurt your knee?"

He raised onto a thick arm to send me a chilling look. "Do not worry about the knee, Artist. Keep your head down. Did you not notice every disc is aimed at you?"

"I'm out of here," said Bob, army crawling out of the stall. He waited until Jeff had shot another clay pigeon to dust and hunker-ran for the pavilion.

Peach poked her head up. "Where did Bob go?"

"Pavilion," I said, but didn't add my thoughts about a man who would abandon his gal to save his own ass. "Peach, I'll watch for the next one, so you can get away too. They seem to be timed out." I flinched as Jeff's rifle cracked again. "Go."

Peach scurried off her pad and ducked under the control tower to slide in next to Todd.

"Get down," yelled Jeff. The rifle swung toward the far right tower and blasted another disc.

A shadow fell over the range. I looked up. The field lights brightening the day's gloom had gone out.

"I cut off the breakers," Mike called from somewhere behind the control tower. "The traps are down."

The hunters slowly pulled themselves to sitting and Jeff lowered his rifle. I raced toward Max to check his knee. He sat on the mat with his legs extended.

"Are you in pain?" I asked. "Lord, you could have blown that knee out again."

"It is nothing." Sliding his knees up, he gritted his teeth, grabbed the lattice separating the firing stands, and pulled himself to standing. I ducked under one big arm to support him and he hissed as his weight adjusted to the bad knee.

"That's it," I said. "To hell with this stupid hunt. You're going to a doctor and then home."

"Stop treating me like the child. Give me moment and I will be fine. I have never let pain defeat me and I will not let it now."

"Someone tried to kill us," I exclaimed. Maybe a bit too loudly, judging by the twisting heads and shocked faces.

"Hush," muttered Max. "You'll make this worse. If anyone should go home, it is you. Your head was the only one endangered."

"It could have been Bob Bass," I whispered. "I was standing in his stall."

From the pavilion, Bob's cursing carried across the range, making my ears burn.

"If that is true," Max said, "then these ambiguous messages are meant as a threat to him. Do not say anything yet. Bob Bass will cause much havoc on this lodge and cost them possibly millions, when it may not be their fault. He is known to easily cast the lawsuit. First, we need to know what caused the traps to start. In the case of the criminal act, we will make your suspicions known."

"Any whiff of a criminal act and I'm going to the police. I don't keep secrets," I muttered.

Max slid a hard glance at me and raised an eyebrow. I bit my lip, realizing that statement made me a liar. But this was neither the time nor place to admit a secret love life, so I shot him a look of my own, before turning away to hide my embarrassment.

"The craziest thing I've ever seen," said Todd, hurrying to meet us. "Are y'all okay?"

"I'm fine," I said. "But Max has messed his knee up again."

"Damn," said Todd. "I'm supposed to be watching that knee."

"What is this meaning?" Max growled.

"Nothing," I said quickly. "Let me get you some ice." I hightailed it toward the pavilion.

Inside the pavilion, Bob's publicist tried to match Bob's shouts with soothing words. Peach and her camera stood behind them, offering an occasional word of support. Viktor watched the proceedings from his grill station.

I stopped in front of his counter, my breath jagged with agitation. "Do you have any ice?"

His thick brows lowered. "You still have your head, I see."

"What?"

"The Bob Bass complains his head was nearly taken off. I am watching. The small disks came closest to you, not Mr. Bass." Viktor bent to reach beneath the counter and yanked open a door.

"Barely," I said. "Thanks for your concern. Or were you hoping to serve my head for dinner tonight?"

"I wonder if there is enough protein inside that thick skull for a meal?" Viktor filled a baggy with ice. "I am warning you. You work for the Bear, and you'll be lucky to keep that head attached. Look what already happens."

I gaped.

Viktor slapped the bag of ice on the counter. "Your mouth will draw the flies. You tell the Bear, I am watching him carefully. If I were you, I'd leave him now. Go home, Miss Tucker."

Snatching the bag, I whirled away from Viktor. The Sparks and LaToya had already moved back into the pavilion to huddle around the fire pit.

With his cane, Max hobbled toward the fire, shooing off Todd's attempts to help. He eased onto the edge of the fire pit, his bad leg extended before him and arms crossed.

Long lines on the sides of his face framed his high cheekbones. The slight lift on the edge of his eyelids lengthened with his grimace.

"This should help," I said, laying the ice bag on his knee. I kept Viktor's warnings to myself. The Bear's pride was on the line, and I feared what would happen to his knee if he decided to acknowledge Viktor's threats. I'd have to watch Max's back for him. Like hell I was going home if this Viktor decided to make trouble for the Bear.

But first, I needed to know how skeet traps turn deadly. "I'm going into the control tower to ask Mike for a first aid kit."

"Stop worrying so much. You are like the old woman." Max dropped the ice bag onto the edge of the fire pit. "My knee cannot feel this ice through the wool tweed, in any case."

"You could shove the ice down your pants."

I backed away at the low growl uttered from his throat.

Todd flinched. "Maybe I'll look for the first aid kit too."

I glanced up at the tower. Through the windows, I could see Mike Neeley and Jeff Digby gesturing like they were in the midst of a heated argument. "I'll be right back." With my eyes on the window, I patted Max's shoulder. "We'll fix you up."

Before Max could protest, I dashed out of the pavilion.

Todd caught me in two of his long-legged strides. "You want to find out what happened, don't you?"

"You're curious too. I have to know what happened. Skeet doesn't fly out of those traps like a cannon. They're supposed to arc up in the air like a bird."

"Unless we're talking *Angry Birds*."

I pointed at the tower. "Looks like the manager and the field guide are in the middle of a knock-down, drag-out. We may learn something useful from that."

"Fighting about the skeet screw-up?"

"Mike's good people and I can tell he's worried about the lodge. Especially if someone like Bob Bass threatens to litigate."

"What do you mean?"

"The Bear says Bob's well-known for being sue-happy."

"But he's shrugging off all these anti-hunt demonstrations."

"What demonstrations? Some hog-related messages. We don't even know if they were made by an activist like Bob Bass claims. It could be Lesley Vaughn, off his nut. He's not anti-hunt. He's just pro-pig. I just don't know if he's whack-a-doodle enough to have killed Abel. Did you see anybody else here?"

Todd shook his head. "I was watching the contestants. But none of them went into the control booth."

We had reached the red stilt structure and stood at the bottom of the stairs. Through the open trapdoor above us, I could hear the argument I saw from the windows. Mostly Jeff Digby yelling about safety and liabilities.

I flicked a look at the firing stands. "Where are the guns?"

"Digby collected all the rifles and locked them in a box in his Gator."

"Jeff's probably worried about more accidents. Wasn't it amazing how he shot those targets to save us from getting hit?"

Todd's gaze hardened. "Are you going soft on Digby?"

"Seriously?" I gave him a slight push on the arm. "Let's go up before they kiss and make up. I want to hear what they're saying in the heat of it."

We climbed the stairs and stepped inside the wooden box before either man noticed us.

Muted light flooded in from the narrow sides and floor-to-ceiling front window. The men stood before a long table holding computer equipment and thick binders.

Mike held a hand up to cut off Jeff's rant and turned toward us. "What can I do for you, Miss Tucker?"

"Ma'am." Beneath Jeff Digby's trimmed beard, crimson flared, licking his cheekbones.

"We came to grab the first aid kit," I said, stepping into the center of the room.

"Who's injured?" asked Mike. "I thought no one got hit."

"Don't worry. My friend has a bum knee and he must have wrenched it during your mishap. We mainly need ibuprofen and something for his pride."

"Let me get it for you."

I turned to Jeff Digby. "Do you think someone deliberately set the targets to fly at us?"

"Can't see how. They'd have to mess with the skeet software."

"What do you mean?"

"You can program each tower for the number of clays launched and their speed, angle, and size," said Mike, handing me a bottle of Advil. "The software sends a signal to each tower and triggers the launcher for the kind of throw you want."

"But how can it go off if no one is pushing the buttons?" I said, revealing my complete ignorance about all things electronic.

"I guess it was a glitch," said Jeff. "And if so, I'm going to kick some programmer's butt from here to tomorrow. I didn't know the damn thing was on. Must have started up when we hit the power to turn on the field lights."

"How hard is it to break into this building? Could someone have known how to time the program thingy for when y'all started target practice?"

"You think someone did this on purpose?" Mike pulled in a tight breath. "How?"

Jeff shook his head. "The building was locked tight. Mike and I are the only ones with a key because the equipment is so expensive. Plus the whole area's surrounded by the fence and locked gate. That fence is a ten-foot-high chain link."

"You should check the fence line anyway," said Mike. "I'll call the software company. Maybe they can tell us what went wrong."

"I'll check the fence, but I can't see how or why," said Jeff.

The why was the issue that scared me.

"What else can go wrong this weekend?" Mike leaned against the table. "I don't want to cancel this contest, but this is some bad juju."

Jeff shook his head. "Now or never. I can't keep that hog loose any longer. As far as I'm concerned, the big hunt's this weekend or we can't do it at all."

"Surely the contestants can't want to continue after this happened," I said.

Bob Bass's reedy whine drifted through the open trapdoor, complaining that they wouldn't have time for more target practice. I heard the low murmur of Max's retort. Bob's whine turned to a taunt about catching the hog and Max's gimp.

"Good Lord," I muttered. "They still want to hunt."

"If we don't let them hunt, they aren't going to take it well," said Mike. "You know what can happen, Jeff."

Jeff glanced at Todd and me.

We feigned polite ignorance at Mike's implication, but the consequence seemed clear. Big Rack could face financial ruin by canceling an event this well-publicized. Particularly when an egomaniac like Bob Bass felt gypped of his trophy.

I hated to spell out the other consequence of continuing the hunt. "Bob Bass thinks anti-hunt protestors are behind the pranks. Maybe one's gotten out of hand. Have you seen Lesley Vaughn today?"

"Lesley Vaughn's obsessed with Hogzilla, but harmless," said Jeff Digby.

"But he's been sneaking around your woods, spying." I turned to Mike. "We caught him last night headed for the preserve to track down Hogzilla."

"I think Lesley's harmless too, but his antenna doesn't pick up all the channels, you understand. He drives Jeff nuts, asking to track Hogzilla with him."

"What about other guests?" I thought about the ominous phone conversation I'd overheard that now added to the menacing atmosphere. "There's a guy in the room next to me. Deed. What about him? Is he a hog lover like Lesley Vaughn?"

"Listen," said Mike. "I know you feel involved because of Abel, but this isn't your place. I can't discuss guests like this. Just let it go. Jeff and I will handle it."

"If there's something weird going on, as a guest, I want to know who's rooming next to me. Remember someone broke into my room."

"She's right, Mike, and in this case, not discussing a guest might make it worse. You should have seen her with Lesley." Jeff turned to me. "Jayce Deed's a photographer. We didn't take any other hunters this weekend because of the contest. He's from out west and just here to relax and do some photography."

"Thank you, Jeff." I turned to Mike. "I'm not trying to infringe on the privacy of your guests. But with all that's happened, it feels awful coincidental to me that you've got a sudden software snafu that could have knocked a person's head off."

"I don't think it would have knocked your head off," said Todd. "But it would have made a pretty big dent."

I shot him a "not helpful" look.

Mike's brows came close to knotting. "It had to have been a glitch. I'm going to call the software company now to make sure. But at this point, unless the hunters ask for a cancellation, I'd need a better excuse to call off the hunt."

What more do you need than attempted murder, I thought, and prayed that wasn't the case.

TWENTY

To top off the morning's scare, icy rain began to trickle from sodden clouds. While Mike spoke to the hunters about software glitches and Todd assisted Max to their cottage, I scooted back to the lodge in a golf cart.

Although I felt bad for Mike and the other Big Rack employees, I hoped the contestants chose to cancel the hunt.

Because they were so competitive, I doubted they would.

Back in my room I cursed my lack of dry clothes, changed again, and without hesitation, grabbed my phone to dial up Luke.

To hell with family guilt, I'd almost gained a saucer-sized hole in my head.

"Luke," I said when he picked up. "We might be leaving soon. Can you talk?"

"Just for a quick minute." His voice rose. "I'm watching the lunch rush to pick up speeders."

Considering the size of Halo, I didn't think the chances of a farmer zooming home to check on the state of his winter wheat would hinder us any.

"So there was a mishap at the target practice." I explained the skeet incident, carefully choosing my words to prevent Luke from an apoplectic fit.

"Cherry, that's more than a mishap. If it's not a computer glitch, that could be attempted murder. At the least, it's malicious intent. You better hope the software has a design flaw."

Damn his power to see through my whitewashing.

"Once again, I'm unable to tell if a certain party was the intended victim," I said. "At least no one got hurt, except Max. He messed his knee up, diving from clay targets. I've got Todd on nurse duty, don't worry."

"I don't worry about Avtaikin as much as you do." Luke clipped his words. "You're trying to downplay this accident. Why?"

"I'm not downplaying anything. I told the manager that he should cancel the hunt. What with that anonymous note on my painting, I'm pretty sure someone here doesn't want me asking questions about Abel's death. Although for the life of me, I can't figure out if the peacocks and cake messages have anything to do with it."

"Forget the peacocks," he growled. "What is this anonymous note?"

I sucked in my breath, hoped the note wouldn't freak him out, and blew out my story in one quick exhalation. "Someone broke into my room and left me a message. 'Accidents happen.'"

The other side of the airwave went still. Except for the sound of Halo's lunch rush speeding by and Luke's heavy breathing.

"Hey, baby?" I whispered. "You still there?"

"I don't like it. Not a bit."

"What do you think it means?"

"It means someone wants you to leave this Abel business alone, Cherry. Why'd you wait so long to tell me?"

Because I didn't want to worry him? Or because I was afraid he'd make me stop poking around? "It's not a very explicit message. Kind of vague, if you ask me."

"Someone broke into your room. Did you tell the lodge manager?"

"Yes, I did. And we didn't see anything on the security feed because they have low-rent security for such a high-rent hotel."

I won't repeat the words blasted into my ear.

"Girl, you better know what you're doing, because it sounds like you opened up a hell of a can of worms over there. I'm going to make some calls. You hold tight."

I would hold tight, but I couldn't hold still.

"It's almost time to leave for the bunkhouse," I said, trying to lighten the mood. "Or as Lesley Vaughn would put it, our destiny with the Super Swine awaits. Anyway, I guess my investigation is over. I won't be in my room anymore, so no worries about more break-ins."

"Not funny. Just watch your ass, because if someone dares to lay a finger—" Luke broke off his words. "This is one holy mess. I'm calling Swinton PD. I'm guessing you didn't tell them about the note either."

"Calling Holt was next on my list, and that'd save me some time if you did it for me. They sure as heck don't listen to me anyway." But I sure as heck didn't need an obstruction charge. "Could you leave my name out of it, though? Rookie Holt's a bit touchy about my interest in Abel's death. Until I have something solid to give her, I thought I should lay low on investigative reports."

"I'm buying more Tums."

"Just buy economy-sized," I said. "I'll call when I get back from the woods."

I couldn't stop the hunters from continuing the contest just like I couldn't stop Shawna Branson from ruining my family's reputation. I couldn't even stay away from Luke, when I knew we'd have no future. I was just torturing myself with these calls for advice.

But I knew I couldn't let those people go into the woods alone without knowing who was behind this or why. Someone had to be wary. I came to Big Rack to get away from trouble, and it looked like by avoiding one kind, I had stepped into something much bigger.

I hated that my last words to Luke might be advice on shopping for heartburn medicine.

* * *

From the overhang of the Twenty Point, I watched the hunters ready themselves for the trip into the preserve's back forty. Whereas I wanted to cling to the warmth and aridity of any manmade structure, the hunt contestants trotted about in the drizzle like a pack of terriers, barking excited greetings and occasionally shaking the wet off their insulated rain hats. I squinted at Todd, who looked neither miserable nor excited to stand in the clammy, gray weather. He wore his best poker face, which meant he hid some powerful feelings.

Or was playing poker in his head.

"I guess the contestants didn't call off the hunt," I said. "How do you feel about going out into the woods with a suspicious person on the loose?"

"At least the SEC season is finished. I'm not missing any football today."

I patted his arm.

Mike bumped out the Twenty Point's door, a clipboard in his hand. "Y'all ready to go?"

"Any news on the skeet software glitch? Did Jeff find any issues with the fences?"

"Fences were fine. No break-in detected. The skeet company's going to read through the system log to figure out what happened. Of course, they don't want to admit any fault on their part, which is why someone is coming out to check the towers."

"Mike, think of the consequences if something else happens. You can still cancel now."

"It had to have been an unfortunate fluke. I spoke to everyone individually and they all want to continue. The anti-hunting signs seem to spur them on. They're all determined to win."

"Winning isn't everything. Y'all seem to have forgotten about the death on this property."

Mike blew out a sorrowful sigh. "I really am sorry you found Abel. It's upset you. Are you sure you don't want to go home?"

At my headshake, he nodded and slogged out into the rain.

"I tried," I told Todd.

"Do you want to go home?"

"Are you kidding? Who's going to watch over this crew?" I waved my hand at the happy hunters. "Besides you, of course."

"Thanks." Todd gave me a heart-tripping smile. "But I'd rather do it with you than by myself. Watch over the crew, I mean."

"I wish I could find this Jayce Deed before we leave. He wasn't in his room when I checked. He might have seen something." I turned toward the restaurant door. "I'll check here one last time. I could use some coffee anyway."

Like a harbinger of doom, Viktor passed through the Twenty Point door, carrying a large plastic tub. "No coffee. The hog will smell you."

"Pigs don't like coffee either?"

"I see you did not take the advice I offered."

"To go home?" Too many people wanted me homeward bound. "My friend, Mr. Max, is determined to win the hunt. I'm not abandoning him."

Viktor delivered me an eyeball full of bitter repugnance. "What is the saying? It is your neck in the line."

"On the line. Not in."

"I think you get my meaning." He dipped his head and hurried to load his tub in the back of one of the utility vehicles.

I tried not to think of his meaning. My nerves couldn't handle many more portentous messages.

"Artist, are you ready to mark this day in history with the canvas and paintbrush?" Max limped through the Twenty Point door, a thick walking stick in hand. "What has happened to your coat?"

I glanced down. "The chartreuse puff paint is running. I don't think it's waterproof."

Contrary to most of the Big Rack population, Max didn't wear camo weather gear. He was outfitted in a gentlemen's field coat, matching tweed slacks, knee-high rubber boots, and a tweed flat cap. He pulled a silver flask from an inside pocket. "Here, warm yourself with this."

"I'm not taking a shot and then climbing in a Gator for a bone-shaking two-hour drive. I'd rather keep my lunch, thanks." I eyed his getup. "You do realize we're stalking a hog in the rain, not pursuing a fox on horseback?"

His glacier eyes increased my shivers. "Englishmen hunt in such weather. I find traditional clothes the more comfortable."

"Glad I'm not English. I miss the sun." A frenzy of icy raindrops increased their spatter. "I didn't bother to bring my oils. I brought my soft pastel kit and sketching gear instead."

"Excellent." By the arc of Max's chin, I had a feeling the English field outfit had more to do with posing than hunting.

Max turned and I followed his line of sight to the Gator where Peach Payne and Bob Bass waited. Bob had also dressed for the occasion. His usual peacock-feathered cowboy hat accompanied a thick, charcoal-colored wool field coat with a sheepskin collar. Catching Max's eye, Bob held out his arms to shoot him with a mock rifle, then flashed his whitecapped smile.

"Considering all that's going on, I don't find fake shooting very funny," I said.

"Lighten upward, Artist," said Max. "Bob Bass will be defeated today."

With a laugh too hearty for a soggy afternoon, Bob Bass shot Peach with a finger Uzi.

"I can see why some anti-Bob Bass fanatic might have done those pranks," I remarked. "He would incite the most harmless into crazed stalkers."

"I agree. But the stalker will have much difficulty following us so deep into the wood. Now we can focus on the competition and not the hijinks." Max clapped me on the back and limped toward the group of utility vehicles, calling out to the Sparks and LaToya.

"I don't have a good feeling about this."

Todd rubbed my shoulder. "It's probably all the trail mix and Funyuns you've been eating."

We followed Max, lugging our bags into the rain. Between the five UTV side-by-sides, Jeff Digby barked orders to his crew of outfitters. The contestants handed over their rifles to Mike to place in the long, cushioned fire box strapped in the back of the Mule, the only two-seated vehicle.

Once again, Rick clung to the sidelines. Darting a look toward me, his eyes met mine then flew away. Hunching his shoulders against the rain, he trudged to the far end of the parking area to smoke.

"I wonder if the skeet accident shook up Rick," remarked Todd.

"That man's more jittery than a cat in a room full of rockers. But considering what we just went through, it makes sense. I'm not sure why everyone else is taking it in stride. You'd think they had clay pigeons shot at their heads every day."

"You seem fine."

"You know me. The school psychologist suspected I have an underdeveloped amygdala. How about you?"

"The school psychologist warned me not to hang out with you. But I didn't listen then either."

A yelp carried across the drive. From the front seat of an empty Gator, a brindle with expressive eyes and a stocky body rose on her hind legs, then barked a greeting.

"That's Abel's dog." I hurried to meet her. Dumping our bags in the rear cargo space, Todd and I swung into the back bench.

"Hey girl, good to see you again," I said, leaning over the seat to pet the excited creature. "I met your comrades. Don't you worry, I'm on the case. You know that, don't you?"

Mike walked toward us carrying a bungee cord and hooked it over the mounded gear behind us. "That's Buckshot. She sure has perked up. Real miserable in her pen, but now that we're headed for the hunt, she's back to her old self."

"You're not going to let Buckshot go after this behemoth hog, are you?" I rubbed her soft, floppy ears. "With the purported size of that monster, it's liable to eat her."

"No, ma'am." Mike circled to face me. "Buckshot's a bayer. If we need her to track, she'll holler when she scents the hog."

"She's a sweet dog," said Todd. "Are you hunting too, Mr. Neeley?"

"I'm just along to make sure everything goes to order." Mike adjusted his gaze and waved to someone behind us. "I've got to help. Talk to y'all later."

A hand grasped the roll bar and Jeff Digby swung into view. Jeff wore the rain clothes of normal hunters, Mossy Oak Gortex. A heavy five o'clock shadow accentuated his features.

"Y'all set?" Jeff asked.

"Did you find Lesley Vaughn?"

Jeff rolled his eyes. "No. But I told the staff to look for Lesley. He's meant to check out today. But someone did try to sneak through the reserve gate before dawn. The alarm went off."

My personal rain cloud magnified and grew stormy. "Dadgum, I should have stayed on that guy. I could've camped outside his door."

"Not really your job, is it?"

"What if Lesley's intent is to do us harm?"

Jeff eyed my troubled features. "Don't worry. Lesley's spent plenty of time here at Big Rack. He can be a nuisance, but he wouldn't hurt anyone. I don't think he went anywhere, even if he tried. He can't get far without a vehicle. These woods are thick as molasses. If he's on the trail, we'll spot him." With a nod, Jeff turned to bark more orders at his crew.

I looked at Todd. "If Lesley or someone else is trying to stop this hunt with 'accidents,' that hog is not the only thing that's going to be stalked in those woods."

TWENTY-ONE

The trip to the bunkhouse included two plodding hours of bumping and jerking through the cold and wet, plus an extra hour tacked on for pushing the side-by-sides out of deep mudded ruts. The forest seemed devoid of any life, including one Lesley Vaughn. I hoped he had given up his hog tracking and gone back to his room to dry off and warm up like any sensible person would. Unfortunately, Lesley didn't strike me as sensible.

The roar of the UTV motors and churning of wet clay made discussion impossible. In the first hour, the hunters and guides hooted joyfully at each tree-root bump and fling of mud. By hour two, we huddled miserably, fearing each mud bog might be a side-by-side's last. No one wanted to end our travel with a long trek through steady rain, even if it meant the possibility of sneaking a peek at the Great Pig.

I gave up on friendzoning and clung to Todd for warmth and for fear that I might get bucked into the downpour. Huddled betwixt Todd's amply muscled pecs and guns, I grasped his damp coat with one hand and the edge of the seat with the other. He held me tight with both hands. I could only imagine such stability derived from clenching the seat with his well-defined glutes.

A picture I tried to pass from my mind unsuccessfully.

After too much time alone with my thoughts, the path curved and presented a break in the forest. A tin-roofed cabin, wide and long with a low overhang and deep porch, appeared. White Christmas lights had been strung along the rafters and a fresh wreath hung on the door, welcoming us with a bit of holiday cheer. My heart, sore butt, and stiff spine gladdened at the sight. Immediately, my stomach woke, shouted, and scared Buckshot into a barking frenzy.

The side-by-sides slowed to a stop, spitting mud against the porch railing.

Max turned in the front seat and eyeballed us. "So cozy."

The man didn't suffer a drop of mud splatter and had remained as cool as whipped topping through each jostle and mud stick. Beside him, Buckshot also turned to observe our backseat clinch. She gave a happy yelp of approval and climbed over Max to bound into the surrounding bushes.

"Very funny," I replied, prying my stiff fingers off Todd's coat. "And now I understand why we're staying in the bunkhouse. But if this place doesn't have hot water, I'm walking back."

"It's got hot water all right," muttered our outfitter. "I suppose y'all might call it roughing it, seeing as how we'll share bedrooms and there's no TV, internet, or cell phone service out here. Other than that, most folks could live pretty comfortably. Better than my kin, anyways."

"It is these comforts that make me happy to be American," mused Max. "At home, the hunt weekend means to sleep in open air. Maybe a tent. In America, you have the house for sleeping everywhere. Even in, as you say, the middle of nowhere."

"Only Americans with your size of wallet, Bear." I turned to our bearded driver. "I've been thinking you look real familiar. Hard to tell staring at your back and with you covered in camo. But didn't I meet you at the Double Wide last night?"

"Yes, ma'am. Caleb Guterson." Hopping from the Gator, he ducked his head against the rain and followed the cluster of outfitters to the porch, where Jeff Digby stood, handing out orders.

"A Guterson working for Big Rack?" I said. "That doesn't make sense. Don't they hate the Woodcocks' takeover of this area?"

"I reckon a paycheck's a paycheck," said Todd. "The lodge probably called out to local hunters as extra guides for this weekend. And if they poach, I imagine he knows the lay of the land pretty well."

"I don't like it," I said. "All these weird incidents, with the last one almost killing someone. Lesley Vaughn could be on the loose, looking to protect his monster pig. The Bob Bass haters haven't come out of the woodwork to protest, but there's always that possibility. And now one of the Big Rack enemies is employed for the hunt? What is Mike Neeley thinking? He should have called this off."

Max turned to study the man working a key in the lock of the door. "Mike Neeley strikes me as the man with the concern for others more than himself. He must keep Big Rack going. Too many lives depend on the jobs. He has not worked here long. Less than a year."

"Mike Neeley is going about this all wrong. With a cancellation, Bob Bass might have spread bad press for Big Rack, but the lodge may never get over the publicity of two deaths."

The Bear twisted to shoot me a hard look.

"Two deaths?" said Todd.

"Don't you see?" My voice worked into a furious whisper. "It's all I could think about on this ride. Now we're out in the wilderness, where someone can easily hide. And unless we turn around and go back as a group, we're trapped. We'll be spread out in the deer stands like sitting ducks."

"Artist, you must save your creative expression for the artworks." The Bear reached over the seat to rub my knee. "Do not worry so much. I will not let anything harm you. Besides, we're all armed."

"That's exactly why I'm worried. Everyone's armed and there's a nutjob on the loose."

As promised, before sundown we found ourselves sitting in deer stands with enough night vision equipment and arms to supply a CIA mission. After deliberating over whether to stay in the warm bunkhouse with Viktor or huddled next to a space heater in a deer stand with Max's team, I chose the stand as my first watch. I didn't like leaving Buckshot behind but trusted her to remain vigilant with a whispered word to watch Viktor.

After thirty minutes of non-hog sightings, the walkie-talkie squawked.

My ears perked and I listened to the garbled, whispered report from the Group Two guide.

Our team outfitter, Tennessee, reported our status and fell back to watching the quiet forest through thermal imaging binoculars.

"Tennessee," I said, scooting across the wooden box to his side of the blind. "Please translate that message. Did someone get hurt?"

"Mrs. Sparks twisted her ankle, ma'am." Tennessee gave Max a look of marked impatience. Having tired of shushing me himself, Tennessee looked to the other male group members for assistance. Max and Todd knew me better than to try. This was the very reason my brother had rarely taken me hunting.

"Twisted her ankle running away? Or fighting off someone?" I listed ten other desperate means one might twist an ankle until Tennessee interrupted to call the Sparks team leader for more information.

"Mrs. Sparks twisted her ankle jumping out of the deer stand when she went back to the Gator to get a thermos of coffee," reported Tennessee. "The ankle's swelling and they're taking her back to the bunkhouse."

"She has coffee?"

"Maybe you'd like to join her, ma'am."

"If only it was possible, Tennessee. Somebody's got to remain alert for intruders."

He delivered a look that told me Tennessee would have trouble maintaining female companionship. Turning back to the window, he resumed his pig watch.

Max snorted. "It is for this reason I am glad I persuaded you to not bring your gun, Artist."

"An oversight on my part, Bear." I looked at our guide. "I've got a Remington Wingmaster, Tennessee. My daddy's shotgun. She's a classic."

"You could use a twelve gauge, but I wouldn't try for more than a hundred, hundred fifty yards."

"I'm not interested in shooting Hogzilla. This would be for protection."

This seemed to only increase Tennessee's irritation. He jammed the binoculars into his sockets with an intensity that would cause bruises.

"Cherry," whispered Todd.

I crawled to the opposite window.

Todd also had binoculars trained through the blind's opening. Scooting close to him, I squinted through the window. "Do you see anything?"

Todd dropped the binoculars, slung an arm around my neck, and set his mouth to my ear. "No. Actually I've been thinking about what happened at the clay shoot."

"You don't think it was a glitch either?" Relief whooshed through me. Knowing I'm right amidst naysayers was a cross I often bore, but this weekend's cross had become a heavy burden on my small shoulders. I scooted closer to face him. "How could they have done it? Jeff Digby and Mike said the building and fence hadn't shown signs of breaking and entering."

"Their system could have been hacked from the outside," said Todd.

"They can do that? I thought that sort of thing was just done to big sites."

"I think so. I know somebody who hacked into an online poker site."

"Why?"

Todd shrugged. "Mess with the odds, I reckon."

I studied his relaxed expression. Often used at poker tables. "It wasn't you that hacked into the poker game, was it?"

Todd started a "now baby, of course not" lament.

I placed a finger to his lips to stop the frenzied whispering. "Can the skeet software people find evidence of a hacker?"

"If they know to look for it, I guess."

"I think we need to tell Mike and Jeff Digby so they can report it. Why didn't you say anything earlier?"

Todd cut his eyes away. The skin covering his sculpted cheekbones darkened.

"Lord Almighty, Todd. Since when did you let men like Jeff Digby shake you up? I've never seen you like this."

His clear blue eyes swept back to mine. "I don't like the way he looks at you."

Vanity shot an electric current through me, causing my pulse to speed and my hands to creep up Todd's shoulders. I leaned toward his ear. "Really? Like what?"

"Like you're crazy. I didn't want to mention hackers because it would set you off and he'd never believe another word out of your mouth."

I pushed off Todd's shoulders, forgetting to whisper. "The hell."

A sound much like a cat suffering strangulation emanated from Tennessee's position.

"Artist, perhaps you and our mutual friend would like to take the coffee break in the bunkhouse?" said Max. "The rain has slowed. Take the small jeep-like vehicle. Mr. Tennessee and I can radio when we want to return to camp."

I glanced at Todd, my pride-induced anger ebbing. "We do need to report some important information to Mike Neeley."

Crossing the small room, I stopped next to Max's chair, my eyes fixed on the leg he had propped on a tub of supplies. My heart squeezed, cinched by the thought of ruining Max's weekend in my desire to root out a criminal. "I hate to leave you. What if you need something? I don't want you running up and down this deer stand. Just look what happened to Jenny Sparks and her ankle."

"Thank you, but Mr. Tennessee can assist me. I insist you leave."

Placing my hand on his shoulder, I bent toward his ear. "Please be careful. I know you don't believe me, but there's a nutcase out there. Maybe they're just a crank, but I fear the worst."

"You often do." Max's lips slid into a wry smile. He took my hand and squeezed. "If I see the psychotic, I promise to shoot first."

"Are you crazy? Don't shoot anybody." I gripped his hand. "I'm thinking about worst-case scenarios and in them, there's a gun fight."

"I make the joke. Much shooting will scare the boar." Max gathered my other hand in his large paws. "Artist, you must calm yourself. The pranks were most likely made by the Bob Bass agitator. Bass said they will not make the scene unless it is public. We are deep in the woods where no one can see us. Go to the bunkhouse. This weekend was to relax you."

Todd approached and settled a hand on my shoulder. "I'll see she gets some rest, Mr. Max."

Max quirked an eyebrow. "Good luck to you then, McIntosh. To make this one rest is the Herculean task. You may have a similar strength, but I fear this weekend makes for stimulation not relaxation in the case of our artist."

I rolled my eyes and climbed out of the stand. Back into the shroud of cold and wet that now accompanied darkness. Perfect weather for hunting hogs.

And those that might hunt hog hunters.

TWENTY-TWO

Dreary weather had absconded the daylight. The dark swooped in and swallowed the forest, like the burgeoning darkness in El Greco's *View Of Toledo*. The arduous drive back to the bunkhouse meant a crawl, searching for tree markers in the gloom that felt as ominous as Hansel and Gretel's missing bread crumb droppings. I tried the thermal imaging binoculars, but the forest became even murkier but for the bright spots of critters hiding in the trees. Mud sucked at the tires and the engine whined. Todd parked the Gator to better examine the overgrown path.

"I guess we're not helping the hunt with all this noise. That hog will surely have hit the county line by now," I said. "Jeff Digby better have sweetened those feeders with something pretty remarkable to keep Hogzilla around."

"Do you see another marker?" Todd cut the Gator's lights to shine a flashlight on the surrounding trees.

I picked up the binoculars again, adjusted the focus, and skipped my achromatic vision from tree to tree. White fuzzy movement in my horizon line caught my attention. I scooted forward on the seat and searched for the darting form. "Something's out there."

I felt Todd's muscles tighten. "Is it the hog? How big?"

My binoculars caught the object. I followed its zig-zagging path between trees. "It doesn't move like an animal. I think it's human."

"Can I look?"

I handed him the binoculars and directed his gaze where the form had moved. "Do you see it?"

"Yeah." Todd adjusted his seat to follow our prey. "He's coming closer. Kind of round."

"It's got to be Lesley. Give me your phone. Maybe I can reach Rookie Holt. We may need the police out here."

Todd plucked his phone from inside his coat. "No bars."

I tried 911 without success. "We've got to do something. Haul ass and catch him."

Todd dropped the binoculars. "Are you kidding me? This thing doesn't haul ass. Between the mud and the trees, the best we can do is mosey."

"Then I'm going after him on foot." I scooted toward the side of the Gator and hopped out.

"Wait. You don't haul ass very well either." Todd slipped off the seat next to me. "I'll wear the binoculars and guide us. I'm taller so I'll be able to spot him easier."

"You don't have to rub it in." I handed him the binoculars. "What is that man up to?"

"Okay, got him. Lesley makes a pretty good target."

We took off, stumbling in a jerky gait after a figure I could not see. Prickly weeds snagged my jeans and wet branches slapped my face. Trees suddenly loomed as Todd jolted me to and fro between the dense vegetation. Granite erupted from the clay, stubbing our toes and threatening our ankles.

Todd jerked to a stop, yanking me back. "The land falls off a bit. I almost missed it."

I inched my boot forward and lost my toe to empty space. "Falls off a bit? Thank the stars you caught us in time."

"Lesley's leaning against a tree over there." He pointed to a dark spot in the dark. "We'll have to go around this gully, but I think we can catch him. He must be dog tired."

He wasn't the only one dog tired.

We continued our journey, more stumble than trot, following the edge of the low ravine. At a gentle slope, we crossed. In the ankle-deep water, mud sucked at our boots. Flashes of quicksand memories left from my childhood's Saturday morning television viewing had me clinging to Todd's arm, ready to climb him bodily to reach some overhead Tarzan vine.

I hopped out of the ditch minus a boot. Todd retrieved my boot while I stood on one foot, cursing Lesley Vaughn for attempting to save ridiculous hog monsters from their villainous fate. Shoving on my boot, I took a step and fell over a tree branch.

"Cherry?" Todd yanked me to my feet. "What do you plan to do with Lesley once we catch him?"

"Probably sit on him. At least until I catch my breath." I swiped at a wet leaf stuck to my face. "I hope Lesley gets chiggers. It'll serve him right."

"I was just thinking..."

Previously, I had held dubious feelings when Todd uttered that portentous sentence starter. However, having been elucidated on Todd's basic computer-hacking knowledge (which eclipsed my own), I raised my hopes. "Yes?"

"Instead of grabbing Lesley, maybe we should just follow him. We might catch him in the act, so to speak, and then you won't look so crazy."

I narrowed my eyes at the man I could barely see. "You have a fair point, although I do think you're overstating the crazy part."

"Besides that, I don't know if I can find the Gator, and I haven't seen a tree marker in ages."

"You mean we need to follow Lesley because we're lost and he might know where he's going?"

"Yep."

We continued our trek. Unable to mask our heavy tromping or my reflective clothing, we kept our distance. After another thirty minutes, a glimmer of light shone in the distance. The light grew to reveal a familiar building and the growl of an approaching UTV.

"Lesley's headed for the bunkhouse," I whispered, now pulling Todd back into the trees edging the drive. "Let's hide a bit and see what he does. But if it looks dangerous, I'm rushing to stop him."

We hurried to the clearing, halting behind a thicket of pines. A Gator pulled in the drive, slamming to a stop before the bunkhouse porch. A guide jumped out and ran around to the passenger side. Holding his arm, Rick slid out, scooted past the outfitter, and waited while the guide fumbled with the doorknob.

"What happened there?" I said. "Looks like Rick got hurt."

I worried my lip, scanning for Lesley, who had disappeared at the approach of the side-by-side. "Where's Lesley? I am not searching these woods for him again."

Backing out of the pine thicket, we followed the edge of the tree line to the far side of the clearing. No Lesley Vaughn. Defeated, we turned our back on the wet, cold treachery of the forest and headed toward the bunkhouse.

"You know what I'm thinking?" I looked up at Todd. "If you're right about the skeet system hacking, Lesley Vaughn would get my vote for most likely to know how to hack."

"If it was Lesley, he was aiming for Bob Bass's head." Todd grabbed my hand. "Or yours."

Todd and I slogged across the gravel drive and met another side-by-side pulling away from the bunkhouse. Clinton Sparks hollered a hello, explaining their return to the lodge. Jenny Sparks reclined in the back, her ankle wrapped, iced, and propped on the seat. Caleb Guterson slouched in the driver's seat, jiggling his leg and refusing to make eye contact.

"How bad is the ankle?" I asked.

"Viktor thinks it may be a fracture." The fret lines crisscrossing his face betrayed Clinton Sparks' hearty voice. "These things happen, but I wanted to get Jenny back before the mud gets worse."

Viktor thinks?

"Good luck," said Todd. "Be careful on the drive back."

"Thanks," said Clinton. "It's a shame. We've had many happy weekends here. Jenny and I had been thinking about buying Big Rack. Retirement investment. This weekend's soured us some."

"I didn't realize the owners were interested in selling," I said. "With all the changes they're making, I thought the Woodcocks had dug their heels into the lodge for good."

Clinton shrugged, then turned in his seat at Jenny's wince.

"We best get," said Caleb Guterson. "It'll be slower going in the dark." He peeled out, spraying mud.

I glanced at the dismal state of my jeans, now dirtier thanks to Caleb Guterson. "I spied a washer and dryer in that bunkhouse and I think it's going to get some use this weekend. I'm about out of dry clothing."

"Wonder if Caleb's ticked because he can't participate in the hunt," said Todd.

"Wonder why his momma didn't mention her son was acting as a guide for the tournament," I said. We continued our trudge toward the bunkhouse. "You don't think Caleb planned on causing trouble, do you?"

"If the Gutersons were behind any of those hog head messages, Caleb doesn't get the chance to do anything now."

"I hope you're right, Todd." Reaching the porch, we shook off the wet and wiped off our boots.

"And wasn't that fascinating," I continued, "learning the Sparks were interested in buying out the Woodcocks? You think folks around here knew that? Do you think that's the reason Mike has been so determined to continue with this hunt?"

Todd pushed open the front door. My brooding over Caleb Guterson and the Sparks fled. Although warm and dry, the bunkhouse was steeped in tension only out-thickened by Viktor's bubbling soup. Buckshot charged forward, barking an anxious greeting. I bent to pet her while casting a sidelong glance at Rick. He sat on a bench at the long pine table in the center of the room. A bloody shirt and thermals had been tossed aside and a first aid kit lay open on the table. His rangy, pale torso revealed a barrage of old scars and his left arm lay on the table, oozing blood from a long cut. Behind him, his guide hovered, ashen and fidgety. At the opening of the door, Rick had glanced in our direction, flashing a face marked with a dozen bloody cuts, before dropping his gaze back to the table.

Viktor looked up from the package of sterile bandages he held. “Ah, good, a second vehicle has returned.”

“Sorry, Chef. We hoofed it from some point between our deer stand and here.” I peeled off my wet coat and hung it on an antler hook. “What’s going on? Looks like a field hospital.”

“His rifle exploded,” said Viktor, dabbing the gash with a wet cloth. “The Little Joe has done an admirable job. He brought Rick here quickly.”

Todd and I exchanged a long look.

Another accident. This one more dangerous than the clay shoot.

“I swear I didn’t touch the Winchester, other than to hand it to him,” said the green-faced guide.

“They said it was a new rifle.” Rick ground the words between his teeth, sucking in his breath at each touch of the cloth. “Lil Joe, you must have dropped it. Got some mud plugged up in the barrel or something.”

Lil Joe mopped his face with his hand. “I swear I didn’t do anything. I was real careful with all the firearms.”

“Misfires happen,” I said cautiously. Leaving my boots and wet socks at the door, I barefooted it to the young guide and jerked my thumb toward the first set of bedroom doors. “Why don’t you clean up? Maybe a quick hot shower? That’s my plan when you’re done.”

Lil Joe obediently slipped into the bedroom and disappeared.

“I don’t like that guy,” whined Rick.

“I’m sure he didn’t do anything to the gun,” I said, trying to calm Rick. “Where’s Mike?”

“Mike Neeley left before Mr. Miller arrived,” said Viktor, dabbing ointment on one of Rick’s bigger facial cuts. “He hiked to Team Two’s deer stand. It’s not so far. The Sparks left, so Mike goes to clean it out.”

“You’ve got a good touch, Viktor. Maybe you should have been a doctor instead of a cook.”

Viktor cut me a sharp glance. “The good chef must know the first aid in the case of a kitchen accident. How is it you arrived without vehicle? Where is Avtaikin?”

I glanced at Todd, who still worked at peeling the bibs from his long legs. I wanted to wait for Mike to talk about Lesley’s appearance. “Does Rick need to go to the emergency room too?”

“No. No hospitals.” Rick cringed.

I felt annoyed at my distaste for his weakness and sought to change the subject. “What were you shooting at?”

“We saw the hog.” Rick’s voice rose and his trembling subsided. “Tusks as big as my arm. I fired a round at him.”

“Rick, you’re lucky to be alive,” I said. “My uncle told me about a similar accident where the man died. Used it as a gun safety story. Are you sure it wasn’t the ammo you used? The casing could have had a flaw.”

“It nearly would have killed me.” His shoulders relaxed and Rick warmed to the story. “I let go when the gun blew up. The Winchester fell out the window and busted to pieces on the forest floor. Scared that hog away too.”

I glanced at the wall clock made from interwoven antlers. “Maybe you better hang it up for the night. Take some painkillers and rest.”

“I agree,” said Viktor.

“As soon as Lil Joe cleans up, we can send him back to gather up the busted gun and whatever else y’all left,” I said, hoping the misfired rifle might offer some clues.

Todd ambled through the bedroom door to explain the plan to the guide.

“I could join LaToya and her guide,” Rick said. “She’s really sweet, don’t you think?”

“Quiet now.” Viktor threaded a needle then applied it to a deeper cut in Rick’s face.

I winced. “Stitches? I doubt that’s a skill most chefs have.”

Viktor glared at me. “And not many artists organize hunt activities. Leave me so I can concentrate.”

Cleaned up, Lil Joe reentered the main room in his weatherproof bibs. Donning his coat, he slipped out the front door. Buckshot trotted from her fireplace nest to prowl between the front window and door. A few minutes later, Lil Joe reappeared in the doorway.

"Close the door, Little Joe," said Viktor. "You make it cold in the room."

The guide's paled features stood starkly against his dark beard. Like a squirrel caught in traffic, he hesitated, stuck between entering the room and looking out into the dark, clammy drive. He glanced from our expectant faces and back to the drive. Buckshot yipped, then paced between Lil Joe and our spot near the table.

"What is it?" I felt ready to explode from tension.

"The Gator." Lil Joe took a last look, then stepped inside and shut the door to lean against it.

I let out a deep breath. "What happened to the Gator? Did you leave the lights on? Battery dead?"

He worked his jaw, then spoke. "The tires. Slashed. Every last one of 'em."

TWENTY-THREE

While Viktor and Lil Joe discussed radioing the remaining hunt parties, I pulled Todd into an empty bedroom. True to the cabin's name, bunks lined both sides of the room, each covered in thick quilts pieced from hunting motif fabric. I recognized my bag among the others stacked against the wall, and while I talked, I stripped off my soggy jeans and pulled on my last dry pair.

"Todd, we've got to find Lesley," I said. "I thought he had a screw loose, but I underestimated his level of wingnut. I saw Lesley's pack last night. It didn't look like he had any weapons, although he obviously carries a good knife. Do you know how hard it is to cut a Gator tire? Those are off-road jobs, not some worn-out Michelins."

Todd stared at the ceiling. "Yep."

"And then there's Rick's gun exploding on him. I don't see how Lesley could have messed with any of the hunting equipment, though. Mike and Jeff supervised putting all the weapons in those safety boxes themselves."

"Right."

"Should we risk waiting for everyone to get back and then spend time organizing a search party? Lesley's watching the bunkhouse. He can't be too far away." I hopped on one foot, pulling on a dry sock. "I say we scout his location while we're waiting. You saw how he moves. It's not like Lesley's quick on his feet. I think we could take him, although that knife makes me nervous. What do you think?" I tore off my damp top and tossed it to the floor.

Todd continued to check out the ceiling beams.

"Todd? Are you even listening? How can we get Lesley's knife from him? If the guy wanted to behead us with clay pigeons, he's capable of anything."

My finger struck the air. "I know. The guide, Lil Joe, must have his own rifle. I bet they didn't leave his weapon in the deer stand."

I strode to the door, my quick plan ready for action.

"Wait."

I turned back. "What? Let's get going before the others get back and make it even harder to leave. I can just hear the Bear. 'Artist, you jump into thee action without taking time to theenk.' He'll probably insist on going too, and with that bum knee, I can just see him slip-sliding in the mud. And *wham*. There goes his ACL."

Todd dropped his head, cut a quick glance toward me, and let his gaze fall to the floor. "You're forgetting something."

"What? I've been piecing this together. Lesley playing GI Joe. Since hearing about Hogzilla, he constantly stays at the lodge, searching for his beloved Super Swine. He probably did all that stuff to scare us from the hunt and now that we're out here, he's really trying to stop us from getting that hog. Maybe he thinks we can't get to the deer stands if he sabotages the side-by-sides just like he did the skeet software. Hate to think what else he'd try to sabotage."

I turned back toward the door. "Lesley was at the Double Wide the night Abel died. We need to get him to confess. I thought it was accidental. But now I'm not so sure. Abel might have said something that angered Lesley and Lesley followed him into the woods. Lesley's a big guy. Abel was small. One hard shove by Lesley and Abel could have easily fallen into that ravine. I ticked off Lesley too, and look what happened to me. After I ignored his warning, I nearly got my head taken off by an orange disk."

"Stop."

I looked over my shoulder. "Sakes alive, Todd. What is it? We've got a monster hog-lovin' fruitcake to catch."

Without peeling his gaze off the pine flooring, he waved in my direction. "Clothes."

I glanced down at my cinnabar green bra. "Right. Guess the Bear is right about taking time to think."

Todd shook his head at the floor. "I've been asking you to do that very thing all weekend."

Rick had disappeared into the second bedroom. While the guide Lil Joe sat at the pine table, fiddling with his walkie-talkie, Viktor chopped vegetables on the small kitchen counter. After donning our damp coats, Todd and I claimed the need to check out the Gator for ourselves, figuring Lil Joe's gun was likely strapped in the back of the UTV.

At our announcement, Viktor turned and pointed the knife toward us. "Just one moment."

He strode forward, the knife gripped in his hand. The polished metal caught the light shining from the antler chandelier.

A bright spot bobbed along the paneled walls with each of Viktor's steps.

Lil Joe scooted around in his seat, eyes following the knife. His finger hovered over the walkie's talk button.

Beneath the long table, Buckshot lowered her head and growled.

"We won't be gone long." I yanked the zipper up my coat, but sidled closer to Todd.

Todd maintained his placid poker face, but his fingers began to tap a slow tempo against his jeans.

"I think you two should stay put in the bunkhouse. I do not trust you to leave." The knife moved as Viktor spoke, jabbing the air to accentuate his points.

"Why?" I tensed, watching the knife. My hands dropped to my sides in loose fists.

"You arrive with no vehicle. After you arrive, we find the UTV tire is cut."

Lil Joe watched us, scooting around on the bench to slowly push to his feet. Buckshot followed, sliding forward on her haunches and flicking her ears back.

"We didn't slash the tires," I said. "That's ridiculous. And we arrived without a vehicle because we had to park it to walk."

"Why park? Why should you walk in the rain? Your deer stand is not so close. It makes no sense." The knife pierced the air before me. "You carried the disgusting cake. You are at the target practice when the clay pigeons attack."

"Same as everyone else," I said. "And if you remember, they were aimed at my head."

"But they missed you." Viktor's eyes narrowed. "And you found the dead man."

"That kind of thing happens to Cherry all the time," explained Todd. "We're not sure if she attracts trouble or if she's just brave enough to not run from it."

"Not helpful, Todd," I muttered.

"You are not answering the questions," said Viktor. "Why did you leave the utility vehicle?"

"Did it get stuck?" asked Lil Joe.

"We thought we saw something." I reckoned their reaction if I explained a knife-wielding Lesley hiding nearby. Lil Joe might take off with his gun. Viktor too. Then the rest would return, revved up from the stillness of a deer stand and eager to shed their built-up adrenaline and hunting prowess. After all, my scheme had been just as half-cocked and eager. Too many accidents had happened already. I wanted Lesley taken alive. We needed his confession for killing Abel. "Hogzilla."

The guide shook his head. "It took off in the opposite direction of your deer stand."

"Maybe it circled around?" said Todd.

I reached to squeeze his hand in approval. "We had to follow on foot. Then we got lost."

Viktor waved the knife. "You followed a thousand-pound animal without weapon? For what purpose?"

I gripped Todd's hand. "For fun?"

"I do not believe you." The knife whipped to the side, pointing to the fireplace at the far end of the room. "You will wait for the others. Because you decide to track the boar, the deer stand three has no vehicle. Number four must drive in the wrong direction to retrieve Avtaikin and the guide, Tennessee."

"Dangit," I muttered. "That's right. We're down to one side-by-side and the Mule until we find ours."

I closed my eyes, feeling guilt kick me in the gut. A feeling I'd like to relieve by kicking Lesley Vaughn in his hindquarters.

"They'll probably find our Gator on their way back," I said, reorganizing the plan in my head. "Don't worry. I'll go out and investigate the tire slashing."

"There is nothing to investigate," said Viktor. "The tire is slashed. You will stay here until Mike Neeley returns."

I paced the back bedroom while Todd watched, drumming his thighs in time with my footsteps. Buckshot trotted behind me with perked ears and tail pointed at the rafters.

"Why didn't you just tell them about Lesley?" His drumming slowed as I pivoted before the piled duffel bags.

Buckshot dropped on her forelegs to wag her tail at Todd.

"I wanted to tell Mike first, and everyone's so nervy, I don't want any shooting-first-asking-questions-later scenarios."

"What are we going to do now?"

I paused my circuit of the room and squatted to scratch Buckshot's belly. "Wait until everyone arrives, I suppose. Talk to Mike and Jeff Digby, who know about Lesley. Hopefully, they can calm everyone and organize a search party for him. It'll just take longer than I wanted."

Thunder rolled in the distance and the patter of rain on the tin roof turned to pounding.

I glanced toward heaven. "This is just not my weekend. Why didn't Mike cancel this damn hunt? Wasn't finding Abel's body enough of a hint that everything would turn to—" I stopped myself, ashamed. "I need to count my blessings, Todd. I may be suspected of perpetrating malicious acts here and accused of low morals and trashy DNA at home, but at least I'm not dead or in jail."

"Yet," said Todd unhelpfully. He patted the edge of the bed and Buckshot leapt beside him. "You aren't doing any good wearing out the floorboards. I know waiting's hard for you, but if we're going to search for Lesley, your feet'll appreciate a bit of a rest."

"You're right." I dropped next to Buckshot, then fell backward to stare at the upper bunk's slats. She turned three circles and laid her head on my belly. I stroked her ears while Todd scratched her haunches.

"Better?" said Todd.

"I'm jumping out of my skin, but my feet do appreciate it, hon."

"You could use the break. You've been nonstop nerves since you got here, baby."

"I swear something's been bothering me ever since I met Abel Spencer. I just can't put my finger on it."

"Maybe you sensed he was sly, like people have been saying."

"I don't know." I ran a finger under Buckshot's collar. "I was so struck with admiration for his relationship with Buckshot here. Abel seemed nice. His questions about the hunt didn't seem particularly intrusive. Just the usual neighborly nosiness. Maybe I misjudged him."

"What questions did he ask?"

"I've been trying to remember exactly. I couldn't really answer, so they didn't stick in my brain. Something about how the weekend was organized and how they chose who got to hunt."

The sound of boots clomping on the porch startled Buckshot into leaping off the bed. I shoved to my feet and shot to the door where Buckshot stood barking.

As I pulled open the door, Buckshot tore through and galloped to the front window. Viktor and Lil Joe had disappeared. I strode across the floor, snatched my coat, and headed outside.

Evening had evolved into dead of night darkness. Rain soaked the seats of the vandalized Gator. At the porch's far corner, Viktor and Lil Joe had surrounded Mike Neeley. While Viktor explained how I had sabotaged the side-by-side, Lil Joe reported Rick's accident. Ignoring Viktor, Mike turned on Lil Joe.

"I can't believe you didn't call me on the walkie," he bellowed. "You need to report everything."

I flinched, feeling bad for Lil Joe. First chewed out by Rick, then his boss. I had yet to see Mike lose his cool, but everyone had a tipping point.

Thunder rumbled, drowning out their voices for a moment. I decided my Lesley Vaughn defense could wait until everyone had calmed. Instead, I attuned to Lesley sightings. Too dark to see into the forest, I watched the edge of the drive lit by the bunkhouse floodlights. I half-expected to find Lesley crawling out of the tree line, readying to throw ninja stars at the remaining tires.

Shivering, I ran my hands along my arms and turned my attention back toward Mike's group. Having given up on gaining Mike's attention, Viktor stood to the side, arms crossed. He slid a hard glance at me and I volleyed one in return.

Looked like we were going to have a showdown.

In the distance, an engine rumbled. Mike's harangue subsided and Lil Joe took advantage and slipped away. Taking a deep breath, Mike grabbed the porch rail in his hands and ducked his head. Viktor watched him for a long moment, then looked at me.

I walked the length of the porch, stopping between the two men. "Don't be too hard on Lil Joe. Viktor fixed up Rick. Misfires do happen."

Mike raised his head, but kept his eyes on the rain-soaked drive. "Nothing's going right this weekend. And everything was planned so carefully. I should have cancelled when I saw the forecast."

The walkie on his belt squawked and he lifted it without tearing his eyes from the driving rain. "Come in, Team Three. What's going on? Over."

Tennessee's garbled voice sputtered, "...no vehicle."

"What was that, Team Three?"

"Still waiting for Team Four." Tennessee's voice grew clearer. "Can't reach them on the walkie."

A stone the size of Gibraltar dropped to the pit of my stomach. Bob Bass, Peach, and Jeff Digby made up Team Four.

The wind shifted and the rain smacked the porch railing. Mike took a step back, adjusted his channel, and held the walkie to his face. "Just a minute, Tennessee. Let me get Team Four on the line. Team Four, respond please. Jeff, are you there?"

The line crackled. I held my breath. The whine of a UTV grew and headlights shone in the darkness.

"Team Four? Digby, what's your location?" Mike's voice trembled.

A massive splash accompanied the Mule's entrance into the lighted drive. I squinted beyond their headlights and saw the two-seater held Team Five's outfitter and LaToya. The UTV swung around, spewing an arc of water and orange mud, then pulled before the bunkhouse. LaToya reached between her feet, pulled up her gun case and backpack, and dashed up the porch stairs.

"Oh my, is it getting bad out there," she said. "We could barely see and got stuck twice. I hope this storm blows through quickly. I thought I sighted that hog coming to our feeder, but thunder cracked and it bolted."

I tried to smile. "Go on in and warm up, LaToya."

Her excitement shone through any disappointment or discomfort. "I'm starving."

Shaking off the water, her guide hurried up the porch steps and set their supply tub on the floor. He looked over at Mike's pacing and agitated barks at the radio, then at me. "What's going on?"

"Team Four is not answering their calls."

"Shit," said the older man. "We've got another problem. I didn't want to use the walkie because I didn't want to scare the girl."

"What's wrong?" Goosebumps flooded my skin and I wrapped my arms tighter around my body.

"I need to grab a couple men and go back out there." He reached for his rifle pack and slung it over his shoulder. "Who's all here?"

"Lil Joe, Mike, and Viktor. My friend, Todd. Rick's injured," I said.

"Shit, I really need Jeff Digby." He glanced over at Mike. "What in the hell is going on?"

"What happened?" I asked. "Don't worry about scaring me. I've grown up with hunters."

"This is different."

I eyed his fidgeting, the worry lining his face, and the grim set to his mouth. "I've also helped on some Forks County Sheriff's Department cases."

He looked me over, drawing a quick character assessment the way older men do, and somehow found me worthy. "There's a man out there."

"Watching the bunkhouse?"

"No." The outfitter shot another side glance at Mike, still pacing and shouting in the walkie. "The man I saw was dead."

TWENTY-FOUR

A second body in the woods. I couldn't help the comparison between Abel Spencer and Lesley Vaughn. Both had fallen into a rocky gully. Although, while Abel's upturned body had blocked a gentle stream, a torrent wrapped Lesley like a flowing shroud. He lay like a large, dark rock in the foaming rapids.

With the rain splattering our hooded heads, we stood, shining our flashlights over Lesley's still form at the bottom of the steep hill. Buckshot trotted along the edge, ignoring the rain and burying her nose in accumulations of wet leaves at the promise of each enticing new scent.

LaToya's outfitter, Big Clem, had pointed out the broken branches and the washed-out section where Lesley must have slid or skidded back and fallen.

"Caught my eye," he said. "Thought maybe the hog had done it, so I stepped out of the Gator to check."

"God Almighty." Mike covered his eyes with one hand and squeezed his temples. "Big Clem, go farther down the embankment and see if there's an easier way to get to him."

"Better wait for the police before you touch the body." I flashed my light on Big Clem's generous-sized boots. "Maybe you could throw a tarp over him for now. And keep your eye out for evidence while you figure out how to get to the body."

"Evidence of what?" Big Clem's gruff voice sounded confused.

"Of what caused him to fall." I thought again of Abel and his hat. "And where his pack landed. I don't see it on him."

"I can't see the police getting out here anytime soon, but I guess that makes sense." Big Clem threw an uncertain look toward Mike.

"You called it." Todd glanced at me, and I tapped my finger against my lips to keep him from continuing.

"She called what? This artist is some diviner?" Viktor leaned around Mike to serve me a vicious glare. "Why can she boss around the outfitters like the police? She's not the police."

"Diviner? Cherry does like to eat," said Todd. "But I meant she said someone else was going to die."

"Thank you, Todd," I mumbled. "So, so helpful."

Mike dropped his hand and jerked around to face me. "You thought someone was going to die?"

I blew a loud sigh through my nose. "This weekend feels jinxed, is all. With everyone on edge and Lesley skulking around, I feared he might get accidentally shot."

"How did you know this Lesley is creeping around the woods?" Viktor's flashlight beam caught me full in the face.

I blinked back the spots. "We caught him sneaking into the preserve last night. Then Todd and I saw him after we left the deer stand."

"You followed this Lesley? This is why you left the utility vehicle in forest? You lied."

I raised my hand to block the beam. "I wanted to see what Lesley was doing. I thought he was behind the pranks back at the lodge and I was worried what else he may do."

"And you did not tell us this?" Viktor's flashlight beam swung to Mike Neeley. "I suspect this woman of cutting tires. She also abandons the utility vehicle and chases this man. Who is now dead. And she finds the other dead man. Who died in the same way."

Evidently I wasn't the only one to draw comparisons between Abel and Lesley.

"What are you getting at?" Mike shoved the flashlight away.

The beam of light smacked me dead-on in the face. "I find this woman much suspicious."

"She does get pretty suspicious," said Todd. "She's been real suspicious of Lesley, poor guy. And of what happened to Mr. Abel."

"Abel Spencer's death was an accident," said Mike.

"Maybe for one lil minute, y'all want to focus on the dead man lying at the bottom of this hill and not on me?" I stepped toward Viktor and swatted his flashlight. "Point your beam on the forest floor and see if there are any footprints that haven't been washed out by the rain or trampled by the Cherry Inquisition."

"You are not police." Viktor flipped the beam back toward my face. "Mike Neeley, place this woman under house arrest. If she is chasing this man in woods, maybe that is why he fell. And who else could slash the tires?"

"Miss Tucker, maybe we should take you back to the bunkhouse. Just stay there until we get some of this figured out," said Mike. "I still can't get Jeff Digby on the walkie and Avtaikin's team is stuck at his deer stand. I need to think. This feud between you and Viktor isn't helping."

"I'm not the one trying to feud," I gasped. "Todd's been with me the whole time. Ask him. We didn't chase Lesley, we followed him. Lesley didn't even know we were tracking him. I don't think. And I didn't slash those tires or do any of those other things."

"No sign on peacock coop?" sneered Viktor. "Artists have paint."

"Viktor, you are slandering my very name."

"I know who is your sponsor, artist. Max Avtaikin. The Bear. You are the associate of the known criminal. He worked for the casino boss. I was cook at the same casino restaurant. You think I do not know what he does?"

"Dammit, I don't even know what the Bear does."

"Calm down." Mike waved his hands. "Cherry, go on back to the bunkhouse. Viktor, go with her."

"Are you kidding me?" I said. "I'm liable to find myself at the bottom of a ditch with my neck broke."

"If I want to break your neck, I would not do it without an alibi."

"That's comforting." I snatched Todd's hand. "I'm bringing Todd."

"Actually, we might need Todd," said Mike. "With Lil Joe back at the bunkhouse with LaToya and Rick, I could use him. Todd's got some heft and we may need it to move Lesley."

"Do not mess with the crime scene," I cried. "It's a suspicious death until the police rule it an accident."

"Cherry." Mike sighed. "The poor man deserves to be hauled out of that gully before the water carries him away or buries him. I'm sure this is real upsetting, seeing two accidents in one weekend. Unfortunately, coincidences happen."

But coincidences were something I found difficult to believe. I struggled to grasp, let alone assume, that two men were fated to fall to their death in the same area, on the same weekend, and in the same company.

I made Mike promise to radio the police upon reaching the cabin, then insisted on Buckshot's accompaniment. As awkward and uncomfortable as it was, I refused to speak to Viktor on the long, rain-soaked hike back. I liked to think Max had reformed his ways, but I sure as hell didn't trust his past associates to have settled old scores.

Viktor had just written his name on my shit list in indelible ink.

The bunkhouse should have been cozy and comforting after the raw, wet woods. A fire hissed and sparked in the stone fireplace. A small Christmas tree blinked. The antler clock ticked, proving my stomach right in thinking the time was near dinner. However, I felt anything but comfortable.

LaToya kept her eyes on a book. Lil Joe entertained himself by tossing trash into the fire. Rick, I assumed, still slept in the second bedroom. Viktor, having returned to the small kitchen, occasionally shot me malicious looks as Buckshot and I prowled the area near the front door.

Could Lesley have slashed the tires before his accident? The steep hillside where we had found him wasn't far from the bunkhouse. In different weather, it would have been a pleasant walk.

Was it an accident? That question nagged me more than the first. What would have caused him to tumble over that ridge? Lesley's spill made more sense than Abel's. Heavy rain, slippery conditions, unknown territory. The ridge wasn't far from the bunkhouse if he was spying on us. But why did Abel wander off a path known to him since childhood? I hadn't gotten any closer to learning the truth. I hoped Rookie Holt had found something.

I almost wished I had never seen that spot of blue.

"Artist, sit or go in bedroom," called Viktor. "You are driving peoples crazy with the pacing."

I snatched my coat, more comfortable with the wet and cold outside than the chill I felt from the guests indoors. Buckshot pawed the door, ready to accompany me.

"You cannot leave," said Viktor. "We do not trust you where we can't see you."

My face flamed. "I'm going to wait on the porch. If I do something suspicious, I'm sure Buckshot will alert you."

Outside, the rain had subsided, but the damp and dark still seeped beneath my layers. Buckshot bounded off the steps, then slunk back to the drier confines of the porch. Smoke from the bunkhouse fire hung heavy, reminding me of past campfires. Back at Savannah College of Art and Design, I had often joined friends for bonfires on nearby Tybee Island.

There had been a night like this in late fall. Windy, cold, and damp with the mist from the ocean. Someone had introduced me to a tall, dark, and gray-eyed criminal justice major from Southern. He had a girl hanging on his arm, some idiot who had worn a bikini top with her jeans but refused to put on a sweatshirt. We had ditched her behind the pylons at Tybee's pier and walked the length of the beach before heading back to his truck for romance that didn't include angry turtles or sand fleas.

After coming up for air, Luke had brushed the hair from my cheek, twining a cornsilk strand between his fingers. "I remember you from high school. You were a freshman or sophomore when I graduated."

I ran a hand up his arm and toyed with the string from his hoodie. "I know. You're Luke Branson."

"I'm no Branson. I didn't take *his* name when he married my mom. My dad fought in Iraq." The fingers released the strand.

"That suits me fine," I said. "Because as much as I'm enjoying this night, I couldn't date a Branson."

"Who said anything about dating?" His low voice teased and he lowered his head to my earlobe. "And if you're so against dating Bransons, how'd you end up in my truck?"

"Poor judgment after too many beers." I sucked in a breath and held it until his mouth had moved from my ear to my neck. "I liked talking to you. I had previously thought all Bransons self-involved and self-serving."

His lips moved slowly, following the curve from my chin to shoulder. "I told you I'm not a Branson. Besides, Ballards have a reputation too. I always heard y'all were easy to sweet talk into trucks."

I jerked upright, popping him in the nose with my shoulder, and slid off his lap. The chuckling behind the hands holding his nose irritated me even more than his words.

"I'll tell you something, high and mighty Luke 'I'm-no-Branson.' If you think all it takes is some lively conversation and good looks to charm your way into my pants, you've got another thing coming."

The hands had dropped from his nose and I was pleased to see a smear of blood on his finger. "Lighten up, sugar. If I was looking to score that easy, I wouldn't have ditched Dee back at the pier. I'm just showing you why you shouldn't judge someone by their name."

The memory faded.

Now that I was older and a bit wiser, I wondered if Luke and I had hooked up just to prove that statement true. If that was the case, I hadn't done well in proving him wrong about the questionable moral standards of my family name.

But at least we were ethical.

That these people believed I would slash a vehicle's tires for no apparent reason ticked me off to no end. Couldn't they tell the difference between a curious, albeit willful, gal asking pertinent questions and someone with malicious intent to scare and possibly harm folks?

I halted my front porch pacing, causing Buckshot to perk her ears and raise her head. Why would someone want to flatten all the tires on the Gator? If it was Lesley trying to prevent hunters from getting to their blinds, wasn't there a simpler method?

Pulling the flashlight from my coat pocket, I hopped from the porch to the Gator. I squatted before the first flat tire, beaming the flashlight over the slick rubber. No cut appeared in the sidewall. Surprised, I held the flashlight against my knee to catch my balance. Tread would be much harder to cut. Why go to the trouble and not just do some other stupid act?

Reluctant to stand and expose myself to more chill, I gazed at the mud-splattered rim for a long second. I moved the flashlight beam to circle the metal rim. Pulling my left hand from my coat pocket, I felt along the wide lip, closest to the tire, until my fingers touched the rough edge of a rubbery protrusion.

"He cut the valve core." Startled by my own words, I dropped the flashlight.

Buckshot yipped and rushed to save me, knocking the flashlight under the Gator. The beam illuminated a rocky puddle beneath the tire. Dead set in the circle of light lay the jagged remains of the tire valve. An efficient means to quickly flatten a tire. The tire-cutting idiots I had known in my youth generally tried a puncture in the sidewall. Usually in revenge against an ex who had gone looking for love in the wrong places.

I grabbed the flashlight, received a face lick for my efforts, and used the side of the Gator to hoist my stiffening legs to standing. Bending to pet Buckshot, I murmured praise for finding the tire valve while my mind worked on a motive. This tire cutting didn't seem like a mere act of vandalism. More of a means to hamper our transportation back to the lodge. Which made no sense, since Lesley would want us out of the woods. Not trapped in the forest.

Maybe cutting the tire valves was meant to trap us at the bunkhouse.

Maybe whoever had cut the tire valves wasn't Lesley.

I shivered.

Buckshot pawed at my jeans, craving more comfort.

"Lesley had denied his involvement in any of the lodge pranks," I told Buckshot. "Maybe he was telling the truth."

The pranks took a sinister turn in my mind. Was someone else out in the woods with us or had one of the hunters or guides turned on the party?

I started toward the porch steps and halted. In my peripheral, I thought I saw a light flicker.

Turning to face the drive, I squinted past the ring of light streaming from the porch. The flicker had glinted in the timber northwest of the bunkhouse, the opposite direction from where the party rescued poor Lesley's body. The wall of trees loomed in the thick gloom, concealing what lay beyond our small bastion of civilization.

Buckshot's ears flattened. Drawing back on her haunches, she pulled her head back and uttered a low growl.

Another light flickered in the murky depths of the forest. I dashed for the porch with Buckshot on my heels. Cracking the door, I felt for the light switch. Inside, a barrage of "heys" rang out as I hit the wrong switch. Correcting my mistake, I cut the lights to the porch. The Christmas lights lit the rafters but left the porch floor in darkness.

At my feet, Buckshot tucked her tail, snarling.

I squatted to stroke her and squinted into the dark.

The solar-powered security lights offered a dim glow onto the drive. The starless sky shrank, binding the bunkhouse and surrounding forest in the cold, damp skin of early winter.

The flickering light had disappeared. Other than the hum of the bunkhouse generator, the forest sounds had stilled. Inside, I could hear the clink and rattle of bowls and imagined the tick of the antler clock, hammering long minutes. I tuned my ears to the dark, hoping to hear a Gator.

Instead, the dark projected a dull thudding accompanied by the soft squelch of footsteps. Quickly drowned out by Buckshot's deafening bark.

Twenty-Five

I'm not normally spooked by what my deceased Granny Jo called the boogerman. I relished Flashlight Tag and Ghost in the Graveyard and never needed a nightlight to sleep. However, these malicious pranks and deadly accidents made me hesitant to expose myself, not only to some evil trickster, but also to a thousand-pound hog with tusks the size of my leg.

My first thought was to grab a gun from inside the bunkhouse, but Viktor would try to stop me. It would also rile the hunters into action. And something other than a monster hog might get shot. Like poor Buckshot.

Safety first, as Uncle Will always said.

Whatever crept toward the bunkhouse approached slowly. I continued to squint and squat on the dark porch, avoiding the light pouring out the windows where I could see the small crew enjoying Viktor's soup. Someone had thrown new logs on the fire and the smoke billowed from the chimney, luring night travelers toward our small beacon in the woods.

Buckshot had calmed.

I stroked her and murmured happier thoughts. We huddled and watched the dark for a good ten minutes when light bobbed along the rutted drive.

The indistinct form seemed to clump, then break. I wasn't sure if I saw it with my eyes or my imagination. Strains of a familiar brassy whine caused me to pop from my squat. Buckshot burst off the porch, baying. I ran after her, sloshing through the drive.

"Where is everybody?" hollered Bob Bass, beaming his flashlight on me. He wore two rifle packs slung over each shoulder and his fleece collar had grown dingy and matted.

Buckshot danced a circle around the group, panting and stopping before each newcomer in turn.

"Man, what a night." Jeff Digby carried a large duffle with his rifle pack. Setting the duffle on the ground, he gave Buckshot a quick ear scratch. However, the grim set to his features betrayed a chink in his stoic armor.

"Where's your Gator? Mike's been trying to reach you." I left the latest emergency for a later discussion. "I was on the porch and heard you coming."

Looking more bedraggled than a wet cat, Peach trudged behind Bob. In the beam of my flashlight, her back bowed with the weight of her pack, and I reached to take it from her. She clamped a hand on the strap. "I've got it, thanks."

"You look exhausted," I said. "Let me help you."

"I'm good."

"Here you go." Bob shoved the two rifle packs at me, took Peach's arm, and hurried her toward the bunkhouse.

Buckshot yapped and trotted after them.

While I hoisted the heavy packs over my shoulders, Jeff watched the pair escape. "We tried to get to Team Three, but a tree had fallen, blocking the easiest route there. Tried another way to get through and got stuck. Ended up leaving the Gator for now. Bass pitched a fit, but I didn't know what else to do."

"What happened to your walkie?" Another tendril of worry unfurled within me.

"Damnedest thing. I thought I had left it in the Gator while we got out to move that fallen tree. Couldn't find it when we got back. Hunted around by the tree, but it was too dark to find my own feet, let alone anything else. Plus Bass was bellowing to get moving."

"Someone took it from the Gator?"

"Took it? This isn't the city. You think a raccoon's gonna want a walkie-talkie?"

"Somebody's up to something." I explained the tire valve cutting and Lesley's fall.

Jeff uttered a few curses, apologized, then cursed more. "Damn fool. I told him it was too dangerous to hike around in these woods."

He stared at the bunkhouse. "Mike's gotta be beside himself. Did he radio the lodge to tell the sheriff's department? It'd take them a good while in this weather. Not until tomorrow at least, and it smells like we'll get more rain. Damn forest is clogged in mud. No one wants to hunt in this shit." He expelled more curses. "Pardon, ma'am. I should have talked Mike out of this hunt, lodge be damned."

I waved away his apologies. "It gets worse. I don't think Lesley cut the tire valves. It doesn't make sense. Besides, before we reached the bunkhouse, Todd and I saw Lesley disappear into the woods not far from where we found his body."

Jeff shone the flashlight near my face. "What are you saying, girl?"

"That someone else might be out in the woods."

"Nobody's out in the woods."

"Then someone in our party cut those valves. It wasn't me or Todd. Lil Joe and Rick were the only team at the cabin. They had returned because Rick had a rifle accident. The Sparks and Caleb Guterson left when we arrived." I hesitated. "There is Viktor. He was alone at the bunkhouse all day. Everyone else was with their team."

Jeff's silence made me talk faster.

"I know you think I'm crazy. But look at what all's happened. Abel's fall. Signs and threats warning us away from the hunt. The clay shoot accident. Rick's misfire. Tire valves cut. Lesley's drowning. That's a flippin' lot of accidents in one weekend." Not to mention I had been personally warned to stop questioning Abel's death. If only I could see the connection between Abel and the other incidents.

"It had to have been Lesley."

"I don't want to malign the dead, but I certainly hope so. Because it looks like we're going to be trapped here until some of this mud dries."

"Let me get on the horn with the lodge."

I hurried my steps to follow him, my shoulders aching under the heavy packs. "They're moving the body. I told them not to, not before the police could examine Lesley."

Jeff stopped and spun. "Why are you so concerned about all this?"

I jerked to a stop before I smacked into his chest. "I just am. Why wouldn't I be?"

He waved an arm toward the bunkhouse. "Do you see anyone else creating conspiracy theories? Telling grown men how to do their jobs? Giving opinions on police procedures?"

"No."

"Then why you?"

"I just want to help." I chewed my lip. That was a lame reason. "Growing up, I saw my uncle wanting to help victims but getting frustrated that even as sheriff, he was limited by the law. As a citizen I can go places he can't, talk to people who usually clam up at the sight of a badge."

"But why would you want to?"

"Because I'm not afraid to cross boundaries to do what's right. Or care much if crossing those boundaries ticks people off."

Jeff snorted and turned toward the bunkhouse.

Maybe I had said too much. "Liking to help" sounds much nicer than not caring about ticking people off. And after what had happened thus far, maybe I should worry more about ticking people off. I feared this time I had gone too far, but it was too late to back out now.

Both here at Big Rack and back in Halo.

I scurried after him, dumping the wet rifle packs and shedding my coat in the entrance. I followed Jeff to the kitchen area, where he questioned Viktor on Lesley's fall, then opened a closet door at the far end of the kitchen. Instead of a pantry, a small desk had been built inside. On the desk sat a black box with a glowing LED panel and a CB-style microphone.

Jeff grabbed the mike, pressed a button, waited, then pressed the button again. After the third unsuccessful check for a signal, Jeff began calling on each channel. "Bunkhouse to Lodge. Come in, over."

"I don't think you're getting a signal," I said, leaning against the edge of the closet door.

Viktor peered over my shoulder. "No signal."

Jeff extended a look that made no bones about what to do with our mouths. Pulling the box forward, he examined the wiring in back, then fiddled with more buttons.

"Dammit." He tossed the mike on the desk, shoved his hands on his hips, and stared at the ceiling. "Antenna must have gotten hit in the storm or knocked over. I'll have to climb up and check it in the morning."

"That sounds dangerous," I said.

"Maybe something happened to your connection." Viktor looked at me. "Maybe someone sabotaged this radio."

"You better not be implying I had something to do with this." I folded my arms. "I'm the one who wants to get the police out here."

"Enough." Jeff dropped to a squat and hunkered beneath the desk for a long minute. Crawling out, he stood, shut the closet door, and leaned against it. His voice lowered. "The connection looks fine. I don't know what happened. But we're not contacting anybody tonight."

He glanced across the room to where LaToya, Peach, and Lil Joe rested before the fireplace, listening to Bob Bass's bombastic account of their nighttime trek. Pulling his gaze off the guests, Jeff's eyes fell on mine. A gleam of maybe-the-crazy-girl-is-right brightened his deep brown ochres.

"I think we should go out and examine the antenna wire," I said. "If it's intact, then we know there's an issue with the antenna itself and it's just a coincidence."

Jeff blew a sigh out of his nose and Viktor nodded.

I still didn't believe in coincidences. But I also didn't want to believe that someone didn't want us to call for help.

TWENTY-SIX

It felt like I'd never again be dry or warm. Or clean. Once again, I donned my coat and exited into the cold and wet. We circled the bunkhouse past the noisy diesel generator, tramping in the weeds and muck. On the back wall, we found the kitchen exhaust, then located the antenna cable running from the closet outlet to the roof.

The cable had split.

"I wonder if we've got electrical tape?" Jeff fingered the shredded end of the black tube emerging from the wall.

"Does not matter." Viktor waved his flashlight beam between the split pieces of cable. "These ends would not touch."

Jeff reached for the cable dangling from the roof and pulled the halves together. Six inches gapped the divide.

"Shit." Jeff dropped the cables and rubbed his hands on his bibs. "Unbelievable."

I glared at Viktor. "I did not do this. Stop looking at me like that."

"I am just thinking of the difficulty of cutting this wire. Maybe you cannot do such a thing."

I caught myself before I did my usual sass-ridden, "I can do whatever I set my mind to," and realized the defense resting before me. "Well, I didn't. And wouldn't want to. Whatever you think of my friend, Mr. Max, you should know that I have practically grown up in a sheriff's office."

Viktor shrugged. "Where I am from, police are corrupt. Who knows what you have learned in this sheriff's office."

"You're a real horse's patoot—" I stopped at Jeff's growl.

"I need to talk to Mike about this. Not another word between you. You're both driving me crazy."

I offered Viktor my fiercest glare. Combined with my customer service smile for Jeff's sake. "He's right. Instead of throwing accusations around, let's get my sketchpad and a map and figure out if Lesley could have done this or if we've got an even bigger problem on our hands."

Either way, we were trapped for the night.

While Jeff hiked to the scene of Lesley's accident, Viktor and I retreated into the empty bedroom where we wouldn't be overheard. With the map of the preserve spread out on the floor and with the occasional lick from Buckshot, we plotted the bunkhouse, the five deer stand positions, and the area where Lesley fell. An empty bowl of mushroom and rice soup sat at my feet. I ate to stave off hunger, but found pleasure in the savory and thick yet delicate broth. That still smelled slightly of dirt.

Buckshot agreed after sniffing the empty bowl. She backed away, leapt on a bunk, and settled on a pillow.

"Approximately is here, your all-terrain utility vehicle lies abandoned." Viktor made a dot on the map. "In the morning, you can fetch."

I flipped open my sketchbook to the page of illustrations I had made of all the lodge crew and guests.

Viktor sucked in a breath. He pointed to a beady-eyed, giant-mustached chef wielding a Psycho-styled knife. "This. It is me?"

I slapped my hand over the characterization. "Let's just jot down your schedule over the last few days. How long were you alone in the bunkhouse? We left for the deer stands before four. That leaves you and Mike Neeley here until Jenny sprained her ankle. Wasn't that around four thirty?"

Viktor smoothed his mustache. "Correct. Mike left to clear their deer stand around five. Their stand is close. Rick and Lil Joe arrived before half-past five, just as the Sparks leave, and you and your friend soon arrive. So I am never alone."

"No time to go out and walk around the bunkhouse?" I raised my brows.

He lowered his. "No. I do not enjoy tramping about in this weather. I let Mike Neeley do the tramping while I amuse myself with the baking and the cooking."

"And drinking." I touched my nose. "Vodka doesn't hide as well as you think."

"It settles my nerves. The hog is not repulsed by fermented corn or grain," he replied stiffly.

"The hog is no longer our concern. Our concern is preventing another 'accident.'" I made quote signs with my fingers. "By the way, why are you so suspicious of Max Avtaikin?"

"I told you. As cook at the casino, I see all. Your friend and I began working there about the same time. We were children. I scrubbed the pots. The Bear ran notes between croupiers and pit boss. Soon, I am training as sous chef and he is training under the big boss."

I shook my head. "You have him confused with someone else. Max doesn't know you."

"Your friend pretends not to know me. And he knows I know him. He is the dangerous man. I am fearing for my life."

"You don't need to be afraid of Max. He's reformed. I couldn't be friends with a real criminal. I even made Todd quit card sharking and he's got a serious poker addiction."

"I am not believing this for the second. Where is your friend while these accidents occur? I saw the pig's head and 'squeal' message on the peacock cage. I know this American expression. The Bear sends that warning to me. If he didn't send you to cut the tires and trap me at this bunkhouse, then he did it himself. How do we know he is still in the deer stand? Only from the guide, Tennessee. You think this Tennessee is impervious to bribes?"

"No way. Max blew his knee out a few months ago. He's not leaving that deer stand in this weather, much less lurking in the timber to corner you. Although, I wouldn't put it past him to skulk around the woods to bag Hogzilla before Bob Bass gets it." I worried my lip, wishing my brain had halted my mouth before stating the last bit.

"Aha," cried Viktor. "You admit the Bear would leave the deer stand to win this contest. Think how much more motivated he would be to stop me."

"Stop you from what?"

A sly look slid from Viktor's raw umber browns. "I know many things about the Bear. Information that could cause him much trouble both here and in the old country."

I rolled my eyes. "Y'all need to get over yourselves and your 'old country' shtick. Max's already been investigated by the IRS and Homeland Security. Mostly thanks to me. And here I am, invited on a cozy weekend by the Bear. Do you see me worried?"

"Maybe he's not just after me." Viktor raised his heavy brows. "Maybe he's thinking of the accident in the woods for you too."

I gave Viktor my best you're-crazier-than-a-sack-of-wet-cats look. "Anyway, I'm ruling out the other guests too. How would they know about the antenna cable? Although, the Sparks hunt here often enough." I put a question mark under their names.

"Jenny Sparks' ankle has the sprain."

"But they want to buy the lodge. And they could get it cheaper if word gets out about a bunch of accidents."

Viktor raised his brows. "The Woodcocks are selling?"

"Let's focus on suspects. You can worry about your job later."

"As for the antenna, anyone might have asked," said Viktor. "The cell phone signal does not reach this far. As a guest, I would ask what is the equipment for the emergency."

"Most Americans trust the people in charge will take care of them. I doubt anyone asked if there would be a radio with a wire to cut. Let's look at the lodge staff."

"You are too suspicious of the lodge staff. They have all worked for some time. Why act the crazy now?"

"Mike's fairly new. You're new staff too."

"And what is your point?"

"I don't know." I tapped my pencil on the pad. "It seems everyone has an alibi since we've been in the forest. Each guest has been with an outfitter."

"Except when you and your friend, Todd McIntosh, were alone to abandon the necessary vehicle and chase the dead man."

"And you and Mike Neeley were alone in the bunkhouse," I spat back.

"Touché." He rolled his eyes.

"Someone else could be stalking us." I pointed at the map, north of the bunkhouse. "We saw Lesley here and followed him to about here." My finger dragged to a point farther southeast, closer to the bunkhouse. "This is about where he fell. Big Clem saw his body just before he and LaToya arrived around seven. Would Lesley have had enough time to cut the tire valves and get to this spot to fall?"

"Possibly."

"But he wouldn't have reached Jeff Digby's Gator to steal their walkie-talkie, which I don't believe for a minute Jeff Digby lost." I leaned back against a bunk, reaching behind me to scratch Buckshot's muzzle. "And if someone did tamper with Rick's gun, I can't see how it could have been Lesley. Maybe if they find Lesley's pack, that will tell us something."

"What is the motive?"

"For Looney Tunes Lesley? To stop our hunting of his precious super pig."

"No. For other peoples."

"I don't know, but the accidents are becoming more and more dangerous. Rick's already been harmed. Bob Bass or I could have been killed at the clay shoot. And now Lesley."

In the main room, the front door slammed. Excited voices clamored. Buckshot bounded off the bed and scampered to the bedroom door.

I hurried my words. "I think you're right about the accidents. They are meant to scare all of us or one of us. Bob Bass thought it might be one of his fanatics. Rick didn't believe it was protestors. The Sparks wanted to buy the lodge until this weekend. Or maybe Max is the target."

Viktor's voice dropped. "If there is other people in the forest, Lesley may have seen them and for this, they could push him off the ridge."

I met Viktor's eyes. "If that's the case, we need to find this mysterious person. Because he's not just stalking us. He's intent on killing again."

TWENTY-SEVEN

The bedroom door swung open. Buckshot yipped and bounded out the door. Like guilty high-schoolers hiding their vices, Viktor and I scrambled to stuff the map inside my sketchpad and shoved the lot under the nearest bunk.

Todd stepped inside, casting a curious gaze on our floor sit. "What're y'all doing?"

"Reckoning a possible killer." I hopped from the floor. "How'd it go with Lesley?"

"Messy." Todd pointed to his mud-splattered form. Mud suited some men. One of God's crazy gifts. "But we've got Lesley wrapped in a tarp in the back of the Mule. I need a shower and there's a line forming."

"Listen, Todd. Don't mention this to the rest of the guests, but someone's messed with the radio to the lodge. We can't call for help. As you well know, until we find the Gator we lost, right now we've only got the two-person Mule left between thirteen people."

"Perhaps we can radio on the walking-talking and speak to Max Avtaikin. We should send someone to get them and find your utility vehicle. It would also settle my doubts that he is still in the deer stand," said Viktor.

"Sure." I folded my arms over my chest, annoyed Viktor had abandoned our short detente. "Besides, we need to get them back here. We aren't hunting the hog anymore anyway."

Todd's head swiveled, following our exchange. "Mike said we can still hunt."

Viktor and I abandoned our mutual glower to pivot toward Todd. "What?"

"Mike said that although he's sorry about Lesley, we can't all get to the lodge tomorrow morning. He's going to send some folks back and figures the rest can stay to finish the hunt."

"But the police will want to cordon the area," I said. "They need to investigate Lesley's death."

"Mike said it looked like an accident."

"Mike's not the police. He promised me he would contact the sheriff's department."

"He cannot contact police if radio is broken," said Viktor.

"Mike doesn't know the radio is broken." I paused. "Does he?"

Viktor started toward the door and I scurried to catch him.

"Hang on," said Todd, grabbing my arm. He bent down to whisper in my ear. "What's with trusting Viktor? I thought you two were about to kill each other earlier."

"You know what they say about keeping your enemies close," I whispered.

Appeased, Todd righted. "That's a good idea. You work on your enemies, I'll work on mine."

I left that dubious statement for Todd to reconfigure in the shower and caught up with Viktor in the main room. Arms crossed over his chef's jacket, he leaned against the bedroom wall next to Jeff Digby and the two remaining outfitters. In the far corner, Rick fidgeted with his bandages. Bob, Peach, and LaToya sat at the long table, listening to Mike's explanation of Lesley's demise and the evacuation plan for the morning. After swapping the Gator's flat tires for the two-seater Mule's, Big Clem and Lil Joe would drive LaToya and Lesley's body back to the lodge. Jeff would hike out to locate my missing Gator, then rescue Team Three from their deer stand.

"I can't see why I have to return if Mr. Bass, Mr. Rick, and Mr. Avtaikin can continue to hunt," LaToya said. "I'm as good a hunter as those men. I have awards to prove it. I'm eighteen. It's not like I'm a kid."

Mike held up his hands. "I understand, Miss LaToya. The contest is over. I'm not going to present the big prize or trophy. And I will refund your money. I'm just allowing the remaining participants to continue to hunt while they wait to return."

"If they don't shoot that hog tomorrow, I've got to take care of the beast before he does more damage to the area," said Jeff Digby. "LaToya, won't your parents be worried sick about you in this weather?"

"My parents know me well enough," LaToya fumed. "They know I'm an expert shot and likely to have a spot on the Olympic team in a few years. They know I keep a cool head. I'm not some girl who gets shook up by a little rain and cold."

I slipped to her side and wrapped an arm around her shoulders. "Your parents would be proud of how mature you've been this weekend, particularly with all the weird stuff going on. You act better than some adults."

She shook off my hug. "Pardon me for saying so, ma'am. But I'd think you're a better candidate to go back. Considering how most of us think you might be behind this 'weird stuff' going on."

Under the table, Buckshot barked her assent and pushed her nose into LaToya's hand.

"Et tu, Buckshot?" I gritted my teeth and turned to center Viktor in my fiery gaze.

"I may have made haste in the accusation of Cherry Tucker." Viktor accompanied the statement with an Eastern European-fueled sigh. "We have examined the map and it is possible Lesley Vaughn cut the tires. I am sorry to speak ill of the dead, but Lesley wanted to protect the giant hog. Perhaps too much."

LaToya dropped her gaze to the table. "Sorry, ma'am."

"Anyway, I've got to stick around to help my friend, Max." I patted LaToya's shoulder. I recognized her attitude stemmed from a competitive nature combined with teenage stubbornness. "I won't be having much fun, hanging on here. Chock this weekend up to 'hot mess' and grab hunting time somewhere less jinxed. You're braver than me if this weekend hasn't given you the heebies."

"Nature doesn't give me the heebies." Her Mars Brown eyes glared at me. "Only people."

"I want the guides to drive so they can bring back another ATV. Caleb Guterson doesn't realize we need a return vehicle," said Mike. "We could squeeze one more person in. Miss Tucker?"

I realized I could send a semi-reliable messenger to Rookie Holt. One who was currently showering and unable to defend himself. "Take Todd. Mr. Max would rather have my help than Todd's. And I'm sure Todd won't mind accompanying Lesley's body."

"Yes," agreed Viktor, fixing his eyes on Jeff Digby. "I think the artist should stay. She is of no importance to return early. Send other guests first."

"I guess by important guests you mean me," said Bob Bass. "But I want to hang out and finish the hunt. Avtaikin and I have our own little competition that doesn't involve any of y'all. And that artist gal still needs to paint my picture."

"I should stay with Bob," piped Peach. "No way can you get me to ride with a dead body. Gross."

"What about Rick there?" said Bob. "He's hurt, after all."

"I'd rather have Todd, I mean, Mr. McIntosh, accompany me." The rush of her words darkened LaToya's cheeks.

Rick flicked his gaze between Bob and LaToya, but remained silent as usual.

Eyeing Rick, I thought about Mike's statement about Caleb Guterson. Had Mike tried to reach Caleb on the walkie-talkie and failed? Or tried to radio the lodge and failed?

Wait a minute, I thought. Could a Guterson have pulled these tricks to ruin the lodge's big event?

Caleb would have known about the radio antenna. He and the Sparks had left just as Todd and I arrived at the bunkhouse. Rick's Gator had already been parked.

All Caleb would've needed was a minute or two alone to cut the tire valves. That kind of stunt was more fitting to Caleb's background than Lesley's.

Caleb also could have followed Abel into the woods from the Double Wide. But why? Did Abel overhear plans by the Gutersons to disrupt the hunt?

I dropped onto the long wooden bench next to LaToya and used my finger to trace designs on the wood's surface. The idea of Caleb sabotaging the radio and Gator made more sense than a mysterious stalker. I could see the Gutersons planning pranks meant to scare the guests. Had their intended pranks turned into deadly accidents? Or were the Gutersons driving toward more malevolent acts?

It was hard to imagine that kind of evil, but in the Gutersons, I recognized the viciousness that often came with self-preservation.

"I am serving more soup now," announced Viktor. "There is also the corn soufflé, honeyed fruit salade, and barley tea."

The crowd dispersed into the kitchen. I scooted down the bench toward Mike, waiting for Jeff Digby to join us.

"Did you find Lesley's backpack?" I asked without segue, because I was not a segue kind of girl.

While Mike appeared momentarily perplexed, Jeff seemed to have adapted to my repartee. "Found it beneath him. It had gotten tangled around his legs in the fall."

"That makes more sense for an accident," I said.

"More sense than what?" asked Mike.

"Abel's hat." I waved that aside. "I'm glad you decided to send LaToya back. Makes me feel easier about this business." I looked at Jeff. "Did you tell Mike about the radio antenna?"

He nodded.

"Damn shame," said Mike. "It'll be okay, though. Viktor's first rate at nursing and we've got food and fuel. Big Clem and Lil Joe will get back tomorrow afternoon with more transport. That'll give the last guests a chance to hunt tomorrow morning if they want. Then maybe we won't have to refund everyone's money." Before I could speak, Mike hopped up from the bench. "Thanks for your help, Miss Tucker. Boy, do I need a shower. I'm going to grab one while everyone's eating."

We watched Mike walk toward the kitchen, where he complimented Viktor on the food. I glanced at the lines tightening around Jeff's eyes.

"Is Mike in denial?" I asked.

"He's a good guy," said Jeff. "Takes things to heart. Maybe a little too much. I'm going to suggest he take a vacation after this weekend."

"You don't like this plan of letting the hunt continue tomorrow." I dropped my voice as the guests took their seats at the other end of the table.

"Nope," said Jeff. "It's not worth the money. Everyone's keyed up and we don't need more accidents. I'd just as soon have everyone sit tight and wait for the rescue. I'll stay and get rid of that hog myself."

He rose from his seat and I placed a hand on his arm.

"What about Caleb Guterson?" I whispered. "He had the opportunity to cut the tire valves. Possibly the antenna wire too, while we were getting ready to depart for the deer blinds. You know how the Gutersons feel about the lodge."

Jeff kept his eyes on my hand clamped around his wrist. "I guess it's a possibility."

Behind us, the bedroom door opened and the fragrance of hotel shampoo mixed with the funk of wet dog, mud, and mushroom soup.

Todd emerged with his wet locks slicked back, long and water-darkened. I heard Peach's sharp intake as she beheld the amazing sight of the freshly showered, shirtless Viking. Even LaToya gasped. As he lived in my home, I had become mostly desensitized to a wet and partially nekkid Todd.

Mostly. After all, as an artist, I could never become completely immune to beauty.

Next to me, Jeff grunted. "I thought he'd never get out of the shower. I'm next."

I pulled my hand off Jeff's arm to wave Todd over. "Do you want some dinner?"

"In a minute." Todd shrugged on a flannel, plopped onto the bench next to me, and began buttoning the flannel over his muscular glory. "I want to talk first."

At the other end of the table, Bob dropped a spoon in his empty bowl and resumed his constant prattle that had ebbed while eating.

Rick abruptly pushed away his bowl, yanked his cigarettes from his front pocket, and stood. Despite the bandages spotting his face, he appeared to have recovered from the misfire.

"Going out for some fresh air? I'll join you. Who else's coming?" Bob glanced at his dinner companions.

LaToya kept her eyes on her food, but Peach jerked from her internal musings at Bob's statement.

From his pocket, Bob pulled out a metal cigar case and waved it at Rick. "Bet you'd like one of these Cubans. I betcha never even tried one before. I like to share little privileges with my fans. Try a Cuban."

"I'm fine with the Pall Malls," said Rick. "Thanks anyway." He scurried toward the front door, grabbed his coat from a hook, and flew into the dark.

Still sharing his cigar knowledge with the room, Bob followed Rick. Peach snatched her GoPro from the table and hurried to grab her coat from the drying rack beside the fireplace.

The front door swung open again and a belt of cold and damp snuck into the room.

Finished with his buttons, Todd refocused on delivering his speech. "I thought about that idea you had about enemies."

I kept my expression neutral as I searched my brain's outbox for comments about enemies.

"You know how spy movies usually have a double agent?" said Todd.

I dropped neutral for bewildered.

"So I'm fixing to do that for you."

"Fixing to do what for me, hon?" Poor Todd. I took his hand in mine and squeezed.

"When we get back, I'm going to ask Shawna Branson out. But I'll do it as a double agent."

I dropped Todd's hand and planted my face in mine. "Oh Lord, of all the bad ideas."

"It's a great idea. From what I hear, Shawna's been kind of lonely. She's hot and all, but she's got a reputation for being high maintenance."

"Lordy." Remembering my self-comparison to Shawna, I peeked out between my fingers. "Wait, do I have a reputation like that?"

Todd shook his head. "You're known to be easy..."

My head jerked from my hands.

"...going. But a little scary."

"Scary? How am I scary? I'm five foot and a half inch." Despite my protestation, I couldn't help but feel pleased. My fierceness preceded me.

"Not physically scary," said Todd. "You're cute as a bunny. Scary like a guy might begin a date with you at Red's and wake up in jail the next morning."

"That's ridiculous. No one I've dated has gone to jail." I paused. "Except Dewey. But he doesn't count. I didn't know he was on probation."

"Anyway, I thought taking Shawna on a couple dates might work. I might learn something that could help y'all."

"That's a terrible idea. First off, Shawna knows you're my roommate and Cody's best friend. Second, if she finds out you're dating her to help me, she'll throw a hissy so epic, it would literally rip the town in two. Like an earthquake. With spewing lava. And some of Lesley's mythological creatures flying right out of the crack in the earth. Therefore cementing my brother in prison for eternity."

"I'm confused," said Todd. "Does Shawna cause earthquakes or volcanos?"

"You need to eat because your brain is tired," I said. "I will get you some of that tasty dirt soup."

"I think you should sleep on this idea," said Todd.

"I've got plenty of ideas that need sleeping on." I swung my legs over the bench. "Right now, I'm more concerned with rescuing Max and keeping Viktor from going wacko from paranoia. Then there's the Gutersons. Considering they are now my most likely suspects for scaring everybody."

As Viktor had been gifting me with the evil eye since our initial meeting, the one he offered at my request for Todd's soup held no meaning.

"You are wrong," he said, shoving the bowl of piquant brown liquid at me.

This remark, so oft repeated in my presence, left me unperturbed.

I asked on which account I was now wrong.

"Big Clem called Team Three on the walking-talking."

"Walkie-talkie," I corrected.

"Whatever," he said. "And the guide Tennessee answered. He says Avtaikin is safely in the deer stand."

I beamed.

"But when I insist on speaking to the Bear, Tennessee does not give the good answer. Big Clem forced Tennessee into the confession."

My beam dimmed. "Max isn't in the deer stand. He's out stalking that damn hog, isn't he? He's going to rip out all that fancy surgical work."

"He is not stalking the hog," seethed Viktor.

"Good." I tucked the bowl against my belly and grabbed a plate of cornbread fluff. "Because I was just imagining the Bear lying at the bottom of a hill like Lesley and Abel. If Max slips and dies, I'm going to kill him."

"No, you misunderstand. Avtaikin is in the forest. But he is not stalking this hog. He is stalking me."

"You're crazy."

"I am not crazy. I grew up with this man. The Bear hunts me. I feel it. If Maksim Avtaikin allows me to have knowledge of his whereabouts, he is not the man I know."

"Then he's not the man you know." I tromped back to Todd and handed him the soup and corn soufflé. "Unbelievable. That Viktor will not let up about Max. He suspects the Bear of everything."

"Does he suspect Mr. Max will cause earthquakes and volcanos?" Todd laughed.

I replied with a well-honed stink-eye.

"Have some more soup," said Todd, holding up his spoon.

I scowled at the thought of Max creeping about in the cold, damp woods. "I've got to look for him. I wonder if I could take the Mule. I know Lesley's in the back, but—"

A splintering crack bit the night air and the light in the room dimmed. Buckshot broke the millisecond of stillness. With short, frantic barks, she scooted from under the table and galloped for the front window.

Someone hollered from the porch. Viktor whipped around to face the room, forgetting the dripping ladle in his hand. Before the fireplace, the two outfitters shot simultaneous looks at the rifle packs lining the wall.

I ran for the door and yanked it wide. Behind me, feet pounded on the pine flooring.

The porch light remained on, but the light had disappeared in the drive.

In the distance, a faint pop preceded a splashing thump. The next shot hit wood with a splintering crack and the Christmas lights blew. A hand shoved me to the floor. Darkness swallowed the porch.

"It's a sniper," howled Bob. "They're trying to assassinate me. They've got a silencer."

"Stay down and crawl into the house," growled Jeff Digby, whose powerful hand still flattened me to the porch floor. "I cut the porch lights. Big Clem, shut the house lights so they can't see in."

The bunkhouse darkened. Heavy paws dug into my thighs and butt and someone licked my ear. "Jeff Digby, I hope to God that's not you."

Jeff's hand released my back. "Dadgum, Buckshot. Get inside, girl. Lil Joe, grab her collar and get her on the leash before she gets hurt."

"What's going on?" Todd called from behind me.

"I didn't hear a bullet hit anywhere too close," I whispered to Jeff. "Unfortunately, I've had some experience with bullets in my vicinity and am alert to the sound of one hitting near my person."

"They must have missed," said Jeff. "Holy shit, who's shooting at us?"

"It's the Bear," called Viktor. "He's come to finish me off."

A boot rammed into my side and I cried out.

"Are you okay?" asked Jeff.

"Bob Bass just kicked me."

"I'm trying to get into the house and you're blocking the door," hollered Bob.

I belly scooted onto the wet porch and let Bob slither over my legs. Craning my neck, I saw Peach hunkered behind a rocking chair, clutching something against her chest. "Get in the bunkhouse. Don't be scared, just crawl inside."

The object in Peach's hand fell to the ground with a clatter. She scooted out from the rocking chair to feel along the floor.

"Leave it. You can get it later. Where's Rick?" I squinted, but darkness had enveloped the far end of the porch. "What happened to the security light? Rick, are you down there?"

Another pop sounded in the forest. "Get down," I yelled. Somewhere in the drive, the bullet smacked into the ground with a loud whump.

"What's going on?" called Mike.

Scuffling sounded in the doorway.

"Get your butts inside," hollered Jeff. "Get out of my way."

"Stop blocking the doorway," said Todd.

Bullets smacked the drive.

"Is it you, Avtaikin?" shouted Viktor. "Give me a gun. I will take care of this now."

"Absolutely no guns," I yelled. "Rick's missing."

From the back bedroom, Buckshot began to howl.

Lord, I thought, you've got to help me. Because these men are about as useful as a trapdoor on a lifeboat.

I glanced back at the rocking chair. "What are you doing?" I asked Peach. "Do you want to get killed? Get inside."

"Stop it," she screamed, crossing her hands above her head. "Enough."

Figuring Peach for meltdown mode, I drew into a squat and leapt to her aid. We slammed onto the slick wooden floor and slid into the chair. Her head smacked the rocker with a crack. We held eye contact for a long second before she bucked and shoved me off.

"What the hell?" she screamed. "Get off."

"Calm down," I said. "You're in shock. Let me get you inside and we'll get you some tea. And ice for your head."

"Oh my God. I don't want tea. Just leave me alone."

"Peach, is that you?" called Bob. "Babe, what's going on?"

"That girl attacked me." She crawled past me. "I'm coming, Bob."

"Cherry, hurry inside," called Todd.

"Where's Rick?" hollered Mike. "Let me out, Jeff."

"Not until you put down the gun, Mike."

The door slammed shut. I glanced over my shoulder, satisfied Peach had gotten inside but feared the panic would lead to more shooting. "Rick. Where are you?"

Footsteps thudded nearby. I gave up on Rick and scooted backward, sliding on my belly toward the doorway. The footsteps stilled. My elbow struck an object and sent something sliding toward my hip. I grabbed the small box, shoved it in my back pocket, and continued my scoot. My foot struck the door, and I hammered the wood with my toe.

Next to the porch, boots hit a puddle with a soft splash. The door remained closed. I pushed back onto my heels, eased my back against the door, and reached for the handle. Beneath me, the wooden floor vibrated with a heavy thud.

"It's me," whispered Rick.

I placed a hand against my heart, trying to shove it back into my cold chest. "Get over here. I'm at the door. What're you doing?"

"I ran behind the house at the first shot." He scooted toward me, panting.

"Did you see anyone?"

"No." Rick's bandaged head bobbed near my hip and he crawled into sitting.

I turned the doorknob and we fell into a pile of bodies. Someone hauled me backward, the door slammed shut, and a flashlight blinded me. "It's just me and Rick."

"Why'd you stay out there? What in the hell is the matter with you?"

I blinked toward Jeff's voice.

The flashlight winked out. "I wanted to make sure Rick and Peach got in safely."

"Holy shit, are you crazy?" Jeff's voice quieted. "Who the hell is out there?"

"Did anyone try to call Tennessee and Max to make sure they're all right?"

"It's Avtaikin," said Viktor, somewhere behind me.

"Max wouldn't shoot at us. It's someone else. Who's got hold of me?" I struggled against the arms that had wrapped around me. "Is that you, Todd?"

"Just making sure everything's where it should be."

"I believe my parts are just fine, Todd. Let me up."

The glow of the fire illuminated ten bodies hunkered near the doorway. Eleven shadowed faces glanced warily at one another. In the back bedroom, Buckshot whined and pawed at the door.

"We have a situation," Mike spoke slowly. "I'm not sure what's going on."

"No one goes outside tonight," said Jeff. "No lights either. And I'm locking the guns up."

"I have a right to defend myself," shouted Bob. "Someone's trying to assassinate me."

"Or me," said Rick. "You weren't the only one outside."

"Why would anyone want to assassinate you?" said Bob. "Besides, you weren't on the porch. Where'd you go?"

"Y'all hush," I said. "Someone radio Max and Tennessee and make sure they're okay. Warn them to be on the lookout for an armed and dangerous suspect. Now."

Twenty-Eight

Jeff Digby and Mike took the first watch. The remaining nine filed into the two bunk rooms, dividing the men from the women. Buckshot was released to prowl the main room. As I took my turn in the bathroom, I realized I still had Peach's video camera shoved in my pocket. Leaving the camera on the toilet tank, I eyeballed the tiny box while I changed into my Talladega t-shirt and chili pepper boxers. The back of the camera had the touchscreen Peach had used to replay footage. Not that I was nosy, but Peach might have caught the shooter on camera.

And I was nosy.

I pressed the largest button on the front of the camera and the back screen lit, displaying a series of tiny pictures. I chose one and a video began to run. Peach's production had a hidden camera look and played surprisingly well. I snorted at her capture of Bob's more bombastic comments and realized the scene took place on the porch just before the shooting.

"Where'd the guy go?" Bob had asked Peach of Rick. "Poor man deserves a little treat after having his gun blow up. Amateur. I wanted to teach him how to smoke a very fine cigar. These local yokels don't know quality. You'd think Rick'd stick around when a star like me offers him a Cuban. Ol' tar head probably couldn't appreciate it anyway."

"Sure, Bob," piped Peach from behind the camera.

The video panned back, skimming the dark woods.

"What's that?" said Bob.

The camera centered on Bob once again. He leaned forward on the porch rail, squinting into the night. “Did you hear something?”

“What?”

“Something’s out there.”

The security light blew. Bob fell to the ground howling. “Someone’s trying to kill me.”

The camera followed him to the ground, focusing on Bob’s face. Tears bled from his eyes and his nose ran.

“I don’t think it came near us, Bob,” said Peach.

“They killed the fat guy and now they’re after me,” Bob blubbered.

Offscreen, footsteps pounded and the porch door squeaked open. The air popped and a thumping splash sounded in the distance. The screen had gone dark, but the camera continued to roll, switching to backlight. Bob’s grainy face returned. He appeared to be wiping the tears and snot, bravado returned.

“It’s a sniper,” howled Bob. “They’re trying to assassinate me. They’ve got a silencer.”

A moment later, I heard myself calling out, then Jeff ordering Bob to crawl into the house and for others to hit the lights. My whispered communication to Jeff continued amid shouts by our housemates. On camera, Bob began to crawl. Reaching my spot in the doorway, he kicked me. I had curled up and yelled.

The video cut off.

I slapped a hand over my hot cheeks. That ass had deliberately kicked me. Caught red-handed. And I had been caught hollering like a stuck pig at his measly kick. If that video went viral, I’d never live it down. Lord, how embarrassing.

I set the camera back on the toilet and prepared to get busy with a toothbrush. In the mirror, my cheeks remained splotchy and I pulled in a deep breath to calm myself. Unfortunately, my self-image was a lot bigger and tougher than my on-camera image. With certain realities, I preferred ignorance.

While I brushed my teeth, I couldn’t help but mentally replay the video. If I had been embarrassed, I couldn’t imagine how Bob might feel. Why on earth had Peach taken that humiliating footage? No woman could be that stupid. Could she? I had reckoned her dumb brunette routine as a gold digger stunt. I wasn't sure which was worse. Hooking up with someone like Bob out of true idiocy or conniving someone like Bob into believing you were stupid.

I felt my blood pressure rise and decided to leave those irritating thoughts to focus on the shooting. Most of us had been in the main room. Jeff had gone into the front bedroom to shower. Mike was doing the same in the back bedroom. Rick, Peach, and Bob were the only guests outside. One of the first shots had hit the security light. Only one shot had gotten close to the porch and that had hit an eave where the Christmas lights hung. So why shoot near the bunkhouse? Had Bob, Peach, or Rick been an actual target? Or were the bullets just meant to scare them? Or scare someone else?

I refused to think about Viktor's accusations of Max. I shifted my focus back to Bob and Rick. Except Rick hadn't been on the porch. He had hidden behind the house when the shooting started. And had reappeared on the porch when the shooting stopped.

I stared in the mirror, catching the curl of my lip as I thought about Rick. Toothpaste dripped out the corner of my mouth and wisps of blonde frizz had escaped my ponytail. Where did I get off feeling high and mighty about slightly creepy Rick? The poor guy was injured. Did my intuition think Rick had slunk into the woods and shot at the bunkhouse instead of sneaking off to smoke?

Or was someone else out there? Another Guterson, working with Caleb? Someone else entirely? Someone who didn't want to scare the group, but actually wanted to harm one of us?

Too bad Peach had focused on Bob and not on the shooter.

I grabbed the camera and watched three more videos. Each one focused on Bob acting the fool. Not helpful. And probably bad for his TV ratings.

Before I could get more irritated with Peach, I rinsed out the toothpaste and stalked from the bathroom. LaToya was huddled in an upper bunk with her headphones. Peach had curled up on her side in the bunk beneath her. I slipped out the door. In the main room, the fireplace glow highlighted Jeff Digby's form gracing a bench before the window.

At my entrance, he turned from his window peep, then peeled the night vision goggles off his face. "What are you doing?"

"What'd you do with the rifles?" I whispered and drew closer. "Were any missing?"

"Don't you ever stop? Or sleep?" He continued at my headshake. "We have another storage closet in the kitchen. I locked them in there."

"Did Rick have access to a rifle? Weren't some rifle packs left on the porch?"

"Why?"

"Rick wasn't on the porch when the shooting started," I said. "Probably, he wanted to get away from Bob Bass and smoke in peace. But I want to know if a gun is missing."

Jeff shook his head. "Can't see Rick doing something like that. He's got issues, but going postal in the woods isn't one of them."

"What kind of issues?"

"I don't know if I should say," said Jeff. "But I've been keeping an eye on him. Making sure he's not hanging around LaToya too much or anything. But Rick's not violent."

I sucked in a breath. "He's a creeper. I knew there was something off about him. Y'all should have told us."

Jeff cut his eyes to the window. "It bothers me enough that Rick's here this weekend. I'm trying to keep my distance, but watch him at the same time. Flippin' shitty luck he got picked in the raffle."

"How do you know he's a creeper? Has he been convicted?" I rested my hand on the windowsill, angling closer to listen to the story.

Jeff's pitch dropped. "About ten years ago, he was arrested for statutory rape. He was about twenty-three, the girl was fourteen. Did his time and moved back a couple years ago."

"I thought his whole loner act was weird. I noticed how he hangs back from everyone."

"Used to being ostracized, I guess."

With the fire behind him, Jeff's features were difficult to read. His low voice hardened. "You can imagine how everyone reacted when Rick won the raffle."

"That's why the staff's been so tense."

"Gutersons are about the only ones who'll serve him. Fear of getting fired by the Woodcocks is the only reason the lodge employees are dealing with him. There's only one person in town who'd give him the time of day."

"Abel Spencer," I whispered. "Because he wasn't liked either. Town drunk and snoop."

"Yeah." Jeff swallowed hard. "You met Jessica at the lodge?"

"I tried. She refused to come out and meet the guests. Because of Rick?" I matched the tremor in Jeff's voice with my knowledge of Jessica. "Merciful heavens. Jessica had a daughter who died. And that's why she's hiding in the kitchen. Doesn't want to see Rick."

Jeff nodded. "Ruby overdosed on her mom's meds one night when her mom was at work. Autopsy showed she'd been...you know. We don't know how long it was going on."

"Was Rick charged?"

"No evidence other than he lived on their street. The lawyer said they'd have a hell of a time proving anything with Jessica as a single mom and Ruby a latchkey kid. There wasn't a diary or note or anything.

"Ruby was physically mature for her age," he continued. "Rick probably gave her attention, and she was unsupervised a lot. They ruled her death as accidental. Couldn't prove Rick had anything to do with it, but Jessica suspected him. They didn't even arrest him. Nothing to go on."

I blinked back tears. "How old was Ruby?"

"Thirteen." Jeff cleared his throat. "Anyway, Rick's a miserable son of a bitch who deserves something worse than death. I can't stand to look at him. But he's not the type to shoot at anyone."

"Why in the hell did you allow him to win the raffle? Why didn't they throw it out and pick another damn ticket? Good Lord, there's a teenage girl in this tournament." Angry tears threatened to wet my eyes and I balled my fists to dig my nails into my palms.

"Dammit, I don't know. The Woodcocks announced his name on the news before I even knew about it. LaToya's eighteen, so the police couldn't do anything either." Jeff's anger cooled mine. "This whole damn weekend's screwed. I'm just trying to keep everyone safe."

I gazed at Jeff, his eyes unreadable in the dark.

In the fireplace, a piece of wood popped then flared. Buckshot grunted, rolled over, and returned to sleep. The antler clock jumped a minute forward. Beneath my palm, the windowsill felt clammy. I clenched my hand into a fist.

I needed fresh air. Cold, wet air. "I'm going outside to look for bullet casings."

He shook his head. "Not a good idea."

"That's never stopped me before."

Hugging the wall of the bunkhouse, I watched the timber a few long minutes. Without the stars, the sky felt compressed, heaven a little closer than felt comfortable. Through the window, firelight licked abstract patterns on the porch's flooring. I knew Jeff watched for trouble with his thermal binoculars, probably wondering what in the hell I was doing. I didn't know what in the hell I was doing, other than I needed to do something.

I missed my family. The cold and dark made me afraid for my brother. Although jail did guarantee some degree of warmth and nourishment that I was not getting in the woods.

And I worried about Max. In my imagination, he lay dying in a stream of muddy water. I longed to kick Tennessee's sullen butt for letting Max trip around the forest for something as dumb as a super hog.

Mostly, I felt achy over the dance my heart played with Luke. I had a giant-sized wedgie lodged inside my chest where guilt had constricted my heart and lungs. I wished Luke had never moved back to Halo, so I couldn't have fallen for him again. My family harbored grudges almost better than Luke's stepfamily. Were we even going to get a chance at a happily ever after?

Was this why my mother left her kids? Skipped town with Billy Branson rather than deal with a Ballard-Branson grudge match?

Maybe Todd was right about giving up on Luke. I couldn't abandon my family for a man.

Before I could do something even more stupid, like cry, I snuck in the direction where I had heard the bullets hit. With my flashlight, I nosed around the Christmas lights, but the pulverized bulbs gave me no leads. I struck off the porch, pointing my flashlight on the mud, and searched for a clue beneath the broken security light. Bits of glass and plastic littered the ground. I skimmed my flashlight up the light pole. If the bullet had lodged near the light casing, it was too far away to see.

I cut the flashlight's beam and stared into the gloom, following a rough line from the pole to where I thought the shooter had hidden. My sight adjusted from nothingness to vague shadows. In keeping with the season, not a creature stirred.

Figuring the marksman already had his chance to shoot me, I aimed my flashlight on the ground and began to tread toward the forest.

Ten yards from the security light pole, my flashlight beam winked, catching a gleam of metal, then sparked again. I leaned over to examine the mud. The soft clay had ruptured, creating a polka dot effect of small tunnels. I continued my track, following the trajectory into the soggy forest. In a small clearing protected by a thicket of buckeye and backed by a cropping of vine-choked trees, I stopped and swiped the beam over the dense carpet of wet leaves. The rain had pounded the star-shaped leaves into an effective mat. Scattered over nature's carpet, tiny bits of lead glinted in my beam. I examined one eraser-sized, hollow slug that looked like it would make a good finial for Barbie's staircase. The pointed dome tapered to a thin waist with a rifled, hollow skirt. As a child, I often stole these from my brother and drew tiny faces on the tips.

"An airgun pellet?" I muttered and shoved a few in my pocket. "Who's using a pellet gun?"

Nothing made sense. Another prank meant to scare us, not kill us.

I tromped around, flashing my beam on the forest floor, but could find no other evidence of the prankster. I trudged back, switched off the flashlight, and stood at the edge of the forest, listening. Behind me, the porch door creaked. I glanced over my shoulder, expecting Jeff Digby. A tow-headed man ducked through the doorway, pulling his parka closed with one hand. The door shut behind him, and he stood in the shadows, searching the porch and drive. I clicked on my flashlight and shined it under my chin.

Todd started, backed up a step, then trotted down the porch stairs and through the drive. His unlaced boots clomped through puddles and the mud without regard to the silence or dark. "What're you doing out here? I about had a heart attack when you flashed that light. Thought you were a ghost."

"I'm just getting some air," I said, clicking off the light.

"No, you're not. Something's bugging you and you're trying to keep yourself busy because you can't sleep."

"You know me well, my friend." I smiled, then checked the grin. "Look at this."

I dug the pellet from my pocket and shined a light on my palm.

Todd picked it up to better eyeball the small slug. "A diablo. I used these as a kid. That hog will think it's a horsefly, not a bullet. Who's hunting with a Daisy?"

I shoved the pellet back into my pocket and switched off the flashlight. "Tonight's sniper. Who wasn't actually sniping. I'm feeling awful confused."

"Better get out that sketchpad. That's the only way you get unconfused."

"You're right. And it's much warmer drawing than it is trying to find clues in the dark." I reached for his hand. "I'm sorry I've been such a pain. I know my love life's been driving you crazy. You just want what's best for me, and I appreciate that."

"Baby, you're driving yourself crazy." He squeezed my hand, but before he could continue, I jerked him to the ground.

"Listen," I whispered.

The door to the bunkhouse scraped against the threshold and soft footsteps fell upon the planking. The culprit skulked against the shadowed bedroom wall, away from the front window. My eyes flickered from the creeping body to the window. Jeff Digby's form, previously backlit by the fire, had disappeared.

I tapped Todd's hand and pointed toward the porch. Half-bent, we tiptoed to the flattened side-by-side and hunkered behind it, watching the porch. The shadowed body had reached the far end of the porch, hopped off, and slunk around the side of the bunkhouse.

"That's not Jeff Digby," I said. "Too small."

"Why'd you think it was Digby?" whispered Todd.

"He's not at the window."

"I didn't see him when I came out, either."

"He was on guard duty." I cocked my head, then shot to standing. "Shit. Rick."

Forgetting the skulker, I ran for the porch, leapt the stairs, and dashed into the bunkhouse. The fire blazed with a new log. The girls' bedroom door was cracked, and I poked my head inside. The sound of LaToya's even breathing eased a small amount of tension. The bathroom light exposed the empty bunk below. I checked the bathroom, then hurried to the men's room.

Cracking the door, I slipped inside and was immediately assaulted by raucous snoring and the stale, musty scent of men. Jeff stood with his hands on his hips, staring at the sleeping man in an upper bunk. In the bunk across from Rick, Viktor rose on an elbow and looked from Jeff to me.

I placed a finger to my lips and tugged on Jeff's arm to lead him from the room. Behind us, I heard the soft thump of Viktor's feet hitting the floor.

Viktor closed the bedroom door behind him, looked from Jeff to me, then at Todd standing before the front door. "Well?"

"Peach snuck out," I said. "And the weapon used tonight was a pellet gun. I found a handful of dropped pellets. Most of the shots peppered the mud. They weren't really shooting at anyone."

"Where'd Peach go?" asked Jeff.

"Around the west side of the house. She's been taking a lot of unflattering videos of Bob. Now her little movie camera's gone."

"What does that mean?" said Jeff.

"Don't you want to find her?" I asked. "Where's Mike? Let's get him to watch the window."

Jeff shook his head. "I don't want to wake him. A pellet gun doesn't sound too dangerous. Let him sleep."

"I'll watch," said Viktor. "I am not sleeping."

"If we've got to trek into the woods, let me get some supplies," said Jeff, turning toward the kitchen.

"We're wasting time." I bounced on my boot heels, then hurried after him. In the kitchen, I found him unlocking the pseudo-gun cabinet. "What were you doing in the bedroom?"

"Nothing," he growled.

"You were thinking about Jessica's daughter and Rick, weren't you?"

He turned to shoot a look back at me. "You brought it up. I wasn't going to do anything."

"Then why were you in there?" I settled my hands on my hips.

"I was just..." He turned back toward the cabinet and grabbed a rifle pack. "Just checking on him."

"Bullshit," I whispered, but changed the subject. "Know any reason why Peach would sneak out? Bob's sawing logs in the bedroom."

"No." Jeff swung around with the open pack in hand. "I've got some medical stuff, just in case. We'll take thermal goggles too."

"And you've got a rifle." I cut my eyes to the Marlin he had strapped in the backpack's carrier.

His brown eyes met mine. "That hog is still out there."

"And whoever Peach is meeting."

TWENTY-NINE

With our eyesight reduced to grayscale, we tromped into the dark, cold void like alien monsters. Buckshot was left behind, swapped out for thermal binoculars and Jeff Digby's tracking sense. Through the binoculars, the landscape had an Escher-like quality. Fascinating, yet slightly eerie. Creeping along the side of the bunkhouse ahead of me, Jeff Digby glowed white. Behind me, Todd, bright as an angel, murmured in delight at each scurry of mouse and possum.

"Todd," I whispered. "Cut it out. You're going to give our location away."

"I can't see how we won't spot them first," said Todd. "I love these heat sensors. Did you see that bird flying above us?"

"That's a bat, hon."

Jeff held his arm out then flicked his hand to the right. We followed his point, slogging through the mud and into the woodsy undergrowth. I tried not to think about the dampness wicking through my sweatpants and thermals to my chili pepper boxers, which already felt soggy.

I concentrated on Jeff's abrupt starts and stops as he tracked Peach's movement into the woods.

"How did she know where to go in the dark?" I whispered.

"Two sets of prints," said Jeff, pointing at an ambiguous spot on the forest floor. "Someone's leading her."

We had hiked for an interminable ten minutes, when Jeff held out an arm to stop us, then motioned to get behind a tree. He squatted, pulling me down beside him. I yanked on Todd's pant leg, bringing him into our huddle.

"Can you see that dark object in the distance?" whispered Jeff. "You'll notice the angles. Once you spot it, it'll stand out."

I squinted through the binoculars and found the peak of a tent's rainfly. "Someone's camping in the preserve. I want a closer look at the tent."

"Are you nuts?" whispered Jeff. "If you get shot by an air gun, it's going to hurt."

"She'll do it anyway," said Todd. "You just have to let her do her thing."

"Thank you, Todd," I said, patting his leg.

"He supports your death wish?" said Jeff.

"I don't have a death wish." I whipped my binoculars from the tent, glaring at Jeff's spectral form. "Todd knows I don't stand aside to let someone else do a job I feel needs to be done. Todd just gets me."

The statement was so true, I felt one of the knots in my heart tighten. Todd remained unnaturally quiet.

I wondered if my heated cheeks glowed whiter than the rest of my body. "Let's get back to the business at hand. Stalking Peach."

We turned back to watch the tent. For a longish minute nothing happened. As I'd never been much on patience, I rose from my squat, trying to ignore the loss of warmth our small huddle created.

"Y'all stay here," I whispered. "Jeff, I trust you're a good marksman, but if things get crazy, I'd rather you not shoot. I fear that would increase my odds of landing a bullet near or in my body."

"You are nuts," muttered Jeff.

"I was told I have an uninhibited fear response." I took a step and looked back. "And that does not mean I'm crazy."

Todd gave me a ghostly bright smile.

I picked my way through the trees, moving in a half-circle while keeping the tent in my thermals. Reaching the small clearing where the tent had been pitched, I dropped to crouch behind a stand of trees and studied the camp. Two large plastic gas cans flanked a cooler. The absence of a fire pit surprised me, but made sense with the wet weather. No sign of life showed within the rugged tent, although I couldn't hope for that kind of luck. I crept closer, pausing every few steps to check for movement inside the tent.

Behind me, Todd and Jeff moved soundlessly, flanking my position. I stepped into the clearing, stopping to crouch behind the gas cans and cooler. I flipped up the cooler lid and peered inside. Water jugs, protein bars, and trail mix. Surprised by the lack of beer and wieners, my fingers slid. The cooler lid banged shut. I fell back, feeling mud ooze beneath my seat. I froze, hunkered in the cold muck, waiting for a maniac waving a pellet gun to emerge from the tent.

No maniac.

Grabbing the handle of a heavy gas jug, I hauled up and onto my feet. Then thought about the need for such large gas cans. When camping as a kid, we used small bottles of propane for camping stoves and lanterns. These giant jugs were similar to the ones at the bunkhouse, used to gas the UTVs. Did the camper steal the gas or bring his own? They certainly couldn't hike, carrying these heavy jugs. A hike from Big Rack would take a full day to get to this point.

What an idiot I was. Lesley Vaughn didn't hike through the preserve. He must have gotten a ride. From this camper. Which meant they left earlier than the hunting party, sometime after Jeff and I had caught Lesley sneaking into the forest. Jeff had said the preserve's fence alarm had a breach before dawn.

Was Lesley working with someone else? Some other Hogzilla lover?

Had the camper killed Lesley?

My heart slammed into my ribcage. Adrenaline pushed me past the food and gas stand. I prowled the perimeter, looking for a vehicle. Not spotting one, I studied the ground for the missing vehicle's tracks. Closer to the tent, I found muddy ruts filled with water. Satisfied the camper must have taken off, I stole to the tent flap and listened for the breathing of a heavy sleeper. Yanking off a glove with my teeth, I grasped the tent's zipper pull and slowly slid it up.

Behind me, a tree rustled and a twig snapped. I dropped the zipper, spun, and lost my balance. My butt slammed into the tent pole. The tent shook. My arms windmilled, my heels slid against the mud, and I fell backward into the tent. The pole bent beneath my weight and the other end lifted, extended, and popped out of its arc. I fell flat on my back, covered in collapsed nylon.

"Dammit," I said.

"Nice going, Tex." Jeff Digby's whispered voice drew closer with his footsteps.

"Someone just jumped from behind a bush fifty yards from here," said Todd. "They lit out like their pants were on fire."

A moment later, we heard the growl of a UTV.

"Dadgummit," I said. "That's gotta be our shooter."

THIRTY

In order to nose around the contents of a collapsed tent, you first have to rebuild the tent. Which means bending straightened poles and reinserting them into their assigned slots. Which is hard as hell to do at God-knows-what-time in the morning.

Thermal binoculars do not help at all with tent poles. They are just as black in thermal optics as they are with plain old eyeballs. Which caused a fair amount of cussing from the peanut gallery. It seemed Jeff Digby did not appreciate my helpfulness in scouting the pellet gun-wielding maniac's tent nor my insistence in helping right the tent that had fallen on my body—not his.

And I did not appreciate his flagrant remarks about my posterior that had "tore down the tent and scared away that sumbitch."

"I don't think Cherry's butt could scare away anyone," said Todd, continuing his slew of unhelpful remarks. "It's not big enough to do much of anything. In fact, in high school we had a name for—"

"Get that pole lodged in the ground before it lodges in your keister, Todd. I'm going in that tent."

"Hurry up, then," said Jeff. "I want to get back to the bunkhouse and make sure everybody's safe."

"When you called Viktor on the walkie, what did he say about Peach's return?"

"Peach told Viktor she had gone out for a smoke and not to tell Bob because he doesn't approve."

"Are you sure you tracked Peach to this campsite?" asked Todd. "Maybe she did go out for a smoke."

Jeff drew himself up before Todd. "Are you commenting on my tracking skills, son?"

"Boys, all that grunting is going to attract Hogzilla. Peach is a suspect until proven stupid for wandering around in the dark just after someone shot at her."

Of course, I also found myself guilty of that charge.

I crawled into the tent. Besides the typical sleeping gear, the camper had left two large duffel bags. Camera equipment filled one. The second held clothing and other odds and ends that did not include pig heads, peacock feathers, or threatening notes. But I did find a plastic dish of pellets.

"I bet I know who this guy is," I called to the sleep-deprived, surly men standing outside the tent. "I'd recognize these hipster flannels and expensive camera equipment anywhere. No-Mustache, a.k.a. my lodge neighbor, Jayce Deed."

"Who'd you say?" The tent flapped open and Jeff's head popped into view.

"The guy staying at the lodge supposedly spending his weekend on nature photography."

"He's not supposed to be in the preserve. I coordinate all the hunting trips, including the vehicles. I didn't sign out for the photographer. Or for anyone else to use a UTV."

"Hate to break it to you, but I don't think he's out here to take pictures." I crawled out of the tent and took Todd's hand to regain my footing. "This guy is paying top dollar to stay in your lodge, yet he's snuck into the preserve to camp in a rainstorm just to take photos? I knew plenty of photography majors and even the hardcore nature lovers wouldn't do that."

"Too soft?" asked Jeff.

I shook my head. "Crappy lighting. This cowboy's up to something. He's the one terrorizing the hunting party."

"Do you think Peach is involved?"

"Let's find out."

* * *

Upon our return to the bunkhouse, Buckshot raised a sleepy head at our entrance, then dropped back before the fire. Jeff sped into the men's bedroom, leaving Todd and me to explain our findings to Viktor. I eyed the doorway to the back bedroom, wondering if Jeff's hurry was more to do with Rick's sleeping habits than the call of nature. I decided a possible pedophile's safety wasn't my priority. If Jeff wanted to beat the crap out of Rick, he'd wake everyone doing it anyway.

"The Peach," Viktor droned in his Iron Curtain monotones. "She appears not the smartest lightbulb in the box. When I said to her, 'why smoke in middle of night,' she said, 'I always smoke while Bob's sleeping or he'll give me a hard time.'"

"It could be true," I said. "Bob gives Peach a hard time about everything. Sneaking out to smoke might be a safe little rebellion for her."

"I do not approve of the smoking. It ruins the tastebuds and makes it difficult to taste nuances in my cooking."

"You might have sold me on a new habit, Viktor." I winked. "And by the way, you can tell me I'm right. Max is Hogzilla hunting, not Viktor hunting. Finding Deed's campsite proves that."

"It proves nothing until we learn the truth of what Jayce Deed is doing in the woods," said Viktor. "Perhaps the Bear did not cut the tire or shoot the pellet gun, but I do not trust him. He will attempt on my life, mark my word. And I will be prepared."

"It's hard to mark your words when I can't understand them, Viktor."

The back bedroom door creaked and Mike plodded out. He had pulled his Big Rack ball cap over his tousled hair. "I can't believe how hard I slept. Jeff filled me in on what's going on. I told him to grab some shuteye while he could."

"You are exhausted by the stress," said Viktor.

"I guess so." Mike yawned. "So our photographer is camping in the preserve? And y'all followed Peach to his site?"

"Digby tracked her to the campsite," I said. "We didn't actually see her there."

"The tracks might not have been hers," said Todd. "Digby might have gotten them confused. It's not like he's perfect. He probably makes mistakes like that all the time."

I ignored Todd's green-eyed bluster. "Mike, shouldn't we wake Peach and see what she knows?"

"Will it make a difference if we do it now or in the morning? If we wake Peach, she'll likely wake Mr. Bass."

"Jayce Deed is still out there," I said. "Aren't you concerned he'll do something else? If Peach has anything to do with him, we might be able to use that information to stop Deed. What happens if he cuts the tires on the other vehicles? Or worse? We're trapped out here."

"Please calm down," said Mike. "We're not trapped. The lodge knows we're out here and if they can't catch us by radio, they'll eventually send someone out to see what happened. Someone will radio in tomorrow to check on things. When they can't get through, they'll send someone."

"Perhaps we should wait," said Viktor. "The Peach makes no sense at the best of times. Without sleep, she may be impossible to understand."

"Leave this to Jeff, Viktor, and me," said Mike. "You're a guest, Miss Tucker. It's not your place to question my customers. Particularly at this time of night and after all you've been through."

Todd stepped closer to me, pressing against my back.

I narrowed my eyes. "What are you saying, Mike?"

"You're a bit irrational and excitable right now."

"And Peach is Bob's date and Bob Bass has a lot of money and a TV show, so he deserves some protection. If Bob gets pissed at the lodge, it could go belly up and you're out of a job."

"This is not just about me, Miss Tucker. I have other people to protect."

"Protect them by allowing some crazy guy to terrorize us? Two men are dead, Mike."

"Both accidents. Unfortunate accidents. Do you think I'm not sick with worry about all this? It's not just the lodge at this point. I've got to keep everyone calm. Interrogating Peach Payne in the middle of the night could rouse everyone into a state of panic."

Todd's fingers dug into my arm. "We'll catch a little sleep and talk about this later."

"It is a good idea," said Viktor.

"I'll take over the watch, Viktor," said Mike. "You can get some sleep too."

"I'll take over the watch." My eyes felt dry, my body ached with fatigue, and exasperation hammered the back of my head, but I was not interested in sleep. Particularly sleep ordered by a group of men who would not recognize urgency, even if it was gnawing on their hindquarters.

"Come on, Cherry." Todd tugged on my arm. "Let's get some rest."

"You too?" I yanked my arm from his grasp. "Unbelievable. I'm not some little kid y'all can send to bed."

Mike settled his hands on his hips. "I'll take it from here."

Viktor shuffled to the men's bedroom. "I will use ancient grains to make the breakfast. You will enjoy."

"I sure hope ancient grains is a euphemism for a chicken biscuit." I stomped to the women's bunk room, muttering to Todd, "These people are blind. Blind! How can they ignore facts? Peach did leave tonight. Deed is out there. Lesley is dead. We need answers. Who is the target?"

"Let's take a detour from this. Just for a minute." Todd held open the bedroom door, peering inside.

I slid inside the bunk room. LaToya rolled over in her sleep and Peach snored into her pillow.

I looked up at Todd and whispered, "You can't come in here. It's women only."

"It smells better than the men's."

I glared through the open doorway at Mike. "I'm not feeling too keen on men right now."

"I know that doesn't mean me."

I sighed and toed the doorframe. "It should. You complicate things for me."

"You know that's not true." At the fierceness of his whisper, I glanced up. In the dim lighting, his cerulean blues met my anxious gaze. "I'm about as uncomplicated as you can get."

True. And not true. A complexity I didn't quite fathom lay beneath his mellow surface.

Just like the complexity going on behind the scenes at Big Rack.

"I need to know how Jayce Deed fits into all this. And how he's connected to Peach."

"You'll figure it out. Same as you'll figure out how to help Cody." Todd planted a quick kiss on top of my head. "I believe in you, Cherry."

"I should probably clean up," I mumbled. "And think on this additional complication."

"Go on." Todd placed his hand on the small of my back and gave me a quick shove into the room. "I'll be here when you need me."

That was a solution for a problem I did not want to consider.

In the bathroom, I peeled off muddy clothes until I had stripped to my boxers and t-shirt, then rinsed the mud out of my sweats and began working out the water for a drip dry. With each hand wring, I let my thoughts squeeze out the weekend's perplexities, keeping my focus square on Big Rack and off my love life.

Who gave permission for Jayce Deed to take a UTV and camp in the preserve? Someone who could override Jeff Digby. Who else was there? The Woodcocks? Maybe they hired Deed to photograph the lodge grounds. And didn't know Deed actually planned to terrorize the hunt party and possibly murder Lesley Vaughn?

That hypothesis lacked a few things. Namely, sense.

Sakes alive, this was confusing, I thought. Maybe the men were right and I was overreacting. I eyed myself in the mirror. The circles beneath my eyes matched the deep hue of the weekend's recent storms. Not my best look.

I glared at the mirror. "What's wrong with you? Rookie Holt needs evidence. You said you'd help her."

There was one person who might answer some of my questions. My reflection's grin gleamed with malevolence.

"The men should have thought more carefully before sending me to bed in the same room with Peach," I whispered. I spun from the mirror. Leaving the light on, I cracked the door and slipped out, allowing the bathroom light to cut a wedge across the floor.

"Peach," I whispered. "Peach, you awake?"

She muttered a curse and rolled over.

"Peach, can I have a cigarette? Where's your bag? I'll get them out myself."

"I don't have any cigarettes," she hissed. "Leave me alone. It's the middle of the night."

"That's what I thought." I shook her shoulder. "Get up."

She flung an arm to shoo me. "Go away."

I snagged the arm and yanked. "You're going to tell me all about Jayce Deed and why you let him shoot at Bob and Rick."

Peach flipped over and pulled her arm into her body, dragging me with her. Her tight, gym-built muscles bunched beneath my grip, and my hand slid off her arm. She grabbed my wrist and squeezed. "I don't need to tell you anything. I don't even know what you're talking about. Who are you to tell me what to do?"

I bit my lip from crying out. A lifetime's accumulation of other's disapproval and disdain rushed through me, roaring for revenge. I pulled back my left elbow and popped Peach in the nose.

Regrettably, I was kneeling and using my weak arm. She blinked several times then lunged. We toppled to the floor, scratching and pulling hair. Tussling like a couple of Jerry Springer girls.

"What is going on?" called LaToya.

A moment later, the bedroom light blared, revealing my embarrassing supine position. Peach sat astride me, while I grappled her shoulders. Peach swung at my neck, missed, and smashed her fist into the floor.

I curled up, slammed my forehead into her nose, and shoved her off.

She toppled back, holding her nose.

"Crazy, white trash bitch," screamed Peach.

"You tell me what your boyfriend Deed is doing in the woods." I grabbed a fistful of Peach's overly moisturized hair and yanked until her chin jutted toward the ceiling.

She grabbed my ear and wrenched. I howled in pain.

Fists hammered on the bedroom door.

I swung a knuckle at Peach's chin and missed. She chucked one back and caught my shoulder.

Icy water hit my face and drenched my Talladega t-shirt. I blinked off the water, looked up, and found LaToya standing over us, a cup in her hand.

"You crazy women chill." The stink-eye LaToya delivered held the level of disdain only found in teenagers annoyed with adults.

I ducked my head. Water dripped off my ponytail into my lap.

"Everything's fine," she hollered to Mike. LaToya folded her arms over her chest, reminding me of a stance my deceased Grandma Jo often had taken with me. "What's going on?"

"Peach snuck out in the night and we tracked her to a camp. The camp of a Jayce Deed, who's supposed to be a photographer but is in reality a pellet gun-wielding psycho intent on scaring the pants off someone in this tournament."

"How do you know this?" said LaToya. "Did you see her at this camp?"

"Well, no. But I saw her sneak out. When she came back, she told Viktor she'd gone out to smoke. But she doesn't have any cigarettes." I pointed my trigger finger at Peach. "Ha."

"This girl is a lunatic," said Peach. "I don't know any Jayce Deed. And how did she see me sneak out? Where were you?"

"Finding the diablo pellets your boyfriend, Jayce Deed, shot at the bunkhouse tonight."

"Pellets?" LaToya lifted her lip. "Some guy shot at us with a Red Ryder?"

I stood, dripping LaToya's cold shower onto the pine planks. "Peach, you're going to fess up right now or I'm going to show Bob all those awful videos you took of him."

"Bob's not going to put up with this bullshit." Peach sneered. "He sees you for what you are, you piece of trash. You think playing detective makes you look smart or something? We're laughing at you behind your back. You're just an ignorant hillbilly."

My last nerve hammered.

"Hillbilly? Peach, because you're from California, you may not realize this." For this important lesson, I used a heavenly directed finger point. "In Georgia, we are not hillbillies."

"True." LaToya nodded. "Around here, she's just called country."

THIRTY-ONE

I left Peach with LaToya. I had a feeling LaToya already didn't care for Bob's girlfriend and she hoped Peach's guilt meant a chance for her to stay in the tournament. After borrowing a pair of thermal coveralls from LaToya, I snuck out of the bedroom. Mike dozed by the window. Jeff had locked his rifle back in the kitchen pantry, but the night vision binoculars still lay on the great pine table. I grabbed a pair, a leash, and bent to rouse Buckshot from her hearthrug nest.

"Come on, girl," I whispered. "It's go time."

With a long yawn, she stretched, shaking out each leg. Showing her the leash, I led her to the door. At the scrape of the lock and rattle of the doorknob, I held my breath. I glanced back, but Mike's chin still lay on his chest. A tea cup rested on the windowsill.

"That's what Viktor gets for not bringing coffee," I muttered.

We slipped into the dank and murky pre-dawn. Buckshot's collar jangled and after a brisk body shake, she bounded forward. I pulled her back and led her around the side of the bunkhouse.

"Usually I take Todd with me on these kinds of excursions, but I think it's best not to involve him."

Buckshot cocked her head.

"It's personal," I said. "Besides, Todd has many skills, but tracking is not one of them. I don't want to endanger you, but I could sure use your help. As Abel's faithful companion, you have a dog in this hunt, so to speak. Are you ready to do your part?"

Her bushy tail whipped back and forth.

"Buckshot, we're hunting Jayce Deed's campsite. When we get there, you need to beef it up, act real tough, okay? Pretend you're a German Shepherd or a Chihuahua or something. None of this 'everybody's my best friend' stuff."

She gave a happy yip and swerved into a bush.

"This is serious," I said, hauling her from the bush. "This Deed may have murdered Lesley. For what reason, I don't know, but I do know he most likely has a pellet gun and a knife. I've got to take him by surprise. You're here to let me know if that hog or any other danger's nearby."

Catching a scent, Buckshot rushed forward, pulling me with her.

I scanned the forest with the thermal binoculars, hunting for the unnatural boxed shape of the tent. We threaded through the trees, heading in the general direction I had taken with Jeff and Todd. To plunge into Deed's campsite with no weapon other than a human-loving dog was foolish and irresponsible. I winced, thinking of the harangue I would have received from my Uncle Will and Luke. But action needed to be taken before Deed got away. I'd no luck persuading anyone to mind me thus far. I was tired of being ignored. And feeling stalked made me furious.

And maybe a bit irrational.

At the edge of the campsite, I squatted and pulled Buckshot into my side. The UTV, another Mule, had returned. All appeared quiet in the tent.

"No barking," I told Buckshot, unclipping her leash. "I'm going inside that tent. I want you to wait outside, just in case Deed pulls out a weapon. I'm hoping to disarm him before he knows what's going on. I'll leave the opening unzipped so you can come when I call. Remember, be fierce."

I took her tail wag as agreement and led her into the campsite. I held a heavy-duty flashlight in one hand, the binoculars in the other. Buckshot carried her leash in her mouth. At the entrance to the tent, I sank to my haunches. Buckshot sat, wagging her tail, and dropped her leash. While giving her head a good scrub, I finger motioned the plan, ending with the zip-it lips.

She licked my finger.

I counted to three, said a prayer, then charged in. Swinging the flashlight up like a baton, I crawled forward until my knees hit a body, poised myself above, and tried to determine which end was the head.

"Why're you back?" said No-Mustache/Jayce Deed's sleepy voice.

Pointing the flashlight in the direction of the voice, I turned on the beam and blasted Deed full in the face. He blinked and held up his hand.

"What're you doing?" he said. "I can't see."

"You've been caught. Fess up now."

"Who are you?"

I flashed the light around the tent, snatched the air rifle, then shined the beam in his face. "I'll shoot you and it will hurt like hell."

He rose onto his elbows. "Are you with the hunt party?"

"Who are you stalking? Bob Bass? How do you know Peach?"

"Come on, man." Deed rose to sitting. "Put the gun down. I'm not doing anything."

"Liar. You're not a photographer. What's your real reason for being out here?"

"Dude, seriously. I'm camping. I have permission to be out here."

"The hell you are. You don't even have wieners or beer. You and Peach are working together to terrorize the hunters." I dug myself a hole and hoped he jumped in. "I got her to confess back in the bunkhouse and now we're holding her."

"Wieners?" Deed's nostrils flared and the soul patch rose with his chin. His sneer bared angry white teeth, before laughing. "Her confession should have made my intentions clear."

"So y'all are some kind of activists. But this isn't about processed meat. Peach is taking videos of Bob Bass looking like an ass. To make fun of him?"

"There's more to it, obviously." Jayce raised a manscaped eyebrow. "But humor is an important part of our campaigns. It grabs the attention of those with less complex modes of thinking."

"Huh?"

"My father started Ban Sapiens back in the eighties. Before he was mauled by that grizzly. I had to pick up where he left off." The toothy smile he flashed reminded me of a gator's. Ironic, I thought, for an herbivore. "The first step is always education. Civilization needs to understand the pointlessness of our existence. Humans are destroyers. I'm not just talking existential nihilism. That's old news. Ban Sapiens is a practical effort. The eventual culmination will be eradication."

"You want to eradicate humans?" I felt compelled to point out that absurdity but decided my pearls of wisdom would be wasted on this swine lover.

"Humans are the most unnatural beings on this planet. Do you realize what the world would be like without us?"

"Kind of like that tree falling in the forest with nobody around to hear it. Why aren't you making a fuss of this contest publicly? What's the point of all the guerrilla tactics?"

"Where have you been? Demonstrations are so twentieth century. Who cares about TV news when you can go viral and reach more people? Revolutions start with guerrilla fighters. It's all about using shock campaigns to catch people's attention." His tone reminded me of a preacher's and his hands flew with his speech, eager to share his version of the good news. "This invitation provided the perfect opportunity to ruin Bass's TV show and upload footage that will disgust his fans and show the world what an idiot he is with a few well-timed, startling but harmless gags."

"The skeet shoot incident wasn't harmless. Someone could have gotten killed."

"Peach told me about that incident. Not my idea, but how wonderfully effective. Humans invent a device to train them how to kill and the very device turns on them. So very Frankenstein. Bob Bass goes from hunter to huntee."

"That wasn't you?" I lowered the gun to my lap, but left my hand on the stock. "I don't get it. Do you hate Bob Bass or humans in general?"

"We chose Bass as one example to showcase the inanity of humans. There are others on the list. I could read you our mission statement."

"Another time. You got your footage. Go home and leave the rest of us alone."

"I'm not supposed to go home yet." He cocked his head, drew forward on his haunches, and simian-like, rested his fists on the floor. "Did you hear that?"

"What do you mean, not supposed to go home?" I couldn't get a handle on Jayce Deed's size of screwball. Poor Lesley had nothing on this guy. "Are you planning on chaining yourself to that hog or something? Because I'm telling you right now, that isn't going to work."

"You don't understand. I pity your simple mind."

"Was Lesley helping you? The monster swine guy? Did you drive him out here?"

"Yes. We dialogued, found mutual points of interest, but in the end, our goals weren't aligned."

"So you killed him?"

"Shh." Deed's hindquarters rose with his head. "Something's out there."

"It's just Buckshot. A dog."

Hearing her name, Buckshot whined and scratched the tent flap.

Deed's arms flexed. I swung the lightweight rifle too late. Deed pushed forward, knocking me hard across the chest. I fell back. The flashlight flew, spiraling its beam around the tent. The gun jerked from my hand.

Deed ripped the binoculars from around my neck, then grasped my throat with one hand. His knees pinned my arms to the ground and seat pressed into my pelvis. Releasing my neck, he snatched the flashlight and switched it off.

I now knew where Peach got her moves. Unfortunately, Jayce was much heavier.

Lowering his body, he brought his face close to mine. He smelled of rain and granola. "Quiet."

I squirmed beneath him. "Get off of me."

The tent rustled. Buckshot's brindle nose jutted between our faces. Deed yelped, and the cur gave us a quick face bath.

"Get rid of the dog." Deed's groomed brows spiked and beads of sweat dripped from his forehead.

"Are you scared of Buckshot?"

His white-rimmed eyes flashed and, cobra-like, his upper torso rose, leaving his legs to pin me to the ground. "I'm not scared of animals. That would be ridiculous."

"Because the rest of this is all so sane," I muttered. "I can't very well contain Buckshot unless you let me go."

The pressure on my legs released and I shook them out before rising to wrap an arm around the dog. Buckshot's tail thumped and I stroked her back.

Deed backed into the far wall of the tent and grabbed an object too dark to see. Assuming he had recovered the rifle, I mentally signaled Buckshot to summon a ferocious growl.

She washed my ear instead.

"Here's the thing," I spoke, while trying to calculate the potential deadliness of Jayce Deed. Did his anti-humanism lead toward an eradication of our species, starting with this weekend? "You succeeded in destroying the contest. Well, you and the mud. As far as I know, the hog's still intact. You've got plenty of footage of Bass acting foolish and scared. I assume that's the intention of all those delightful pranks. Mission accomplished. So now you need to come back to the bunkhouse with me and give yourself up."

"Mission not accomplished until I hear differently. I'm supposed to stay until the end."

"Hear differently from who? Peach? What end?" I raised my voice in frustration. "Are you working with somebody at Big Rack? Who gave you permission to camp and to use the UTV?"

"If Peach confessed like you said, you would know the details of my arrangement." He waved the dark object in his hand.

My mind flew through a movie lover's catalog of devices waved by crazy men. "Is that a detonator?" Shoving Buckshot behind me, I began scooting toward the flap.

"Detonator? You've got quite the imagination."

My boot smacked a heavy object and I caught the flashlight before it rolled out of the tent. Aiming at Deed, I clicked on the beam.

Deed's teeth flashed. "It's not just been Bob Bass who's looked like an idiot. You've all made for entertaining programming this weekend. It's been so easy to freak everyone out. And thanks to Peach, now I can track you more easily." He laughed, rose into a stoop, and waved the missing walkie-talkie. "I'm not the one who should be answering these questions. There's someone even more diabolical than me in these woods."

"Who?"

I heard the gunshot at the same time my spotlight caught Deed's collapse onto the tent floor.

THIRTY-TWO

Guilt slowed my speed. I hated leaving Deed, not knowing the extent of his injury. At the sound of the shot, Buckshot had torn out of the tent and after a second's hesitation, I ran after her. Not wanting to give my position away, I killed the flashlight's beam. Into the cold, dark woods I stumbled, afraid of calling out to the dog and attracting the shooter's attention. Lost in a sea of trees, I had no sense of the bunkhouse or Deed's campsite. The gloom magnified every stirring. My heart could have raised the dead with its wild thumping, and my bumbling gait had a thunderous quality I couldn't quiet.

As I slashed my way through cobwebs and tangles of Virginia Creeper, I sorted through the confusion. Had the shooter heard our conversation? Were they Deed's accomplice? Did Deed intend to contact the shooter by walkie-talkie? Another B.S. activist more disgruntled with humans than Deed? One who wanted more than funny videos, but wanted to exterminate Bass? Had Lesley and Abel gotten in the way of their diabolical plan? Was it someone in our party besides Peach? Another mysterious stalker in the woods? Or had Peach escaped?

Somehow the thought of Peach as evil genius filled me with more dread than an anonymous stalker. The depth of a zealot's conviction terrified me. Particularly with a rationality skewed enough to sleep with someone like Bob Bass.

Peach Payne made Mata Hari look like Snow White. Pre-dwarves.

I crashed through a bush, tripped, and fell into a pile of sodden leaves. I lay there, panting and staring overhead into the murky canopy. Dawn had come without a sunrise. Dark clouds had shouldered past my Georgia sunbeams, walling us into a dank, stygian prison.

Lord, how I missed the sun.

A rustling sounded beyond the azalea at my elbow. I tensed, seizing the flashlight in both hands. Curling my body toward my knees, I rose to a crouch, glad for once that the ground was soggy and could muffle my movements. I waited, wondering what caused the swish of branches and squish of wet terrain.

The shuffling movement drew closer. Beneath LaToya's thermal coveralls, my skin grew clammy. I clenched my jaw, puffing short pants through my nose, and considered my options. Running was out. A kindergartner could catch me. Climbing a tree also out. I had no hops and the branches of any hardy-enough hardwood towered above my head. I could spring into attack, which might scare the intruder, but more likely tick them off. Or I could hide and, if necessary, fight them off with a flashlight.

I hoped a better idea would emerge before the being did.

The trampling grew louder. I hunched forward, resting on the balls of my feet and gripping the flashlight. The overgrown azalea shook. I held my breath. A dinner plate-sized snout pushed through the branches. The slimy nostrils quivered and the snout tipped up to reveal protruding razor-tipped, curved tusks. Not as big as Rick's arm as he claimed, but certainly as long as my hand.

This was much worse than a diabolically insane Peach Payne.

The slight breeze shifted and my stomach gripped, seized by the putrid, musky odor. Gagging, I scrambled in the slippery leaves and backed into a hemlock. The azalea's branches cracked as the long snout flexed like a vacuum hose, seeking his next dinner. The great, sloping head broke through, splintering the large evergreen shrub into twiggy detritus. Sharp piggy eyes blinked. He considered me.

I clutched the tree, trying not to vomit or scream.

Behind the monster pig, something crashed through the branches and weeds. A low growl accompanied a string of sharp, excited barks.

"No." My voice pitched in horror. "Buckshot, go home."

The super swine shifted to glance behind him. His ears flicked toward the sound and his jaw worked, scraping his bottom tusks along his flat upper teeth like a grindstone. The massive body turned, rotating like a jackknifed semi, the back end trampling the surrounding bushes. The hog swaggered forward to face the snarling dog.

My heart plummeted and chill bumps broke onto my goose flesh.

"Buckshot," I hollered. "Come here, girl."

I continued to coax and call, unable to see Buckshot's position. The massive hog blocked my view.

The sight would have delighted Lesley Vaughn. The jumbo hog resembled a hatchback in size and could have flattened Alabama's offensive line with its girth. Unfortunately for Lesley, there were no mystical qualities to this prodigious porcine. Unless you counted the putrid stench, which had the ability to knock a person unconscious.

Stiff-legged and body bowed for combat, Hogzilla studied Buckshot. Buckshot continued her litany of barks, ecstatic to have found our prey.

Born to bay, Buckshot had achieved her life's purpose. She'd continue to alert us to this awful beast unless I did something to stop her. I had put the dutiful dog in this terrible position. Sweet Buckshot was no Beowulf to this rank Grendel.

"Buckshot. Come." I gave up on commands, released my grip on the tree, and crept past the hog's back end.

The thick tail swished.

I scurried.

At a cluster of loblolly pines, I swung behind their pencil-like trunks and peered out. Buckshot paused her alert, changed positions, and resumed barking.

The hog dropped his head and swung it side to side, eyeing us. The great jaw popped as he ground the tusks against the whetstone of his upper teeth.

The tension drove Buckshot wild with exultation.

My stand of loblollies offered no more protection than a grove of Q-tips. I had to cover my partner. Praying for the Lord to help this poor, dimwitted dog and the idiot who put her in this situation, I crept toward Buckshot's barks. My boots held firm in the spongey forest floor, but the flashlight shook in my white-knuckled grip.

"Buckshot," I pleaded. "Please come."

By now the shooter would have heard our commotion and I figured the flashlight's beacon would make no difference. I beamed the light on the mess of brambles, vines, and trees between me and Buckshot's baying. She trotted in excited circles not twenty yards from the hog. A quick flash on the monster's face revealed lather dripping from his jaws. I pointed the beam back on Buckshot and ran toward her.

The hog lunged, driving forward like a defensive tackle ready to sack the lithe brindle quarterback.

Buckshot leapt and dashed, ready for the game. Her barks grew frantic as she parried the behemoth's attack. The terrible jaw opened and the hog swung his head to the side, aiming to drive a spiked tusk into Buckshot's hide. Buckshot yelped, but dove away.

Tears blinded my dim vision. The flashlight's beam bounced as my boots pounded the ground, obscuring my view of the attack. Jerking to a stop behind a thick hardwood, I shined the flashlight on the pair. Buckshot had backed against a thin pine, her tail tucked and ears pulled back.

A thin red line dripped off her side. The colossal swine's jaw brushed the ground and its lip curled back, further exposing its tusks, ready to finish off the dog.

I leapt in front of Buckshot and shone the light in the hog's face. Reaching behind me, I grabbed the dog's collar and began to slide backward. The hog grunted and pushed forward.

I turned and ran, hauling Buckshot with me.

Twenty paces in, I felt a puff of air and a block of cement slammed into my back. I flew to the side. The flashlight sailed off. Buckshot's collar twisted in my grip. We collapsed into a pile of leaves, the dog half beneath me. I blinked at the pain rocketing off my spine, shooting through my nerve endings and into my extremities. Beneath me, Buckshot whined and pawed at the mushy leaves, trying to wriggle out.

I lifted my head.

The monster had stopped, drawn toward the opposite direction. The ears flicked forward and back. It turned to glance at us and I dropped my head, hoping what worked for bears might also work on pork. A second later, the hog tore away.

I pushed up on my elbow and then dropped again as a shot rang through the forest and exploded above us.

THIRTY-THREE

Buckshot could walk and I could limp, so we got the hell out of Dodge. I couldn't tell if the shot was meant for the hog or us. We didn't stick around to ask.

Morning had dawned with or without the sun, and that meant hunters could be seeking to eradicate the forest of the vile monster. For that I was glad. But not while I was tooling around in LaToya's camouflage.

My specially designed Day-Glo forest bling was all for naught.

"Buckshot." I staggered forward, massaging the mammoth-shaped bruise on my back. "I believe we have escaped with our very lives. Lucky for you, your scratch isn't a gash. Although I'd worry about pig germs. Who knows where those tusks have been."

She bristled, unamused.

"No time to be sensitive. We are not out of the woods yet. Figuratively and literally. There's a killer on the loose and it is up to us to stop them. And now I have to worry about protecting Bob Bass, of all people."

Buckshot glanced up and returned to her shambling walk.

"Can you smell the woodsmoke?" I sniffed in demonstration. "It's not a very good plan, but it's all I've got. We follow our noses and find the bunkhouse. You know that score. Once there, we might lay low a bit and scout out the doings. Remember, the shooter could be one of us."

One brown eye peered up at me as she continued her dogged creep forward.

I dropped to the ground and gathered her into my arms. "I'm sorry I got you into this mess. Never should have taken you with me. I promise you, I'll figure out what happened to your owner. I'd swear on my love of bacon, whoever shot Deed and killed Lesley also murdered Abel Spencer."

She licked my neck and I rubbed her ears.

"I bet you knew that all along, didn't you, girl?"

We found the bunkhouse almost by accident. The woodsmoke scheme didn't work as well as I thought, but the rhythmic thunk of axe on wood caught Buckshot's ear. Once agreed on avoiding pigs, I allowed her to lead. We followed the sound of the axe blow to the side of the small shed on the east side of the bunkhouse. The two guides, Big Clem and Lil Joe, shared the chore of firewood stacking. Deep in conversation, they took no notice of our peeping from the edge of the woods.

"Let's hurry up, they'll be ready to go in a minute," said Big Clem. "This should hold the rest over until we get back."

"What about the girl who's missing? The artist. Aren't we supposed to take her with us?"

"Shit, we can't wait that long if we've got to turn around and get back to pick up the next group. She's probably lost. What kind of fool goes out in the middle of the night? I'm sore pissed she took Buckshot, but that's likely the only way she'll find Team Three's stand."

"Don't you think it's funny she took off like that? Especially after all that's happened?" Lil Joe heaved a chunk of wood onto the pile and turned to face his older counterpart. "Do you believe that Peach when she says the girl's the one doing all the pranks?"

"I don't know what to think." Big Clem spat on the ground. "I just want to get the hell out of here. I don't even care about getting the hog anymore."

I cupped a hand around Buckshot's ear. "You hear that? Peach's blaming me for all this. The nerve on that one."

Buckshot replied by cleaning out my nostril, and I bit my lip trying not to sneeze. Shushing her, I resumed my watch.

Ensconced in thermal camos and a knit skull cap, Jeff Digby swaggered from around the side of the bunkhouse.

I studied Big Rack's head guide. Wasn't he worried about my disappearance, knowing that Deed camped out in the woods?

He could have lied about giving him permission to camp, I thought. Although I couldn't see a local outfitter supporting Ban Sapiens.

"You done here?" asked Jeff. "I got the tires switched. They're loaded up and ready to go."

"What about the artist?" said Big Clem.

"Let me worry about Miss Tucker." He swiveled his gaze toward the woods.

Buckshot and I shrank back, hovering behind a stand of holly.

While his eyes roamed the dark forest, Jeff continued to speak. "I'm taking Viktor to check on a few things this morning. If Miss Tucker doesn't show up at Team Three's stand, we'll hunt her down."

I rounded my eyes at Buckshot and placed a finger on her mouth. She licked my finger.

Lil Joe tossed the last piece of wood on the pile stacked against the shed. "Mike's staying with the rest of the party?"

"Yeah. It's just Bass, Peach, and Rick until Team Three gets back. Tennessee's going to find that lost Gator now that it's light." Jeff snapped his gaze back to the men and pivoted to leave. "Don't think they'll find the hog around here, though. At least I didn't see it this morning."

Jeff had been out in the woods earlier.

The three men strolled toward the bunkhouse drive. I nudged Buckshot and we crept toward the shed. Peering around the side, we spied the awkward bundle of Lesley wrapped in a tarp and bungee-corded to the rear bed. He hung off the sides like an overstuffed sausage in a too-short bun, a degrading end for someone so sure of future fame. I hoped he got plenty of airtime when the story of his murder finally reached the press. Maybe his book would be published.

Todd and LaToya had squeezed into the backseat with their bags. Big Clem and Lil Joe hopped into their seats and cranked the Gator's engine.

"I sure hope Todd remembers to take all this to the police station," I murmured. "He's probably wondering why I took off without him."

Buckshot licked my hand.

"Max is out there somewhere too," I whispered. "Hopefully he heard I'm supposedly heading to his deer stand. Maybe he'll put two and two together when I don't show up. Although the Bear did miss out on all the real exciting stuff. I doubt he's heard the tally of bodies."

She whined.

"I think I'm becoming desensitized to violence." I apologized for my tactlessness. "But who's telling everyone I've gone to Max's deer stand?"

The Gator backed away from the bunkhouse and began its bouncy ride over the water-filled ruts. The back hung low, loaded with Lesley.

"I didn't get to say goodbye to Todd," I sniffed. "Boy, I'm getting down. Must be the lack of sunshine. I'm going to have to hit a tanning bed if I get through this."

Buckshot pawed my leg.

"Now's not the time for that lecture," I muttered, rubbing my eyes.

She scratched again.

I glanced up and ducked around the wall.

Viktor strode straight toward us.

THIRTY-FOUR

I held Buckshot's collar, flattened against the back of the shed, and prayed for Viktor to go away. He didn't go away, but he came no closer. I could hear him muttering, then a grunt and stacking of wood.

"Hey," shouted Jeff Digby from the bunkhouse drive. "Are we going or not?"

Dangit, I thought. I could probably talk my way into an escape from Viktor, but not the hyper-vigilant outfitter.

"The men did not bring the wood inside," called Viktor. "We need more wood for the fire."

"Let's get a move on. I want to get back to that camp right away. Fog's moving in and it's going to be harder to track Tucker."

"Did you speak to the Peach?"

"Mike did. Peach doesn't know anything. Said that she tried to stop Cherry from leaving last night and the gal went nuts and attacked her. LaToya somewhat confirmed the story. She didn't understand what started the fight, but she let Miss Tucker leave."

I pursed my lips and raised my brows at Buckshot. "Big fat liar," I mouthed.

Peach Payne had a reckoning coming. I still wasn't sure if she was a criminal mastermind or only a willing minion for Jayce Deed. Giving her the benefit of the doubt, I chose evil genius. Could she have snuck out after LaToya fell asleep and shot Deed? I turned my attention back to the conversation between the two men, hoping to learn more about the vile Peach.

"Why would the artist go to the deer stand at that time of night? She must know in the dark it is impossible to find. It's the farthest blind from the bunkhouse," said Viktor. "Perhaps she is working with Avtaikin."

"What do you mean?" Jeff's voice dropped. "I thought she worked for him as an artist or something."

"Yes, of course. It is nothing," said Viktor. "Help me with this kindling."

Wood clacked against wood. Viktor said, "Do you think it's wise for Mike to take the rest of the party hunting?"

"Probably not," Jeff's voice sounded grim. "But Bob Bass has been harping about it all morning. Thinks Avtaikin has an unfair advantage. The fog will provide good cover for them, though."

"Good cover for others too. I don't like this."

"I'll handle it."

I waited for their footsteps to recede, then slunk down the wall to sit on my haunches. Buckshot matched my sit and we exchanged a canine-human tête-à-tête.

"Here's what we know. Someone invited Jayce Deed to camp. Someone who could give him permission and lend him a Big Rack UTV. Could the Woodcocks be involved? Maybe they thought it would be a publicity stunt?"

Buckshot dropped a paw on my knee.

"You're right, how could Ban Sapiens bring good PR to the lodge? Although the owners do sound like they've a screw or two needing tightening." I paused for additional thought. "Could the Sparks have arranged for Jayce to camp? They're friends with the Woodcocks and want to buy the lodge. Bad publicity could drive the price down."

Buckshot flopped to the ground. I swept a hand across her back, inspecting the scratch.

"It does seem a risky and complicated method to get land." I sighed. "One thing's for certain. Peach is involved. I'm going to watch that hunt party. I think Deed was killed to prevent him from revealing who else is involved. Bob Bass is still in danger."

I rubbed the scruff of Buckshot's neck. "I'm going to slip you back inside the bunkhouse for a rest, girl. Your scrape doesn't look too bad. We'll get you fixed up, then I'll do more scouting. I wonder what time it is."

The gray sky didn't allow for any natural time keeping. And as Jeff Digby predicted, although the rain had stopped, the cool air had caused a dense vapor to rise from the saturated ground. Whistler would have loved the landscape for his *Nocturne* series.

I shivered. "I wonder who told everyone I had gone to Max's deer stand. Peach? Did Todd believe it too?"

Buckshot flicked her ears toward the bunkhouse.

"I bet you're right." I rubbed my chin, then examined the dirt that appeared on my fingers. "I think it's about time that Peach and I have another chat. If it comes to it, this time I'm using my right hook."

After Jeff Digby and Viktor had left, I felt more at ease spying on the hunting party, most of whom had no idea that anyone but a prankster had imbedded themselves in our ranks. The hunters exited the bunkhouse. Although the murk of fog now enveloped the forest, the rain had stopped and that alone seemed to lift their spirits. It was as if the fear and suspicions from the previous two days had been sent home with Lesley's body. Despite being terrorized by a shooter after Lesley's death.

Everyone must have learned the marksman had actually been a plinker. Although, in my opinion, reasonable people should still be disturbed by a crazed air gun terrorist.

Too bad this crew didn't include reasonable people.

With his rifle flung over a shoulder, Bob thumped down the porch stairs. The bedraggled peacock feathers on his black cowboy hat drooped and the sheepskin trim on his coat appeared matted and stained, but he maintained a perk in his step that came from a good night's sleep, high expectations, and a willful ignorance to serious issues. Peach followed at a more lethargic pace. She too had a weapon strapped to her back and the ubiquitous GoPro camera hung around her neck.

Back in California, Peach must have been an actress. I always thought her a phony, albeit the gold-digging variety. Looking back at the conversation I had overheard in my lodge room, Deed's argument must have been with Peach. His accusation of "enjoying the benefits" had lodged distinctly in my memory. I wondered how strong her loyalties lay with Jayce Deed.

I drew my attention to Rick, smoking awkwardly on the side of the disabled Mule. His face was a patchwork of bandages, but the tape on his hands had been peeled off. My lip curled and a hot blast of anger surged through me at the thought of what Rick might have done to Jessica's daughter. If we hadn't gone searching for Peach, would Jeff have smothered Rick in his sleep? Pulled Rick out of his bunk and beat the everlovin' crap out of him? I almost wished he had. The very sight of Rick turned my stomach.

But that was not the problem at hand. While Peach and Bob chatted and Rick smoked, I kept my eyes on the foggy woods, searching for odd movement or the glint of a rifle stock. What I lacked in binoculars and scopes, I had in Buckshot, but she lay on the ground, uninterested in serving sentinel to Bob Bass.

I ran a hand over the tuckered dog's head and drew my attention back to the bunkhouse drive where Mike now stood. He pointed toward a section of woods northeast of the bunkhouse, the opposite direction of the half circle of deer blinds and Jayce Deed's camp, where Viktor and Jeff Digby had hiked. Mike's group headed toward the ridge where Lesley had fallen, making my lips twitch in disapproval.

The party trudged through the drive's slop and I scurried from the side of the bunkhouse to crouch beside the porch. Orange safety vests bobbed amid the misty sepias, ochres, and umbers. When I felt reasonably sure they wouldn't see me, I clambered onto the porch. Buckshot pattered after me and together we found the door locked. I leaned my head against the door for a moment, sorry more for Buckshot than my empty stomach, and then checked the porch for a key. One hung from a tiny hook beneath the porch rail. We entered, and while Buckshot sniffed the room for invasive critters, I sniffed out the gun closet. Locked with no key in sight.

"Dang that Jeff Digby. He's probably hiding it in his camo-colored boxer briefs."

Buckshot nudged her food bowl. I filled it with chow.

"Here's what I'm thinking. You could have wandered back to the bunkhouse on your own," I reflected. "Dogs are smart like that. They'll think I lost you, but my name's already mud. I suppose one more screw-up's not going to matter."

She rolled an eye, but continued eating.

"I sure hope no one in Halo hears about this, though. If they think I put a dog in danger, that'll be the last straw. We Tuckers will be run out of town for sure."

Still chewing, the brindle muzzle rose from the bowl to consider my suggestion.

"You're right. I guess when there's someone hunting you with a .30-06, there's not much use worrying about the gossips at home."

In the woods, the bright orange had disappeared into the thickening mist. Leaving Buckshot on the porch, I hurried to follow, scanning the trees as I squelched through the soaked pine straw. Behind the bunkhouse shed, my plan made sense. While the hunters settled into a hollow to wait for the appearance of a critter, I could watch for our stalker. However, I wasn't sure what I would do when I did see an intruder. I had no weapon for deterrent or defense. Plus, with the gloom and my camouflage coveralls, there was always the likelihood of getting shot by one of the hunters.

I shoved that thought away. Instinct had kept me alive this long. She'd have to continue to serve me today.

In the distance, a shimmer of tangerine stood out among the grays and browns. I adjusted my pace, deliberately darting from tree to tree for protection. The orange cluster dispersed into two clumps and I chose the group on the left. It had a smaller blob I assumed was Peach. My hands itched to tackle her and wring a confession from her neck. Revenge made for a violent master.

The orange blobs halted their stroll and settled on the ground behind a screen of bushes. By way of tree hugs, I approached the pair and stopped some thirty yards away. At the sharp blast of Bob's rifle, I dropped to the wide base of a red oak and curled there, then realized he had shot in the opposite direction. When my heart stopped racing, I settled more comfortably and began my watch.

Behind me, Peach remarked on Bob's miss and Bob offered a long, rambling excuse. I rolled my eyes. Each branch creak and pinecone drop made my heart race and chill bumps multiply. The cold and damp pervaded LaToya's thermal suit and I huddled against the tree, fighting misery, sleep, and back pain. The musty scent of decomposing foliage grew with the fog and sneeze prevention became a new priority.

Twenty minutes later, Peach told Bob she needed to tinkle. I peered around the tree.

She was coming this way. With her rifle.

Thirty-Five

Peach trudged past my squat without a glance in my direction. Tromping through the tangle of vines, she disappeared behind a thick cluster of pines. I scooted after her, hoping tee-tee was foremost in her mind. If setting up a sharp-shooting station with a bead on Bob was her mission, I'd be hard-tasked to deal with that dilemma.

I caught Peach with her pants down. Literally.

Unsporting on my part, but as I had no other weapon, surprise suited me.

Her rifle lay a few feet away from the spot where she hauled up her camo rain pants.

I pounced, snagged the sling, and smiled as I gathered the gun in my hand. One of those tactical Smith & Wessons cloaked in Realtree.

A fancy gun for a fancy girl.

"We're going to have a conversation," I said. "I've got some upsetting news. You should probably sit down."

"Well, well. Crazy white trash is back. Guess you're not as lost as they think." She sneered. "Threatening me with a gun this time? Bob's going to love that. In fact, let's do this in front of Bob. Maybe you'll inspire him to write a new redneck song."

"He should be so lucky," I muttered, then cleared my throat. "For the record, I'm not threatening you with a gun. I'm protecting myself. And I really think you should sit down to hear this."

"Sit on this, bitch." She flashed me a choice finger.

"Obviously, we're having a fundamental failure of communication." I gave up on niceties. "Jayce Deed was shot last night. Actually, early this morning."

Her expression didn't change, but her eyes tightened. "What are you talking about?"

"I didn't go to Max Avtaikin's deer blind last night. I went to Deed's camp. I got the scoop on Ban Sapiens. Handy initials, by the way. Jayce told me all about your plan to out Bob Bass online. Then someone shot Jayce."

"What?" She blanched and reeled, catching herself against a pine. "No. That's not possible. He's too smart. Not Jayce. You're wrong."

I shook my head.

All pretense fled. Fat tears rolled and splashed, smearing her makeup and revealing the dark circles she had carefully concealed. She clutched her chest, digging her long fingers into the safety vest. "Who would shoot Jayce? Why would they do that?"

"I don't know." Her reaction removed Peach from my suspect list. I didn't think she could be that good of an actress. "Who gave Jayce permission to camp?"

"Oh my God. Is he..."

I swallowed the golf ball welling in my throat and shrugged. "I'm sorry, I ran. I was afraid of getting shot."

Déjà vu walloped me with her body slam. Once again, Peach had lunged, knocking me to the ground. I gripped the rifle and held it in front of me to ward off her blows, trying to defend without fighting back.

My bruised back did not appreciate this constant aggravation, nor did my hip which ground against a pinecone. Peach's instinctual response did not seem to include flight. Luckily, grief diluted her punches to a weak, half-hearted pummeling.

"Peach, you've got to help me figure out who did this," I gasped, knocking a jab away with the butt of the gun.

"Why would anyone kill Jayce?" Her thick tears splattered my face and she rolled off to curl in a pile of soggy pine straw. "Oh my

God. How could someone do this? Jayce was brilliant. He didn't deserve to die."

"I'm sorry." Abandoning the rifle to the pine straw, I scooted towards her. "It's a shock. But listen, you and Bob could be in danger. You've got to talk to me, Peach. Who invited Jayce to the lodge?"

Shrugging off my comfort, she rolled to sitting. "Some guy called and told him about the contest and said Bob Bass was invited."

"Bob Bass didn't pay for the contest?"

"He paid for me. But no, Big Rack asked him to hunt. It happens all the time. Good PR for them."

Life seemed interminably unfair. Rich people didn't even have to pay the exorbitant fees that kept the riffraff out. "Max Avtaikin had to pay."

"I think Bob goaded Mr. Avtaikin into entering. They're poker buddies or something." She wiped her eyes, then examined her nails. "Anyway, whoever called Jayce had said they'd read our website and knew Bob was on our target list. They said they could get Jayce access to stuff if he wanted to disrupt the hunt."

"Access to stuff like pig heads, cakes, and UTVs?" My nostrils flared.

"Essentially. The cake and signs were my ideas. The air gun was Jayce's. Do you know how long he had to sit out there waiting for Bob to come out? They all worked great. I got lots of footage of Bob reacting like an idiot."

"What about the target practice? Someone could have gotten killed. And cutting the radio wire and slashing the tire valves? Y'all have trapped us here."

"I don't know about those." Her brows pulled together and her lip trembled. "Do you think it was the person Jayce was working with?"

"That's what I'm trying to figure out." I toned down my irritation. At least it was now clear why some of the incidents seemed benign and others malicious. "This would have gone a lot better if y'all just picketed or something. Whoever shot Jayce might have killed Lesley and Abel."

"We don't demonstrate," she said, making me wonder if remorse was even a word in her vocabulary. "Jayce was gifted when it comes to viral shock campaigns. Charities hired him for crowdsourcing advertisement, but his heart is with Ban Sapiens. Was. He really hated people. Hated what people do to the earth. Did he tell you about his dad? Killed in the line of duty, saving a grizzly bear?"

"Crowdsourcing advertisement? Viral shock campaigns?"

Now I knew remorse didn't enter the picture. The words she spoke were in English, but the jargon was beyond my understanding. I rubbed the weary from my eyes to hide my disgust. However, the killer had invited Ban Sapiens to this hunt for a purpose, and for that they had my sympathy. "This throws a different light on things. I thought someone was after Bob Bass. Now it sounds like you and Jayce were lured here to be murdered."

I probably should have softened my words. The blood drained from her face so quickly, I thought she might faint.

"They don't even know about me," she sobbed. "Jayce said he was coming alone and I was already deep undercover, filming Bob when he wasn't looking."

"I think you should go back to the bunkhouse," I said, not trusting the depth of her covertness. I had ferreted out Peach's part and the killer might have too. "It's not safe out here."

She nodded and I helped her up.

"What about Bob?" she asked. "He's going to wonder where I am."

"Bob better go with you to the bunkhouse," I said. "As soon as my friend Todd reaches the lodge, he'll alert the authorities."

"How long will that take?"

"Y'all lock yourselves in a bunk room with some supplies. Can you handle being with Bob a little longer?"

She nodded. "Bob's not a bad guy once you get to know him. He's actually caring and very generous."

I didn't try to reason out the deranged psychology of a radical. But I figured some serious daddy issues lurked beneath her pretty façade.

We tromped through the pine straw to Bob's makeshift blind of piled creeper vines. He lay on his stomach with his backpack shoved under his chest and rifle ready. At our approach, he glanced over his shoulder and rolled over. Spying Peach's tearstained face, he hopped to his feet.

"Babe, what happened?" His eyes lighted on me and his look turned thunderous. "You. What's going on?"

"Bob, I'm so scared. Someone's trying to kill us," cried Peach.

I stared openmouthed as she rattled off a story that involved an ex-boyfriend activist murdered in the woods. The woman's loyalty rivaled a feral cat's. I thought about arguing over the plasticity of her version, but felt too exhausted to care. I just needed them to haul ass to the bunkhouse.

Bob pulled Peach into his arms and she tucked herself inside his shoulder, sobbing and sorry for her sins. I grabbed his pack and hustled them forward, glad he was amenable to the safety of the bunkhouse. The couple confused and disturbed me. I wondered if Peach was up to old tricks, but her cling to Bob seemed genuine. As they walked, Bob murmured comforting phrases about love and forgiveness. Hope blossomed within me. If this flaky pair could make it, didn't I stand a chance for some kind of happily ever after?

I hummed, studying the misty landscape for barrel glints and mad killers. Then realized the tune I hummed matched the phrasings of Bob's words of comfort for Peach.

Lyrics from one of his redneck songs.

If I got through this weekend, I had a lot of music to delete from my playlists.

With Peach and Bob ensconced in the bunkhouse, I breathed easier. Barring a fire or stupidity on their part, they would remain safe until help came. I hid myself in the shadowy eaves of the porch behind a plastic storage bin and worked up my next plan of action. Before locking the pair in the women's bunk room, I had grabbed my sketchpad and a pencil. Flipping the pages, I reconstructed my suspect list. I was rapidly losing members unless a Figure X roamed the woods.

Sheepishly, I crossed out Jayce's soul-patched deer sketch, then Peach's devil-horns and Bob Bass's two-faced caricatures. I was left with Rick, the lodge staff, the Gutersons, the Sparks, and the Woodcocks. The only people I knew for sure roamed the woods were the remaining pairs. Max and his outfitter, Tennessee. Jeff Digby and Viktor. Rick and Mike. And despite Viktor's claims, I knew Max not to be a deranged psychopath.

At least, the Bear didn't normally act the deranged psychopath. I ruminated on this idea for a long minute. Could Max have encountered Deed's camp on his hunt for the hog, heard my distress, and shot Deed in a misguided attempt to save me? Could all these deaths have been accidents?

My fatigued mental state had entered shaky territory. Now I was thinking like Viktor.

Woodsmoke joined the deepening fog to cloak the drive, resembling one of Turner's moody landscapes. Shivering, I reexamined my list of events and checked off the ones meant for Jayce's shock campaign.

At the discovery of the slashed tires and cut radio antenna, I stopped. Those tricks were meant to trap us. But not everyone. One incapacitated vehicle meant most could leave. But no one could radio for immediate help.

One group would be forced to wait for a return vehicle. And in those hours, what might happen?

My heart sped up, warming my cold fingers and toes. Who was meant to stay? If I hadn't lost our Gator and Jeff Digby's hadn't gotten stuck, would we all be on our way home this morning? Sixteen people and a dog in three Gators and the Mule? A tight squeeze with only fourteen seats.

Two people would have been left behind. Which two?

The groups had swapped. Todd and I were expected to stay with Max and our guide, Tennessee. Jenny Sparks had twisted her ankle. If we had all returned to the bunkhouse last night as expected, what would have happened? I chewed my pencil. Jayce's pellet gun sniping. But no one anticipated Peach stealing out to see Jayce. Or for me to follow her. And then slip out again to get Jayce murdered.

Was that intended? Would someone have murdered Jayce without my blowing his cover? And how did Lesley and Abel fit into this scheme?

If all had gone according to plan, the hunt would have started Friday afternoon, gone all day Saturday, and into Sunday. Jayce Deed's antics would have been expected. Mischief that would agitate the group, possibly making us want to return. Peach had given him a walkie-talkie so he could keep tabs on us. All but one group would have gone back to the lodge.

Which group? Peach and Bob? Wouldn't they need someone to drive them?

My brain hurt. And guilt for getting Jayce Deed killed made my eyes smart. I leaned against the wall. When my head tipped into my shoulder, I jerked awake. How long had I slept? I scrambled to my feet and then dropped to the porch floor at the sound of shuffling from the side of the porch.

The scuffling stopped, then receded. My pulse strummed in my throat and the sudden blood flow through my veins stabbed my feet and calves with a thousand pinpricks. I grasped Peach's camouflaged M&P 15, wishing it were something simpler, like a plain old Winchester. I had no experience in tactical rifles. I didn't want to use the fancy gun, but neither did I feel comfortable weaponless.

I crept to the side of the porch and peeked around the corner. Footprints mutilated the mud.

A waterlogged depression shimmered in the damp breeze. Fear cramped my stomach and I hopped from the porch, wincing at the pins and needles in my feet.

I hesitated. No one yet knew that Bob and Peach were in the bunkhouse. Should I return to their hunting position and see who stalked them there?

In the distance, movement caught my attention and I squinted. A spot of Cad Orange broke through the fog, weaving through the pines. It came from the direction of Deed's camp, west of the bunkhouse.

The dab of bright orange grew. The person ran at a good clip.

I darted a look for better hiding spots and rushed toward the tireless side-by-side. Crouching in the muck behind the driver's side, I watched from over the top of the utility vehicle, my cold fingers clinging to the slick metal.

Seconds passed. From my squat, I couldn't see that side of the forest. I tried to slow the breathing that burst from my nose in shots of white vapor.

Who was running? Why were they running?

I could hear them now, crashing through the vines and dying weeds. A walkie-talkie squawked. I couldn't distinguish the walkie's voice or the words, but the person speaking was agitated. Feet pounded and splashed in the mud. I dropped to the ground to peer from under the Gator.

Jeans brushed the top of black boots. They paused in the drive, turned toward the bunkhouse, stopped again, and faced the opposite direction. I wracked my brain to place the boots, then realized the lack of camouflage held the answer I sought. Popping up, I settled the barrel of the gun on the hood of the UTV and called to Viktor.

He started, then spun toward me. "What are you doing here? They are looking for you. Where did you get that gun? Put it away."

"No offense, but I don't trust anyone." I squinted through the gun sight.

"I don't have a weapon." Viktor raised his hands. "Put it away, please. You know I have nothing to do with this."

Sweat broke on my damp neck. "Dangit, Viktor. I've gone in circles all weekend. Everything I think I know has been challenged.

My nerves are close to short-circuiting and my gut is screaming not to trust you."

"You are very tired, I know. You must put the gun down before you cause the terrible accident."

"I'm not putting the gun down," I said, but moved my chin above the sight and my finger from the trigger.

"Where is Bob Bass and Peach? They are missing."

"I'm not going to tell you that."

"Did you kill them?"

"What?" I exploded. "Of course not. I'm trying to save them."

"Jeff Digby found Buckshot's leash at the campsite. And much blood. Who is this blood?"

I leaned my forehead against the side of the utility vehicle and gulped air. Shit, shit, shit, I thought. Where was Jayce's body? Did someone move it? Was he alive? I rolled my head to the side and studied the bunkhouse. Should I have trusted Peach? She said a guy had told Jayce about Bob's invitation to the hunt.

A man wanted to disrupt the contest.

A man? That narrows it down, genius.

Boy, could I use some advice from my Deputy McHottie.

I could also use the backup.

"Dangit." I jerked away from the Mule's cold frame and raised my eyes to Viktor. My head buzzed from exhaustion and I blinked to wet my eyes.

Viktor watched me. He had unclipped the walkie from his belt and raised it near his mouth.

"Don't," I said.

"What did you do?" He lowered the walkie slowly, but didn't let go. "Whose blood is in the tent?"

"Jayce Deed's. Who left the bunkhouse early this morning? Who told everyone that I went to Max's deer stand?"

"Where is the dog?"

I jerked my chin toward the bunkhouse. "She's inside, resting. I'd never hurt Buckshot. I wouldn't hurt anyone. Who told everyone I left?"

He narrowed his eyes. “LaToya told us you fought with Peach. You ran out after the fight. Now we know where you really went.”

“Peach and I are good now. She might have told some lies about me earlier, but that’s all fixed. Sort of. Why were you running?”

“Because Mike reported Peach and Bob Bass are missing. He and Rick wished to move farther out. When he went to tell them this, he could not find them. I ran back to search the bunkhouse.”

“Where’s Max?”

“He is looking for you,” said Viktor. “Or so he says. The Bear has been out all night as well. Did you meet him at this camp? Did he kill the man staying there?”

“No,” I hollered. “Get off your flippin’ high horse about Max. He’s not doing anything.” My feet ached from my squat. Gravity drew me toward the ground, making my thighs and back scream in pain. I shook out a hand, rolled my shoulder, and replaced my hand on the gun’s stock.

“I don’t believe you are a bad person, Miss Tucker,” Viktor murmured in a sorrowful voice. “I think you are tired and confused and scared. I can help you. But you must lay down your weapon.”

“A man invited Jayce Deed to camp during the tournament. He knew Jayce would use pranks and disturbances to scare Bob Bass. They also knew it would disrupt the hunt and we’d have to return to the lodge. But not all of us. One hunter would be left with a staff member…”

Viktor waited.

I jumped to my feet. “Rick.”

THIRTY-SIX

"Where's Jeff Digby?" I yelled, scurrying around the side of the Mule with Peach's rifle.

Viktor's hands flew back in the air. "After we find the leash and blood, we split up. I came back to the bunkhouse to find Peach and Bob Bass. Jeff is tracking you."

"Damnation and hellfire." I clamped a hand on my forehead to stop my head from spinning, then pointed at his walkie-talkie. "Can you radio on separate channels on that thing? Warn Mike and Tennessee that Jeff Digby is dangerous. He wants to kill Rick. He'll probably try and stop me first. I know too much. Just like Lesley and Jayce."

"Cherry." Viktor's voice soothed and he strolled forward, holding out his hands. "Give me this gun. Let's go inside the bunkhouse. I'll make anything you want to eat. Anything at all. And you can rest in front of the fire. It is nice, no?"

"Dammit, Viktor. Like I could think about food at a time like this." I swung the stock away. "If you aren't going to warn Rick and Mike, I'll find them myself."

I spun from him and ran diagonally toward the northeastern border of the drive. Into the dying canopy I dove, not looking to see if Viktor followed. The morning mist continued to thicken with the rising temperature and trapped moisture. I leapt over the olive green roots of shriveling poison ivy and crashed through a raw umber clump of leafless viburnum. My feet pattered over wet pine straw turned coppery Indian Red Lake. While my eyes sorted color and shape in the fog, my ears attuned for the sound of shots, and my mind flashed over what I knew about Rick. The abuse of Jessica's daughter. Jeff slipping into the bunk room to watch Rick sleep.

I shook off a tear stuck on my nose. I didn't want to protect a repulsive piece of crap like Rick. Hell waited for scum like that.

"A miserable son of a bitch that deserved worse than death," Jeff had said.

Justice wasn't served. Jeff burned with revenge. It took a year of planning. The hog would have been the excuse he needed. Charge a ridiculous amount for tickets that no local could afford, but offer one winning ticket in a lottery that Rick would win. Get the Woodcocks to announce it on the news before the rest of Swinton found out and protested. And like a magic trick, provide a big distraction like Jayce Deed's Ban Sapiens to keep everyone's eyes off Rick.

A hunting accident was the perfect cover for an act of country retribution. At the clay shoot, Bob had switched places with Rick and then I had gotten in the way. Had Jeff set up the teals to launch at Rick's position? Rick's borrowed gun had exploded, but he hadn't been killed.

Did Jeff expect these accidents to kill him or only injure? A bullet might be too swift and merciful for Rick's death, but that exploding gun could have maimed him for life. Traveling at ninety miles an hour, a clay disk would have given him serious brain damage if it hadn't killed him.

In the old days, they would have strung Rick from a tree and left him there to warn other men who hungered for young girls.

I couldn't condone his plan, yet I understood Jeff Digby. But somehow his scheme had spun out of control. Why would he kill Abel, Lesley, and Jayce? That wasn't vigilante justice. Was Lesley also invited to the lodge to provide a distraction? Were Jeff's earlier attempts to stop Lesley from entering the forest a ruse? Lesley had made it clear he didn't trust Jeff. But Jeff hadn't expected Lesley to catch a ride into the woods with Jayce.

If I hadn't interrogated Jayce or detained Lesley would they have died?

I cringed at the thought, but continued moving forward.

And what about Abel? Abel had become a splinter lodged deep in my heel. Everywhere I stepped, his death pricked at my conscience.

Vaporous tendrils of fog choked the forest like an invasive case of kudzu. Visibility grew worse and my run became a bumbling gallop. With lungs threatening to explode, I halted my not-so-speedy gait. Trembling, I rested a hand against a sweetgum and searched the milky landscape for swatches of florescent orange. My ears thudded with my heartbeat, and I gulped in moist air that tasted of pine and mildew.

Footsteps pattered on damp pine straw.

My breath caught mid-pant and the hairs on my arms rose, chilling my flushed, damp skin. I swung the harness of Peach's rifle off my back, grasped it in both hands, and lifted it to my shoulder. Sliding behind the tree, I searched the fog for the intruder and strained my ears for the direction of the footsteps.

The padding slowed and stopped.

I dropped to a crouch, my finger on the rifle's safety. With a burst of speed, the footfall slapped against the pulpy leaves. I let out a breath, braced myself against the tree, and steadied my eye through the gun sight.

Breaking out of the mist, Buckshot galloped, charging toward me.

My finger flew off the safety and I almost dropped the gun. Slinging the harness over my shoulder, I stood and wiped the dew from my forehead with a shaky hand.

"I almost shot you, for mercy's sake. Go on home. Get. I don't want you here."

She slowed to a trot, but ignored my order.

"Buckshot," I hissed. "Go home."

Reaching my side, she dropped to a sit and gazed up at me, panting. I sighed, reached to pet her, and pointed once again toward the bunkhouse. "I can't have you here. It's dangerous. This is a one-woman show."

Unfazed by my tizzy, she circled my tree, wagging her tail with doggish glee.

"Seriously," I said. "I don't need nor want a partner. I don't know what's going to happen. We're dealing with a dangerous individual. Jeff could easily take you hostage. Hell, you'd probably jump into his arms willingly, and then what could I do?"

She bent to shove her nose in a thick entanglement of greenbrier and pulled out with a snort.

"You want to chase rabbits, do it on your own time." I kicked a pile of leaves at her. "Get out of here."

Buckshot's head drooped and she fixed me with those sad eyes that reminded me of Abel's other dogs waiting for his return. The knife twisted deeper, but I steeled my gaze and showered her with another clump of leaves. The wistful look continued and her haunches remained glued to the ground. I pushed her and swore. Stomped my feet. Threw a stick. Finally, I leaned a forearm against a loblolly and buried my head in a camo'd crook.

"Why don't you just leave?" I cried. "I'm so flippin' tired. I can't deal with protecting you too."

She nosed toward my belly, wedging her head between the trunk and my legs, then shoved her body into the gap. Her moist doggy breath further dampened LaToya's coveralls.

"Why don't animals ever listen to me?" I wiped my eyes against my arm, but left my weary head to rest. Exhaustion tricked my eyes into closing and I pulled in a deep breath. "Just give me a minute."

Buckshot yipped and darted from the protection of my body.

"Where are you going?" I wearily lifted my head from my arm, stepped back, and smacked into the barrel of a gun.

"Give me that rifle," said Jeff Digby.

He jerked the sling off my shoulder, caught my arm, and freed the gun with a yank that caused pain to shoot from my neck to my fingertips. The barrel of his rifle punched the bruise left by the

Super Swine and I staggered into the tree, smacking it with my forehead.

"Jeff, you've got to listen to me," I said, rubbing my head. "I know how much you hate Rick. I understand. But it's not too late. He might confess."

"Can't you just shut your mouth for once? None of this is your business. Why don't you just do as you're told?" He grasped my arm and whipped me around to face him. Both rifles hung from his broad shoulders and his large hands gripped my forearms, pinning them to my sides. "I don't know what you think you're doing."

The roughly carved face appeared murderous with rage. A flush darkened his bearded cheeks and the set of his jaw reminded me of Hogzilla's horrible grinding teeth.

"What are you going to do?" I whispered.

"I don't have time to deal with you now." His mutterings seemed more for himself than for me. "What did you do with Peach and Bob Bass?"

My hands clenched into fists and I sought to steady my breathing. "Why do you want to know?"

He shook me. "Where are they?"

My vision swam and I bit my tongue. "Just calm down, Jeff. We can work all this out."

"There's nothing to work out. I need to know where they are. You tell me. Now."

I clenched my teeth, shook my head, and popped my knee into his groin. He bent over, loosening the grip on my arms. I jerked my elbows away, turned, and ran. My arms pedaled the air and my boots slid in the mud and leaves. Gasping lungfuls of the cold damp air, I plunged forward.

Buckshot had disappeared. Behind me, Jeff's boots hammered the spongey forest floor. He made no attempt to muffle his footsteps now. They grew closer. I pushed myself into a sprint. The burn in my thighs matched my lungs. The cold air chapped my face. I could hear Jeff's puffing gasps. Fingers brushed my back and a shot of desperation jolted me forward.

His tackle sent me sprawling headlong into a drift of sodden leaves and brambles. A spiky sweetgum ball bit into my cheek and the barbs of a greenbrier vine pricked my hands and wrists. I rolled, but Jeff grabbed my legs and yanked me towards him, then sat on my chest while he hogtied my hands and feet.

"You're not going anywhere. I'll come back for you later."

He left me thumping the ground and cursing.

THIRTY-SEVEN

Buckshot reappeared to lick my face. As friends went, her steadfast loyalty matched Todd's. However, Todd's opposable thumbs would have been more useful in this particular situation. I lay on my back with my wrists tied to my boots, staring into the branches of a sweetgum and praying a spiked seed pod wouldn't fall and put my eye out.

"He used nylon rope, Buckshot. I don't suppose you'd be inclined to chew it?" I demonstrated by gnashing my teeth.

She flopped down beside me, waggled her tail, and laid her head next to mine.

"Do you think Jeff's coming back to shoot me? Is this a pity party? Let me tell you something, Buckshot. I've been in situations worse than this."

I considered my current feet-in-the-air position which resembled the many armadillos dotting our county roads.

"Well, maybe not this bad. But I'm tired of focusing on the negative. I've always been a half-full kind of gal. True, my situation at home has soured me some, but I'm not ready to give up. There are folks counting on me. Peach and Bob Bass. Rick..."

I sighed, staring at my bound wrists and ankles. "Actually, my world view is pretty dim if these are the people worth saving." Wiggling my feet, I tested the nylon wrapping my ankles.

Buckshot scooted closer and edged her nose into my armpit.

"You're right. I don't believe for a minute that Rick is an innocent man. But wrong is wrong. Jayce, Lesley, and Abel sure didn't deserve to die for Rick." I squirmed, chafing my wrists against the nylon while twisting my feet within the boots. My right heel slid into the ankle of the boot. I paused my writhing to rest. "And who knows what's going to happen to the rest of us. Jeff Digby's gone off his rocker."

The nose investigating my armpit had drawn away with my jostling. Buckshot returned to lick my eyebrow, then backed away as I resumed squirming.

"I know you like Jeff Digby, but you like everybody," I said, flopping and heaving against my bonds. "I wish you could meet my Deputy McHottie, Luke Harper. I miss him like crazy, Buckshot, but it's no good. My family hates him and they're going through a tough time right now. How can I choose a man over my family? If Luke doesn't stick around, then where would I be?"

One foot slipped out of a boot. My cramped leg fell into the damp leaves. I wiggled my toes within my sock. Cold and moisture immediately wicked through the cotton. "There's one down. Good thing I don't have cankles."

I worked at the left boot, until that heel also slipped from the confines to fall next to its mate. My wrists remained tied to my boots, but my legs were free. Rolling onto my side, I pushed into a stand then stomped my socked feet.

"Told you I'd be all right." I glanced around, but Buckshot had disappeared into the mist again. Ignoring my disappointment, I used a knee and the tree to pull my boots from their nooses, then shoved my feet back inside. With the boots gone, the rope slipped from my wrists and fell to the forest floor.

Wet socks were the least of my worries, so I disregarded the oozy feeling between my toes and resumed my quest to stop Jeff Digby's murderous rampage.

Their voices alerted me. I had stumbled around in the thickening fog, sure that I had hiked out of Georgia into some alien planet that didn't have a sun.

The ghostly soup dampened my skin and curled my hair, and I began to sweat beneath LaToya's slick coveralls.

The scent of wood rot strengthened as the autumnal colors grew more muted and dull. Beneath my feet, the varying shades of siennas, golds, and umbers became a murky orangish ochre, like someone had mixed in too much Phthalo Green with the red. Tree trunks slashed dark lines through the wispy gray, but other objects remained obscured.

The sounds of the forest were at once distinct and indefinite. It reminded me of swimming in the ocean. Back on Tybee one summer, Luke and I had been body surfing and thought we had heard a child crying and searched to save her, but it had been a gull.

And now I heard bawling. The fog confused me, distorting the sounds and making me spin in circles.

Not a bird.

A man.

The low, shuddering cries came from my right, then the left. I picked my way through the trees, following a drift of voices that accompanied the crying, unable to see beyond a few yards in front of me. I slowed my movement, careful to quiet my footsteps.

"This isn't your place," said a voice who sounded like Mike. "She's my sister. I moved back and I'm taking care of things now."

That's right, I thought. The housekeeper had said Jessica's family moved to be with her. I didn't know she had meant Mike, but it made sense. Mike and Viktor were the new kids at the lodge. But where was Mike? And where was Rick? I looked for the voices, but could only make out the faint lines of trees.

"She was seeing me when that was all going on," yelled Jeff. "It hurt me too."

"You've got no claim on her now. Jessica said as much. If you feel guilty, that's your problem."

"Me, feel guilty?" Jeff bellowed. "Are you comparing me to him?"

Mike's voice remained calm. "Of course not. But if you and Jessica hadn't been sneaking around, leaving Ruby alone so much...it's not like Jessica was at work all that time. Hell, guilt's just about eaten Jessica alive. Why shouldn't you feel guilty too?"

"You son of a bitch. Don't tell me how I feel. You've got no idea what it was like."

"And how do you think I felt? That bastard stole my family." Mike's voice rose above Rick's sobbing. "And who knows how many other families he's ripped apart? How many girls he's ruined?" His words ended in a long, low howl.

His keening cut through me sharper than any knife. I hugged a tree, searching the fog for some movement.

"It can't end like this." Mike's voice returned, choked but more distinct. "Nothing's worked right. The whole weekend's gone to shit. One thing after another, and I can't seem to stop it. And now I've got to stop you too?"

"We can end this," said Jeff. "Let me handle it."

Behind me, something stirred the leaves. I spun, grasping the tree to catch myself from tripping. A squirrel darted up an elm, and I let out a long breath. The squirrel disappeared behind the slithering mist, and as I watched him, a blaze of orange appeared. I crept closer, tiptoeing through the sludgy piles of leaves. The fog shifted, and with it the block of hunter orange. I continued my creep, seeking the color among the dirty gray of the fog, but not finding any orange. I glanced right and the florescent tangerine emerged, half-buried in the leaves. I snagged the vest and fingered the Big Rack label sewn on the front.

Had Jeff forced Mike to take off his safety vest? Or was it Rick's? The lodge had lent Rick a gun and other gear. All the better to set up his accidents.

I had been so busy avoiding looking at the man, I couldn't remember what he wore.

Damn you, Jeff Digby, for making me worry about garbage like Rick Miller, I thought, gathering the vest under my arm.

I stole toward the wall of trees before me, then realized the fog had concealed the steep hillside behind them. Looking up, I wondered if someone at the top of the hill had sent the vest sailing into the fog. I dug my toe into a pile of wet leaves, flexed my foot to push off, slipped, and crashed into a pile of fallen branches. I lay spread eagle, afraid to move and make more noise.

The drone of sobbing cut off. "Who's there?" Rick's voice drifted in the fog. "Help me."

My heart stuttered. "Shh," I whispered, squinting into the fog.

Above me, the blaming and cursing amplified. Mike sounded wild with rage. His anger shook me, bringing back the memory of Lil Joe's reprimand. Mike had been under a lot of pressure. Saving the lodge. Protecting the staff. Keeping the Woodcocks happy. Helping his sister. Organizing the event. And all his careful planning had unraveled. He'd kept calm during each of Jayce's escapades, pacifying the hunt members by keeping them focused on the competition. And now he was losing it.

I struggled up the ascent, slippery with wet leaves, grabbing the thin trunks of saplings to haul myself up the slope. The fog billowed and rolled with me, hiding chunks of granite poking through the clay.

At the top, I clambered through a clump of ferns and found Rick tied to the base of a young hickory. His face was wet with tears, and I felt ashamed by my disgust.

"Help me," he sobbed.

"Did you mess around with Jessica's daughter, Ruby?" I couldn't stop myself. I could see it in his eyes, and yet I didn't want to know. If he said yes, I didn't know what I would do. I felt sick with hatred for this man and the revulsion coupled with exhaustion made my vision roll and my hearing crackle. Nausea punched my gut. I dropped the vest and stumbled away to relieve myself.

"Come back," he called.

"Shut up," I hissed. "You'll get us both killed. Just sit tight. God Almighty, can't you at least keep quiet?"

I rubbed my eyes and gave my head a good rattle, summoning energy and searching for wisdom. Generally, instinct was more my game. Like a hound on a scent, I had kept circling back to that damn Braves cap of Abel's.

Reminding me of that Big Rack cap constantly twisting in Mike's hands.

The hill fell off into another shallow ravine. A soft rush of water splashed over the exposed granite. The same creek that had caught Lesley downstream. Disliking that ominous thought, I left Rick to follow Mike and Jeff's shouting. A chain of trees grew along the ridge, and I moved through them one by one, careful of the roots that spilled out of the eroding hillside toward the ditch below.

In sudden contrast to the wispy fog, Mike and Jeff's solid forms emerged. Mike's hat had been balled up in one hand, an aid for waving and pointing while he raged. A rifle hung around his shoulders. He faced me, shouting almost incoherently at Jeff. Jeff's rifle lay in his hands at the ready, his feet planted and body turned slightly. It was difficult to tell if the stance was defensive or for attack. Probably both.

And what could I do? Two grown men with weapons. Another tied to a tree, like a rabid animal prepared to be put out of society's misery.

Dangit, I thought, all I wanted was a weekend getaway with a side of commissioned painting. How was that asking too much? And where the hell was Max? I hadn't let myself think about him too much for fear of that answer.

How badly I wanted to crawl back to Halo, even with the awful mess of contempt and suspicion surrounding my family.

Crouching at the foot of the tree, I hoped the fog and LaToya's camo would keep me from their notice. I peered out at Jeff and wondered, once again, if such a person could be capable of murder. Maybe in a hot passion, but in this shrewdly calculated weekend?

I watched the two men, studying their reactions. Listened to the growing argument that condemned both in terms of motive.

I liked Mike. But wasn't this carefully planned weekend Mike's baby? Jeff had been worried about safety, whereas Mike seemed more concerned with the lodge's welfare.

Always subdued, Mike fed the hunters' appetite for competition while downplaying the incidents.

Jeff had warned, "Nervous people make mistakes. They'd be a danger to others and to themselves."

A stray skeet. A misfire. An accidental fall or bullet to the chest. Only one was needed to end Rick and the police could be told everyone was keyed up by the odd threats made by Ban Sapiens activists.

I had ruined everything with my questioning of Abel's accident and insistent nosiness into all the lodge pranks.

Why hadn't I seen it? Constantly, Mike had told me I was upset. Suggested I go home. Reminded me the police had ruled Abel's death as accidental. I had believed Mike's insistence that there was no security footage of my room break-in. Mike had the means and opportunity to leave the warning in my room.

But then so had Jeff.

If Hogzilla hadn't found me, would I have been shot like Jayce Deed?

Distant barking broke my concentration. The argument trailed off as the men became conscious of the outside world. The barking grew louder and the fog bore the sound of Buckshot crashing through the undergrowth near the bottom of the hill. Jeff spun to glance behind him and, at that moment, Mike raised his rifle. Grasping it in both hands, he lunged at Jeff.

Without thinking, I leapt out and screamed. Jeff whirled around and brought his rifle up to block Mike's thrust. They struggled at the lip of the ridge, like two goats with locked horns ready to push the weaker off a cliff.

"Mike," I screamed. "Let it go. It's over."

My command had the opposite effect. Mike surged forward, driving Jeff's heels toward the ravine's ledge. Jeff teetered, but regained his footing and pushed back. As the bigger man, Jeff's struggle surprised me, but Mike's wiry build had the strength of desperation. Had Mike honed these skills on similar terrain with Abel and Lesley? Down the hill, Buckshot's baying continued to distract me. I gave up on stopping the hand-to-hand struggle and ran back to Rick.

"Where's your gun?" I avoided looking at him, straining to see the men through the mist. "You must have borrowed another rifle for the hunt today."

"Mike took it."

"Dammit." I glanced at Rick. "What did he do with it? Come on."

"Let me go."

"You don't get it, do you?" I screamed. "You deserve this. But Jeff sure as hell doesn't deserve to get killed trying to stop the man whose niece you destroyed. Now tell me where the rifle is."

"If I deserve this, why are you helping me?"

"Because if we all got what we deserved, this world would be even more hellish than it already is. The law doesn't always work, but we need order."

"Mike wanted me to shoot myself," sobbed Rick. "Held his gun on me. But when he heard Jeff Digby coming, he tied me here and tossed the rifle." He pointed to a massing of the long, fronded leaves of a Georgia buckeye shrub.

I dove at the bush. My hands grasped the wooden stock and I snatched the rifle. I scrambled to my feet and ran through the trees. Ten yards from the men, I stopped. They continued to grapple, grunting and panting with vicious desperation. Without checking to see if anything was chambered, I pushed forward the safety and aimed at the tree line across the ravine.

The rifle cracked. Mike flinched and caught himself, turning toward the shot. Jeff's reaction was quicker. He charged, knocking Mike onto his back, and pinned the rifle against Mike's chest.

"I don't want to hurt you," said Jeff, raising his Marlin. The butt crashed against Mike's skull. His head lolled to the side.

Satisfied, Jeff climbed off his chest to stand and face me.

Damn, I hope I'm right, I thought, staring at the brawny man.

His .45 would make a bigger hole than my .30.

THIRTY-EIGHT

The mist made the scene eerier, less real. Hard-edged and hostile, Jeff loomed over Mike's unconscious body. I tightened my hands on the Winchester, knowing it didn't serve much protection against the adrenaline rush coursing through the giant before me.

"How'd you get away?" Jeff's brown ochre eyes narrowed.

"I have slender ankles." My scowl deepened. "I don't appreciate getting tied up."

"I don't care. You were getting in the way." His shoulders twitched. "I didn't need your help."

"The hell you didn't." I glanced at Mike. "How bad is his injury?"

"He's going to have a hell of a headache."

I blew out a deep sigh and lowered my gun. "Did he kill Abel and Lesley?"

"Not sure about Lesley. Mike found him watching the bunkhouse and said he chased him off. Lesley could have slipped. But Abel?" Jeff paused. "Mike met with him when Abel brought Buckshot to the lodge. Usually I take care of the kennels, but I was busy. I suspected Abel overheard Mike and Jessica talking about Rick. Abel must've said something to Mike. Now I'm sure Mike met him walking home and chased him into that ravine. At the time, I had no proof and wasn't going to rat on Mike to the police if he didn't do anything. I didn't want to believe it."

"Abel was waiting for Rick, who never showed up at the Double Wide. To have Abel leak Mike's plans to Rick would've been a waste of meticulous design. And might have gotten Mike arrested for intent to murder."

"Mike thought he was protecting someone else's daughter from that sicko. He really thought Abel's death was an accident. An accident he caused, but still an accident in his mind. Probably Lesley's too." Jeff flicked his stony gaze past me.

"It'd suit you better if that'd been Rick's skull instead of Mike's, wouldn't it?"

He nodded. "Mike's a good guy. I helped him get his job. Helped him move here. He was under a lot of pressure."

"I'm sorry, but 'under pressure' doesn't cut it. Mike followed me to Jayce Deed's camp. I thought Mike was sleeping. When he thought Jayce would expose him, he shot him in cold blood." I paused. "I thought it was you for a minute."

"We're not all meant for murder." Jeff shook his head. "Never would have thought it of Mike either. Ruby's death's been burning him up. And if anyone deserved to die, it's Rick."

"But not Abel. Or Lesley or Jayce."

"Or me or you, if it had come to that," finished Jeff. "And that bastard's still alive."

Below us, Buckshot's crazed baying had intensified.

"Don't move. I'll be right back," I said, and scurried toward the edge of the hill.

Frantic movement shifted within the denser fog at the bottom and I called out to the dog to let her know I was safe. Slinging the rifle around my shoulder, I skidded down the slope, snatching at branches to slow my momentum. My toe caught a root and I tumbled, sliding on my bottom through the drifts of wet leaves. Buckshot met me with more howls and licks.

"Girl, your timing is crazy scary." I buried my face in her neck and scrubbed her back. "We got him. You and your pack have your justice. And Abel can rest in peace."

Her wagging tail shook my body like an earthquake.

The roar of an approaching motor reached my ears. I jerked my face from Buckshot's fur to grab her collar as she began another spate of crazed baying. A few minutes later, Max limped into view.

"This dog has a fine nose," said Max, grinning. "She leads me to the lost artist like that dog in the old television show."

"Where have you been?" I glowered.

"It took some time to find the vehicle you lost." He pointed behind him with his walking stick, then hitched forward. Offering a hand, he pulled me to standing. "What has happened to leave you looking like this?"

"It was Mike all along. Rick caused his family an unspeakable tragedy and Mike used this contest as a means for revenge. There was an anti-Bob Bass activist invited by Mike to stir up trouble so he could draw attention away from a fatal accident for Rick. Abel Spencer found out somehow. Mike took care of him before Abel could spill the beans and ruin Mike's chance of ridding the world of Rick."

"Accidents to detract from a planned one."

I nodded and wiped away a tear.

"Where is Mike and Rick?"

"Jeff's holding them up there." I pointed at the top of the hill and bit my lip to stop its trembling.

Max studied me, then lightened his tone. "Do you know what I have done? Of course, I am the winner. You have my portrait to paint, Artist."

"You got the hog?" Another tear welled, and I shoved it away with an angry sniffle. His gentleman's hunting apparel had barely dirtied, whereas I looked like I had waded through Rembrandt's palette. "That was probably you chasing Hogzilla and shooting at me last night. I figured you for dead in a creek."

"You wound me. I am invincible, you do not know this by now?" Clasping me in a brief hug, Max rubbed my back, then held my bedraggled self away for further examination. He tucked a frizzy lock of hair behind my ear. "I think you are also invincible. But invincibility is much harder on you."

I sniffed, but my tears had magically disappeared. "Not all of us enjoyed ourselves. How could you cut off communication?"

"Tennessee and I felt to concentrate we must ignore the drama. I'm sorry that I didn't believe this drama was so serious. I thought it was a few pranks to put me off guard." He shoved his hands in his pocket. "Plus there was Viktor at the bunkhouse. It was not a good idea to put us in such close quarters. I heard Viktor had fled to Canada. If I had known he worked here..."

"So you do know him. Dammit, I defended you. Viktor thought you were trying to kill him."

"Viktor was always paranoid." Max's smirk faded. "But I cannot trust him either. He tried to poison me once. Not that it was his fault. He was under orders by the boss. But I will never eat scallops again."

"Huh."

THIRTY-NINE

The low-lying fog was blamed for the inability to send more than one rescue chopper. Knowing small-town police, I figured budget conditions probably trumped the fog. Mike and Rick were flown directly to Swinton's county sheriff's department. An unhappy Peach was forced to join them to give her version of the Ban Sapiens enterprise. I had endured another bumpy, mud-sucking ride back to the lodge with Max, Viktor, and Bob Bass. Buckshot remained to assist the police in finding Jayce Deed, whom Mike had dragged from the camp and hidden. I had left Buckshot's brindle coat tearstained and well-hugged. On the other hand, I left Jeff without any farewell. He stayed with the guide Tennessee to bury Hogzilla.

For this, Max had spent the entire ride in a sulk. He had no good footage of his victory other than a handful of overexposed shots taken with his cell phone.

"Shit, anybody could have doctored these," Bob Bass had said with the graciousness of a man accustomed to buying his wins. "Besides, after the hell we've been put through, I'd think you'd give up the trophy. Not real sporting of you, Avtaikin."

Bob did have a point, I thought, but not one I'd ever verbalize.

"Maybe his reward should be my loyalty." Viktor glanced over his shoulder to catch the Bear's frigid blue gaze and narrowly missed driving into a sinkhole. "I will not pretend I do not remember you. However, I am no informant. I only threatened you to protect myself. I have no interest in the old life."

"You would do well to remember this," said Max, but quirked a smile. "When we return, we should drink to this. I still have the scar where you sewed up my shoulder."

"Bullet wound?" I asked.

"Chef's knife." Max slapped Viktor's shoulder and laughed.

"Well, if y'all are drinking, I'll join you. After this weekend, I need it," said Bob. "And I suppose I should wait for Peach anyway."

I made no plans for a post-murder drink. A shower seemed more appropriate. By the time we pulled into the lodge parking lot, the fog had lifted and weak afternoon rays struggled to break through the clouds.

"Figures," I said, looking at the sky. "Now we'll get some sun."

Max elbowed me in the ribs. "Do not forget to thank Todd for contacting the police."

"Of course not," I said. "Why would I?"

He pointed toward a familiar black Raptor 4x4 parked in the lodge drive. An even more familiar broad-shouldered, lean-hipped man with gray eyes, dusky brown curls, and hidden dimples leaned against the truck. My Deputy McHottie. Next to him leaned my Deputy Rookie. Rookie Holt waved. Deputy McHottie simmered. He didn't need waves to attract my attention.

"Your personal cavalry has arrived. Not a pleasing sight for your friend, Todd McIntosh," said Max. "Nor to me."

I tried to ignore the fluttering in my chest and surreptitiously smoothed my humidity-styled hair. "You don't like law enforcement, period. And you do business with the Bransons, so you don't get an opinion on my love life."

"Artist, this is your problem. We all get to have the opinion on your love life, but you can choose to ignore us. You attribute the opinion to fact, probably because you believe your opinion is thus."

I eyed him. "I can't let my family down."

"They will be angry, yes." He patted my knee. "If you continue a relationship with Deputy Harper, you may find yourself alienated from everyone. But take this from me, you can learn to live as the island if it is important to you."

"What would be important enough to cut yourself off from family?"

"Freedom." The icy blue eyes met mine and he smirked. "Money's not bad, either."

"I don't know if I can do that. Down here, we are judged by our family, because nothing is more important than family. At the end of the day, family's all you got."

The side-by-side slowed to a halt. I vaulted from the cramped seat and into Luke's waiting arms. I pressed my face into the t-shirt smelling of his mother's favorite fabric softener and tried to free myself from the guilt and misery that had become my personal hog wallow.

Pulling myself together, I freed myself from Luke's arms and shook Rookie Holt's hand.

"Good to see you in one piece, Tucker," she said. "From Todd McIntosh's report, he was worried you wouldn't be."

Luke's arm slipped around my waist and held tight.

"All's well when you're alive, right?" My smile didn't convince anyone. "I guess your commanding officer will be happy. You've got Abel Spencer's killer. I'm glad I could help."

Her gaze steeled. "I didn't ask for your help. All you've done is convince me you're a lunatic. Lucky for you, your boyfriend persuaded me not to file charges to teach you a lesson."

"I guess this means no celebratory GNO? I was hoping we could be friends. After spending so much time with Buckshot, I realized I could use more girlfriends. Particularly ones who take victim's dogs into their home."

She rolled her eyes and hid a smirk. "I'll think about it. But I never want to see you in Swinton again."

"Works for me."

She sauntered over to the Gator, calling for Bob Bass. With the officer gone, Max broke his silence to say goodbye.

"Avtaikin." Luke's stiff nod matched his voice.

"The artist is not herself these days," droned the Bear. "Do not add to her stress. She still has a portrait to paint." With a sharp look toward my gape, he pivoted, and using his walking stick, gimped toward the Twenty Point bar.

"That guy drives me nuts," said Luke, then hugged me again. "Holt filled me in on some of her investigation. They were able to lift a clean footprint with Traxtone not far from the ravine where the victim died. Swinton'll get a warrant to search the perp's boots for a match."

"Good. I hope Mike confesses, though." I broke his embrace to peer around the soggy drive. "Have you seen Todd?"

"I heard he got a ride back to Halo."

As we strolled to Luke's truck, I refused to reflect on Todd's lack of goodbye for fear of tears. Our friendship had weathered a few storms, including a three-second marriage. My feelings for Todd were more mixed than a bag of old buttons, but I couldn't hurt him anymore than I could hurt my family. I just hoped he wasn't serious about dating Shawna. That idea was so God-awful, even Todd couldn't pull it off.

I gave Luke a brief account of the tragedy. Before I could finish, he had pulled me off my toes and into another tight embrace.

Pressing my head into his shoulder, he kissed my filthy hair. "Lord, you scare me."

"I didn't expect to see you here." I wrapped my arms around his back and let my head rest in the crook of his neck, seeking a moment's peace between storms. His lack of noise over my amateur sleuthing didn't fool me for a second. The stiffened muscles in his shoulders and neck felt like I hugged a steel column.

Luke released me slowly and stepped back. Scrubbing his short curls, he slackened the clench of his jaw and shook out the tension in his shoulders. "The sheriff and I talked over your concerns about the doings here and I got permission to switch shifts with a buddy. The lodge had thought the radio didn't work because of the storm, but it was Todd's report to Rookie Holt that organized the rescue." He reached into his pocket. "I've got something for you."

"Wait." I placed a hand over his, then shifted my gaze toward the restaurant, where the others partook of vodka. I should have joined them for a shot before taking on this sudden serious sharing of feelings. "I thought a lot about our past while trapped here this weekend. And about my family. I saw firsthand what can happen when a family is ripped apart by tragic circumstances."

"Sugar, what Mike suffered is different from our family feud. He allowed a real darkness to eat at him if he was willing to commit homicide." Luke grasped my hand and brought it to his lips.

"I want to be with you. But silly or not, I can't choose between you and my family. Grandpa, Casey, and Cody are my only blood. I've got to respect and honor their feelings."

"And you've got those who have chosen to be in your lives, like your Uncle Will. Even Red and Todd." Luke shoved his hand into his pocket and pulled out a piece of paper. "And me."

I kept my eyes on the paper so Luke couldn't see the tears I tried to force back into my sockets. "What's that?"

"An address." He placed the slip in my hand, then crossed his arms and leaned against the truck. "Billy Branson's address. I didn't sleep last night either. Spent my free time searching the DMV and warrant databases."

I unfolded the paper and read Luke's scrawl. "What the hell? After all this time, Shawna's daddy is in Georgia?" I glanced up. "What does this mean?"

"Billy Branson's been in the state pen. Got out about a year ago."

"Incarcerated? And now he's out? Did JB Branson know this about his brother?"

Luke shrugged, but his eyes read yes.

"That son of a bitch. What about Shawna?"

"I'm not sure, but I've a feeling she's had a hunch."

"The Bransons have been blaming his disappearance on my mother and all this time Billy Branson's been in prison?" Fury welled inside of me and I tasted a bit of the darkness that had pushed Mike Neeley beyond reason. "And you're giving this information to me because why?"

"We're going to clear up this situation of the disappearance of Billy Branson and Christy Ballard Tucker. I'm tired of the bullshit. This openly declares me on the side of the Ballards." He grasped my hand and the paper crumpled between our clasped fingers. "I understand your commitment to your family. But, Cherry, you are mine, and I'm not waiting any longer."

As he jerked me into his body, my soft frame melded to his hard planes. His finger slipped beneath my chin and tipped it up. My cornflower blues met his stormy grays.

"I only have the address. Haven't had a chance to read his criminal record. You understand what I'm saying? Bringing Billy Branson back to Shawna may not have your desired effect. And there are other implications."

"Implications about my momma." I nodded and stretched onto my toes to kiss him.

Soft lips met mine, but he broke off the kiss before I wanted. "Think you can handle that?"

His concern was justified. We'd be ripping off an old bandage, exposing a wound that had never healed. Besides a hot mess of family feelings, the town would take issue with us for waking an ugly dog that had slept for nearly twenty years. Luke and I would be destroying lines once clearly drawn in the old feud. Local folks needed to know where to stand.

Then there was sweet and loyal Todd to consider. Buckshot had done well as a replacement, but Todd had been my longstanding companion. If I sided with Luke on this venture, what would it do to poor Todd? As a staunch Tucker ally in the war with the Bransons, my secret romance had already threatened to divide his loyalties. This might kill our friendship.

But despite a weekend of death and misery, my heart had not given up on hope. Not on Todd. Or family forgiveness. Or happy endings.

"If you're with me, I can do this," I whispered to Luke. "Bring it on."

Photo by Scott Asano

LARISSA REINHART

A 2015 Georgia Author of the Year Best Mystery finalist, Larissa writes the Cherry Tucker Mystery series. Her family and Cairn Terrier, Biscuit, now live in Nagoya, Japan, but still call Georgia home. Visit her website, LarissaReinhart.com, find her chatting on Facebook, Twitter, and Goodreads, or join her Facebook street team, The Mystery Minions.

The Cherry Tucker Mystery Series by Larissa Reinhart

Novels

PORTRAIT OF A DEAD GUY (#1)
STILL LIFE IN BRUNSWICK STEW (#2)
HIJACK IN ABSTRACT (#3)
DEATH IN PERSPECTIVE (#4)
THE BODY IN THE LANDSCAPE (#5)

Novellas

QUICK SKETCH (prequel to PORTRAIT)
(in HEARTACHE MOTEL)

Henery Press Mystery Books

And finally, before you go...
Here are a few other mysteries
you might enjoy:

PILLOW STALK

Diane Vallere

A Madison Night Mystery (#1)

Interior Decorator Madison Night might look like a throwback to the sixties, but as business owner and landlord, she proves that independent women can have it all. But when a killer targets women dressed in her signature style—estate sale vintage to play up her resemblance to fave actress Doris Day—what makes her unique might make her dead.

The local detective connects the new crime to a twenty-year old cold case, and Madison's long-trusted contractor emerges as the leading suspect. As the body count piles up, Madison uncovers a Soviet spy, a campaign to destroy all Doris Day movies, and six minutes of film that will change her life forever.

HEARTACHE MOTEL

Terri L. Austin, Larissa Reinhart, LynDee Walker

Filled with drag queens, Rock-a-Hula cocktails, and a vibrating velveteen bed, these novellas tell the tales of three amateur sleuths who spend their holidays at Elvis's beloved home.

DINERS KEEPERS, LOSERS WEEPERS by Terri L. Austin
When Rose heads to Graceland right before Christmas, she gets all shook up: the motel is a dump and an Elvis impersonator turns up dead. Will Rose be able to find the murderer and get home by Christmas day? It's now or never.

QUICK SKETCH by Larissa Reinhart
Cherry Tucker pops into Memphis to help a friend who's been hustled out of his savings, and quickly finds herself in a dangerous sting that could send her to the slammer or mark her as a pigeon from cons looking for an even bigger score.

DATELINE MEMPHIS by LynDee Walker
A quick stop at Graceland proves news breaks in the strangest places for crime reporter Nichelle Clarke. When the King's home gets locked down with Nichelle inside, she chases this headline into the national spotlight, and right into the thief's crosshairs.

COUNTERFEIT CONSPIRACIES

Ritter Ames

A Bodies of Art Mystery (#1)

Laurel Beacham may have been born with a silver spoon in her mouth, but she has long since lost it digging herself out of trouble. Her father gambled and womanized his way through the family fortune before skiing off an Alp, leaving her with more tarnish than trust fund. Quick wits and connections have gained her a reputation as one of the world's premier art recovery experts. The police may catch the thief, but she reclaims the missing masterpieces.

The latest assignment, however, may be her undoing. Using every ounce of luck and larceny she possesses, Laurel must locate a priceless art icon and rescue a co-worker (and ex-lover) from a master criminal, all the while matching wits with a charming new nemesis. Unfortunately, he seems to know where the bodies are buried—and she prefers hers isn't next.

CPSIA information can be obtained
at www.ICGtesting.com
Printed in the USA
BVOW06s2200201216
471436BV00016B/231/P